WHO'S KILLING THE LIBERALS

BOOK 1 OF THE JONATHAN SCANLAN SERIES

WHO'S KILLING THE LIBERALS

BARRY SOLLOWAY

CHAPTER 1

Bernie signed off with what had become his trademark slogan. "That's it friends, from the lonely voice of reason in the wilderness of fascism. Nine hundred and sixty more days until the fuhrer will be toppled." He smiled to himself as he removed his headset and pushed his thinning hair back in place. He never understood why conservative callers phoned in to challenge his statements, but such calls were the thing of ratings. Four callers had gone ballistic when he demanded the secretary of defense be shipped off to The Hague to be tried as a war criminal.

The ranting of such listeners provided great theater if scant intellectual repartee. He often wondered why anyone bending to the right would bother listening to his show. However, it was not lost on Bernie that his ability to fire up conservatives had pushed him up into the morning commute time slot in the nation's most competitive market. After the show, he spent two hours at the studio scribbling notes for his next program and glancing through the emails, correspondence, and internal memos piled on his desk. Bernie Fredberg possessed little regard for suggestions from his listening audience but occasionally a gem could be gleaned from the mountain of trivia. Even a blind squirrel occasionally finds an acorn.

As he made his way to the elevator, Bernie noticed the new

receptionist at the entry station. She appeared eminently qualified for the role. Catherine Zeta-Jones' features, a dazzling smile, wasp thin waist and enhanced bosoms. She was even blond, while a feature shared by both his ex-wives and not a deal breaker, she was a definite plus on Bernie's scorecard. He squared his narrow shoulders, sucked in his paunch, and sidled toward the crescent shaped workstation. Offering his most beguiling smile, he waited for her to finish dealing with an incoming call. Bernie's face was beginning to ache from the unaccustomed strain when the woman of his immediate dreams looked up to notice the dumpy middle-aged man with a bad comb over leering at her.

"Can I help you?" an institutionalized smile and a hint of the southeast.

"I'm Bernie, Bernie Fredberg," as in Bond, James Bond.

Perhaps a flicker of recognition but the smile reserved for office supply salesmen remained unchanged, "Debbie Joslyn."

Bernie felt the momentary urge to point out that he could read the nameplate displayed inches from his belt buckle but held back with the wisdom that such response might prove counterproductive to his immediate goal.

"Welcome aboard. Say, I'm meeting a few friends at 7:30 at Gotham City, perhaps you'd care to join us?" Bernie had few friends and no prior plans for the evening, but these were meaningless technicalities.

Debbie turned the wattage up, "I'd love to Mr. Fredberg but I promised my husband I'd be home by 6:00. Perhaps another time." Saved by an incoming call, Debbie turned her attention away from the man sulking toward the bank of elevators.

Bernie's limousine was waiting in the basement garage; its uniformed driver holding open the rear door for the talk show host. The driver's customary greeting was dismissed with a scowl. While thousands of taxis cruised past the Madison Avenue studio hourly the limo was a perk Bernie had negotiated into his contract. Another yardstick that separated him from the army of radio personalities clawing their way up the listenership ladder. His show was miles away from the ratings of the conservatives such as Rush and Hannity, but he held strong positions in New York, New England, and California. Bernie's temporary fugue faded as he considered talking to the station manager about the new receptionist's uncooperative attitude.

His two-level condo in the Upper East Side at 81st and Lexington was only a ten-minute drive from the station. After a miserable winter, the warmth of spring had pushed its way into the eastern seaboard bringing New Yorkers out into its glorious sunshine. As they drove down Madison, the sidewalks swelled with pedestrians basking in the first warm day of the year. Bernie redirected his driver to the Stanhope on Central Park East and only a two-block walk from his condo. It was early enough to secure a table at the hotel's sidewalk café where he settled in with an early lunch and an hour of people watching. As cynical and jaded as he might be, Bernie still found the passing parade of humanity fascinating. Preppies and blue collar, grand dames and rockers, dog walkers, celebrities, and street people in an eclectic flow. School children and adults on their way to or from the Metropolitan Museum of Art across the street provided another color to the landscape.

When he paused from his study of the passing tapestry of mankind, Bernie considered how best to attack the president and his administration. His most recent focus had been on the continued involvement in Iraq, which he repeatedly labeled an illegal invasion, and the amount of money diverted from social programs into military spending. While still a bread and butter issue, he felt it was time to introduce a new battlefield. President Prescott had campaigned heavily on controlling the southern border to protect the country from terrorism and illegal drugs. Thinly veiled but transparently obvious was the promise to stem the flow of illegal immigrants from Mexico. Unfortunately for Prescott's Democratic rival, who predicted dire consequences to the economy and the nation's relationship with its southern neighbor, the issue was enthusiastically embraced by the vast majority of the voting population. Bernie began sketching out how he could frame the administration's plans for increased border security in the most damning light.

As was his usual habit, Bernie ignored his building's doorman, picked up his mail, and rode the elevator to the fourth floor. He was half way across his living room thumbing through his stack of mail when he stopped and glanced toward the windows. He rarely closed the drapes, yet they were now pulled shut casting the room in shadows. His initial thought was that his cleaning lady had pulled them closed for some inexplicable reason. Bernie started toward the windows when he sensed movement to his right. Like everyone, Bernie had experienced fear at traumatic moments in his life. A thrashing by the schoolyard bully, his telephone call desperately trying to secure a date for the junior prom, waiting for an HIV test result, but none of these compared to the primitive visceral fear that now paralyzed him beyond thought, beyond speech.

The first shot hit Bernie high in the chest, knocking him to the floor. The sound was muffled by one of the sofa's throw cushions, and as the talk show host looked up in disbelief white stuffing floated through the room like snowflakes. While his body refused to respond, his mind stubbornly rejected the fact that he was dying. As the figure moved out of the shadows to stand over him, Bernie continued to tell himself that this was not really happening. All such rationalization ended as the second shot passed through his brain.

CHAPTER 2

While Bernie Fredberg's death made the front page of the New York Times, his unexpected demise rated briefer stories and less prominent placement in the balance of the nation's newspapers. Bernie was controversial and pugnaciously provocative but hardly beloved. Fewer mourners attended his memorial service than showed up at the last Tiny Tim Revival Tour.

Statements from the police referred to "promising leads" and "possible witnesses," but the continuing lack of substance gradually drove the story from the news. The cable news shows and the tabloids were briefly atwitter when it was leaked that the killing was clearly an execution with no pretense of a robbery gone bad.

Winnie La Blanc had never listened to Bernie's show, and the mention of his tragic end in the Washington Post failed to catch her attention. Winnie's world centered exclusively around self-promotion and issues facing the black community. It had been eight years since she had closed her tee shirt shop on Bourbon Street in New Orleans and relocated to the nation's capital to found We Are the People. The move to D.C. coincided with legally changing her name from Hester to Winnie (as in Mandela), donning African tribal dresses and appearing at any trial, labor dispute, political rally, or picnic that involved more than five black people.

Ms. La Blanc proved to be an effective fund raiser and quite adept at working the media. While We Are the People did not rival The Rainbow Coalition in scope, Winnie kept her overhead low and found the nonprofit business to be exceptionally lucrative. Most donations came from corporations threatened with charges of racial discrimination. To enhance her national presence, Winnie became one of the most vocal champions for reparation for the sins of slavery. In addition to media exposure, her public tirades on the subject garnered the support of the A.C.L.U. and pro bono legal support. The most immediate challenge facing the civil rights activist was her soon to be ex-husband. Arnie La Blanc found life as the spouse of the female version of Jessie Jackson to be less than satisfying. He detested D.C., and after years of silent displeasure finally told Winnie he was moving back to Louisiana with or without her. The choice was really no choice at all. Winnie was not about to walk away from the position she had carved out of the struggle for racial equality and the high six figure income that accompanied that role. The downside of the divorce was the big bite in Winnie's standard of living that would be coming from the alimony payments that would allow Arnie to live very large in Dixie.

Winnie was seething as she slammed the telephone receiver into its cradle effectively ending her conversation with her divorce attorney. She sat at her desk and briefly considered firing her counsel. It was so unfair that Arnie, who had never contributed an ounce of effort to help her launch her nonprofit career, should benefit to the tune of two hundred thousand a year from her sweat and tears. If anything, the lazy bastard had belittled her ambitions and ridiculed her talents. Unfortunately, Winnie had to admit that her lawyer, Lori Bernstein, was the biggest ball breaker between New York and Miami, and there was virtually no chance of finding a more aggressive replacement. She pushed herself away from her desk and made her way to the coffee machine outside her office. Pearlene Pounds, Winnie's administrative assistant/secretary/girl Friday, took one glance at her boss and became totally engrossed in an email response she was drafting. When Winnie La Blanc was pissed, most found it an opportune time to fade into the background. If the situation called for charm Winnie could lay it on with the best of them, but when a winsome demeanor was unnecessary, Ms. La Blanc could give new meaning to the term mean spirited. And then there was her size. Winnie was big as in NFL offensive lineman big. Even crazed crackhead muggers crossed the street to avoid a possible confrontation with this mountain of womanhood dressed like a tribal chief.

Hunger pangs alerted Winnie to the approaching lunch hour. She decided a substantial lunch at Little Amos's House of Ribs might be the best cure for her foul mood. Summer humidity had not yet arrived at the Capitol, and the restaurant on L was a short walk from the offices of We Are the People. Winnie shouldered her way through the lunchtime crowds as she made her way across Fifth and Sixth. For a moment, she was caught behind a cluster of people waiting at the corner of New York. Just as the light changed and the crowd surged into the intersection, a searing pain in her back dropped the huge woman to her knees. Winnie remained kneeling for a moment as several pedestrians passed, each avoiding eye contact with the black woman in the African print caftan staring sightlessly into the remaining seconds of her life. Only when Winnie collapsed face down on the sidewalk did several people stop to assist the now deceased leader of We Are the People, and none noticed the man who had thrust the thin blade into Winnie's heart.

The murder of a civil rights activist hit the news services like a tsunami. Winnie's killing was front page feature story material in newspapers across the country and television commentators bumped whatever topic they had previously planned to present to speculate on the crime. Several of the totally uninformed legal experts that inhabit the cable stations cited marital discord in the La Blanc household and hinted at Arnie La Blanc's involvement. Fortunately for Arnie, he was knocking back Budweisers with a few friends at the time of Winnie's passing, and more importantly, his gravy train ended with the death of his estranged wife. Several editorials compared Winnie's accomplishments to that of Martin Luther King, and political and business leaders who had truly hated the woman lauded her virtues to the point of sainthood.

The D.C. police were initially tight lipped, but media pressure quickly forced them to admit they had no viable leads. While holding back details regarding the method of the killing, they described it as an assassination and asked for assistance from anyone who had witnessed the murder. Their appeal bore no fruit.

CHAPTER 3

For tax reasons, his accountants had insisted on a permanent residence in a state devoid of state income tax. While several states qualified, Marc Philip Wellstone found Florida the only marginally acceptable choice. Theoretically this meant living in his Palm Beach home at least six months of the year, but when one's wealth stretched into the billions, theory and reality rarely coincided. He found the heat and humidity excessive during the warmer months and the area too crowded with snow birds during the colder seasons. Most of the time he rotated between his modest 35,000 square foot estate in Bel Air, the boutique vineyard in the Napa Valley, and the chalet in Aspen near Snowmass. His wife of the moment was lobbying for an ocean front villa near the Mauna Kea in Hawaii, but he was actively ignoring her arguments. He found the big island boring and the flight back and forth a waste of time, even in the comfort of his private jet.

What Marc did not find boring was the direction of politics in America. In college, Wellstone was drawn into the protest movement. The targets of the marches and rallies changed frequently, but the theme of dissent remained constant. One week it might be the evils of the oil industry and the next the administration's policies toward South America. Frequently, the protest focused on the virtues of socialism versus the greed of capitalism, a debate in which Marc, as a trust fund baby, somehow failed to see as hypocritical. He felt comfortable within the social environment of students and hangers on that held a primary interest in attacking the establishment. After college, the beard and fatigue jacket disappeared, but the distrust of those in power, and most specifically those that fell to the right of the political spectrum, remained. Marc found no irony between his deep-seated alienation of corporate America and making a great deal of money. Several well-placed investments in promising high-tech startups allowed millions to transcend into billions.

Massive wealth brought with it unexpected opportunities. For one thing, it proved to be a powerful aphrodisiac. Marc had never been particularly successful with the fairer sex. He was not so much ugly as unappealing. His features were soft and lacking definition, hair lank and lifeless, and his body thin and flaccid. Clothing hung on his gangly frame like discards handed down by an older brother, and Marc's posture and movements always appeared out of sync. All in all, not an appealing package. However, when Marc passed the five hundred million mark he became much better looking. Women who would never have noticed him in a crowd began hitting on him with gusto. When his net worth shot past a billion, he could not beat them off with a stick. He married Trish, his first wife, after the briefest of courtships. It had, as he later told friends, seemed like a good idea at the time. She was beautiful and bright, fun to be with, and attentive to his every need. While beautiful and bright remained, fun and attentive faded like last summer's roses. In less than a year they were avoiding each other at every opportunity. The marriage was dissolved with little acrimony and a modest army of attorneys. A prenup kept the financial bite quite reasonable. After a brief interval of interviewing, Sandra, an aspiring actress, became wife number two. While still in the happy stage, Marc was beginning to wonder if he would have been prudent to have extended the interviewing process.

Another benefit of virtually limitless financial resources was the ability to nurture and direct political discourse. For several years, Marc had contributed to the traditional liberal causes and to candidates running on the Democratic Party ticket. He was at the top of everyone's list for fund raisers. More recently, he decided to dramatically increase his financial commitment to political and cultural change in the United States and to do so in a far more directed manner. His attorneys formed a series of political action committees through which Marc staged well-funded and professionally orchestrated attacks on the politicians and causes he viewed as the enemy. While the Republican led administration and its policies were the primary focus of the attack ads, challenges were also directed at support for military spending, any change seen as a threat to the environment and to policies he viewed as beneficial to corporate America. Previously, Marc Wellstone's name was only known to the financial community and to professional fundraisers. Once the P.A.C.s began their relentless barrage his name became as well-known as any household product. He was an icon to the far left and a symbol of the misuse of wealth to the right. Marc took equal pleasure from the praise of those supporting his program to shift American political thought as he did the virulent criticism directed at him from the nation's conservatives.

A man in Marc's position surrounded himself with security. State of the art electronics safeguarded each of his residences and a team of former FBI agents offered better protection than that enjoyed by third world dictators. For a self-proclaimed man of the people, Marc spent little time rubbing elbows with the huddled masses. Dining in a restaurant required special arrangements, isolation from the general public and tables strategically located and manned by his personnel. Vacations incorporated all the logistics of the beach landing at Normandy. It was rare that Marc rejected the requirements imposed by Richard Hillman, his chief of security, but one of those exceptions was when Marc wanted to play with one of his toys. The latest was a twin turbo Porsche. Wellstone enjoyed fast cars and driving in the middle of a convoy of vehicles filled with his security personnel provided no rush. When he wanted to satisfy his need for speed, he would tell Hillman his planned route; local police would be notified and Wellstone's security personnel would be scattered along the way. A helicopter filled with well-armed team members would shadow the Porsche until it arrived back in its garage. It goes without saying that speeding tickets were not a concern.

While it may appear hypocritical for a man dedicated to attacking the bastions of conservatism, Marc had campaigned for years to become a member of San Francisco's Pacific Union Club, perhaps for the sole reason that they did not want him in their organization. The P.U. Club was an anomaly, a private men's club whose membership was largely comprised of conservative old money sitting in the heart of the most liberal city in the nation. Wellstone had applied enough financial pressure on two of the members to be nominated and seconded, but the membership committee had, to date, viewed Marc as something they had stepped in on the sidewalk. Therefore, the note he received came as a complete surprise.

Dear Mr. Wellstone,

We would appreciate your attendance at the Pacific Union Club at 7:30 pm on May 14th to discuss your application for membership.

Your meeting will be with Mr. Douglas Brent, Mr. Harold Evens Johanson and Mr. Richard Collins of our membership committee.

Thank you for your interest in joining our organization.
Very truly yours,
Bennett Hayes Ford
President

Marc felt a surge of annoyance when he noted there was no request for a response. Meetings were always set at his convenience, not for that of others. He also knew that a request for a change of date or time would be the same as withdrawing his application. The attraction of sitting in a wing backed chair in the club library, surrounded by cigar smoking conservatives that hated his guts was beyond temptation. There was no way Marc would miss the meeting on the 14th.

———

Wellstone pushed the papers he had been reviewing back into his briefcase as the Gulfstream feathered in for a perfect landing at S.F.O. He had arrived just after 5:00, in time to catch an early dinner before his meeting with the membership committee. A limo driven by one of his security team was waiting on the tarmac. Within minutes, Marc, Hillman, and two other security team members climbed into the limo, drove out of the terminal and onto the freeway. The evening commuter traffic on 101 moved along well until Silver where it came to a virtual stop. Wellstone became impatient as they inched along the last few miles into the city.

"This is bullshit. Take the next exit."

The driver shook his head. "I can take Cesar Chavez and go up Third, but I'm not sure it'll be any faster."

"I don't remember asking for your opinion."

Without comment, the driver exited the freeway and drove up what used to be called Army. Small businesses and light industry lined the street until they turned north on Third where the neighborhood became residential, poorer, and blacker. With signals at nearly every intersection and the street clogged with drivers making their way home, the passing scene became a poor man's version of street theater. Several of the black men standing in clusters along the street turned to watch the limo pass, obviously an alien vehicle in the Potrero Hill District. The landscape began to perk up economically as they approached China Basin and the Third Street Bridge. It was nearing 6:00 by the time they reached Gary Danko's on the edge of Ghirardelli Square, a good twenty minutes past Marc's reservation. Officially the restaurant did not open until 6:30, but special arrangements had been made for Wellstone.

Marc took a table near the center of the dining room as his cadre of security personnel huddled near the bar and entrance. He hated to be rushed at dinner. He interrupted the waiter as the man began to explain the specials of the day. "I'm in a hurry. A small Cesar, the lamb medium rare and a bottle of Harlan cab if you have the '99."

The waiter scurried off to expedite Marc's dinner leaving Wellstone alone to survey the tastefully furnished dining room. He used the time to consider the implications of membership in the P.U. Club. He had always enjoyed San Francisco; perhaps it now made sense to pick up a place in the city. He made a mental note to contact his realtor if the meeting went as planned.

He was on his second glass of wine and only halfway through his entrée when a glance at his watch confirmed he had run out of time. Marc paid his tab and was in the limo within minutes. The Pacific Union Club was perched at the top of Nob Hill, slightly more than two miles from the restaurant. The private club occupied and entire city block and possessed the unique grandeur that said old money and exclusivity. Originally built in 1886 by James Leary Flood, it had served as a tribute to the family's immense wealth and power. The fire of 1906 left it little more than a shell. After the fire, the Flood Mansion, as it is still known, was purchased by the Pacific Union Club and restored by Willis Polk.

When the limo pulled in front of the club's entrance, Hillman and two of his team slid out of the vehicle and began to accompany the billionaire. He dismissed them with a wave of his hand. "Wait outside. I don't know how long this is going to take."

Hillman stepped closer to his employer. "Sir, let me come in with you."

Marc's expression was a blend of annoyance and anger. "Don't be stupid. You think the members here walk around the club with their security people? Maybe I should tell the membership committee that whenever I'm here they need to make accommodations for my bodyguards?"

Richard Hillman wisely assumed the question was rhetorical. He stood on the sidewalk and watched Wellstone disappear behind the club's stately doors.

A uniformed butler appeared as Marc stood in the entry. "Marc Wellstone. I'm here to meet with Douglas Bent, Harold Johanson, and Richard Collins."

The butler nodded politely, "I have not seen the gentlemen, but perhaps they escaped my notice. If you would be so kind as to wait in the library I will try to locate them."

He led Marc to a stately room on the second floor with high ceilings, wood paneling, and a sprinkling of deep leather chairs. A mammoth fireplace dominated one wall of the room. Each cluster of chairs was accompanied by end tables and reading lamps giving the otherwise dimly lit room small islands of light. Two elderly men were seated near the unlit fireplace reading newspapers, otherwise the room was empty. Marc selected a chair in a grouping facing away from the newspaper readers.

He had been seated for a few minutes when the butler reappeared. "Sir, you have a telephone call, the caller said it was an emergency. If you will be so kind as to follow me, I'll show you where to take the call."

He had left explicit instructions not to be interrupted during his meeting. The Pacific Union Club was a sanctuary from cell phones and business calls. This type of interruption was the type of thing that could keep him off the membership list. Unless the call was truly of epic importance, Marc vowed to fire the caller.

The butler led Marc to an isolated hallway and to a remarkably out of date telephone. Wellstone sensed a hint of disapproval as the butler turned and walked away. Marc was sure the call was going to get back to the membership committee. A man dressed as a kitchen worker was walking down the short hallway towards him as he picked up the receiver.

"Hello, who is this?" Marc made no effort to disguise his anger. Before he could hear the reply, his hand that held the receiver was pushed away from his ear and a wire garrote slipped over his head. He tried to shout, but no sound occurred as the wire sliced through the billionaire's vocal cords. Marc stared in confusion at the wall before him as a spray of blood appeared on the dark wood paneling. Then there was only darkness.

CHAPTER 4

It had only been ten days, but the apartment had the feel of abandonment. Jon walked past the pile of mail his landlady had neatly stacked by the door and lugged his gear into the living room. He dumped his pack on the floor and headed straight into the bathroom, stripped, and stepped into the shower running the water as hot as he could stand. Communing with nature might be a near religious experience, but a steaming hot shower after two weeks of bathing in frigid streams had to approach a blessed act.

He left the door to the bathroom open, but steam still filmed the mirror above the sink. Jon threw on a bathrobe and went back into the kitchen to listen to messages on his machine. There were surprisingly few. His mother, who always worried when he made his solo treks into the mountains, had made several calls, but Jonathan had talked to her from his cell on the drive home. Two messages were from his agent, neither leaving an adequate reason to respond; one was from Gale, the woman he was currently spending time with, and one from Cal Hulse. Cal fell into a category somewhere between brother and closest friend. Gale's message was almost institutional, "Hi, call me when you're back from doing your thing."

Cal's was more specific, "Poker game Wednesday night."

Jonathan stared at his image in the mirror for a moment before picking up the razor. He was two weeks past his normal haircut appointment and had not bothered to shave during his trip. He looked like an extra from *Deliverance*. He stayed around his lip first, toying with the idea of leaving a mustache. One look at the mirror and he polished off his upper lip.

He opened a beer, brought his stack of mail over to the sofa in his small living room area, and turned on MSNBC. Jon began sorting out the junk mail as he half listened to a debate over the constitutionality of military tribunals being conducted at Guantanamo. The next feature story captured his undivided attention.

The host adopted an expression of earnest concern as a picture of Marc Wellstone appeared in the upper right corner of the screen. "Yesterday evening Marc Philip Wellstone was found murdered in San Francisco's prestigious Pacific Union Club." A shot of the front of the P.U. Club appeared on the screen. "Details of the crime have not yet been released, but we have been able to set the time of death at approximately 8:00 pm.

"Marc Wellstone has been one of the largest donors to the Democratic Party and to progressive causes over the past decade." The screen shifted back to the host in the studio, now seated next to one of the station's resident legal experts. "Doesn't it seem ironic, Helen, that Wellstone's death occurred inside what is probably San Francisco's last enclave of conservatives? The place had to be filled with people who hated the man. Talk about a room full of suspects."

Helen Wassman smiled into the camera. "Absolutely Ken, and I can add one more interesting tidbit. My sources in the DA's office told me the victim's body was discovered by the club's butler. How many references to *Clue* are we going be seeing as this story plays out? The butler did it in the library with a candlestick."

The host's charismatic smile was replaced with one reserved for grim events. "I'm sure you're right Helen. But in all seriousness, this has to come as major financial blow to the organizations he supported. Without his contributions P.A.C.s like Freedom First and Sound Off for America might not be able to continue. Wellstone's death could change the landscape of America's politics."

Helen Wassman offered a knowing smile. "You could be right. And how about that for motive?"

Ken Fowler turned back to the camera. "We'll be following this story as it unfolds. We also can't ignore the impact on those close to the victim. Marc Philip Wellstone, age thirty-six, leaves a wife Sandra and parents Steven and Bernice Wellstone.

The program shifted to a story about strengthening the levee system in New Orleans as Jonathan thought about Marc Wellstone's death. The billionaire was the subject of the third chapter of Jon's recently released book, *Culprits of the American Culture*. As might be deduced from the title, the chapter did not present the man in a favorable light. Jon had never met Wellstone, his requests for a personal interview went unanswered, but from his research he knew a great deal about the billionaire. Everything he had learned pointed to an unpleasant man consumed by arrogance. Wellstone's most redeeming characteristic was his commitment to his beliefs. The man never wavered in his view of a radically changed America, and he supported those visions with mammoth financial contributions.

Jon knew the billionaire's murder would dominate the news for months. His thoughts drifted away as he found a *Law and Order* rerun he had missed.

CHAPTER 5

Jon enjoyed his morning routine. After his shower and shave ritual, he sat at the kitchen table with a glass of fresh squeezed orange juice, a mug of coffee, and the Chronicle. This morning's edition did not disappoint. Headlines in two-inch type screamed **BILLIONAIRE MURDERED AT P.U. CLUB.** Jon skimmed through the featured story. The article stretched the meager set of facts over two pages. Another article eulogized Marc Wellstone as a progressive, a benefactor of environmental causes, and a man who challenged the fascist agenda of the current administration. The San Francisco Chronicle was never one to confuse reporting with editorializing.

He skimmed through the rest of the paper until he reached the Sporting Green. The sports section's banner was a holdover from when it had been printed on green tinted paper. Why the section was still called the Sporting Green remained a mystery. It took a second mug of coffee to digest the Bay Area's college and professional football, baseball, and basketball news. It was a mixed bag of good and bad stories for the teams Jonathan followed. Cal, his alma mater, was touting the impact of several newly recruited football players, but the highly regarded men's basketball coach had bailed out for a more lucrative deal at North Carolina. The Niners were gushing with self-congratulations over the quality of their draft picks, but more objective voices around the league appeared less impressed and the Raiders were in a legal battle over the rights to the Los Angeles market. Not that much had changed during Jon's week in the woods.

The balance of the morning was spent organizing his notes for the two Contemporary English Lit classes he taught to a room full of uninterested students at San Francisco State. He had issued reading assignments to be completed during spring break, an assignment he was sure most had ignored. William Faulkner's, *Light in August* or a week partying in Mazatlán, not a difficult choice for most twenty-year olds. Jon finally picked up the phone and reluctantly dialed his literary agent, Harvey Balkin. Jonathan had read countless acknowledgements by authors praising the support and brilliance of their agents. While he did not discount the role of agents in the literary food chain, Jon did not care for Harvey. Like most unpublished authors, Jonathan had signed up with the only agent willing to accept him as a client. He found Balkin condescending and pretentious. *Culprits of the American Culture* had been accepted by a small publisher in the Midwest for a ten thousand book print run. The publisher spent virtually nothing on promotion and appeared to use *Culprits* as a filler on its nonfiction list.

Balkin's Beacon Hill accent reminded Jon of Charles Emerson Winchester III on *MASH*. "Harvey Balkin here."

"Hi Harvey, it's Jonathan Scanlan. I'm returning your call. Don't tell me, *Culprits* just showed up on the best sellers list."

"Where have you been?" Humor had never had a strong effect on Harvey.

"I'm fine Harvey, thanks for asking. And how have you been?"

"You know about Marc Wellstone?"

"Sure, it's all over the news."

"How about Bernie Fredberg and Winnie La Blanc?"

"What are you talking about Harvey?"

Balkin paused for a moment before he answered, "They were both murdered last week."

The news jolted Jon into silence. Fredberg had been the subject of the first chapter of *Culprits* and La Blanc the second. Scanlan was having difficulty collecting his thoughts. "Were they together?"

"What…no, of course not. Fredberg was killed in New York and Winnie La Blanc in Washington. Both murders were heavily covered by the media last week. I can't believe you missed it."

Jonathan's thoughts were racing down a dozen paths as Balkin's nasal tones pushed him back into the conversation. "I have no idea how this will affect book sales." The real reason for Harvey's calls revealed.

"We can only hope, Harvey. Hey, I've got to run or I'm going to be late for my class," an excuse to end the call. Jon had hours to spare before he had to leave.

He sat down at his computer and went on the internet. He Googled Bernie Fredberg and Winnie La Blanc, and within twenty minutes knew as much as there was to know about their untimely deaths. If three of the thirty-five people he had written about died within a brief period of time, it could be accepted as a coincidence. To have three people murdered within a two-week period, all execution style, and in the sequence in which they were discussed in the book stretched the boundaries of probability. There was no question in his mind that the killings were somehow linked to *Culprits*, but why? And more to the point, what could he do about it?

Jonathan dialed the non-emergency number for the San Francisco Police Department. He asked the operator to be routed to whoever was handling the Marc Wellstone case.

The operator's voice was emotionless and mechanical. "Were you a witness to the crime?"

"No."

"Are you a reporter?"

"No."

"What is this regarding?"

"I have information that might be helpful to the police."

"What information would that be?" The call screening was becoming wearisome.

"Just connect me with someone."

There was a pause on the line before a recorded message began playing. "You've reached Sergeant Daniel Patriquin. Please leave a message." Jonathan's initial reaction was to mention he had, in fact, not reached Sergeant Patriquin. He decided on a less confrontational approach. "My name is Jonathan Scanlan. My telephone number is 555-3421. I've written a book titled *Culprits of the American Culture.* The first three chapters were devoted to Bernie Fredberg, Winnie La Blanc, and Marc Wellstone. As I'm sure you are aware, these three people were all murdered recently. I don't understand what connection my book has to these crimes, but I can't believe it's a coincidence. I'm leaving now, but I'll be home this evening after 9:30."

The completion of his civic duty did nothing to dispel Jonathan's feeling of uneasiness as he drove across the city.

CHAPTER 6

The blanket of fog covering the western half of the city fell short of the Marina District, but chill winds had dropped the temperature down to the 40s. Carmen Costello sat in her car watching the front of a three-story apartment building on the north side of Green. Every parking space within a two-block radius had been taken when she arrived, forcing her to park illegally at the corner. Her third cup of coffee had worked through her system, and if Scanlan did not show in the next fifteen minutes, she was going to have to find a restroom. Costello was about to abandon her vigil and walk down to Union Street when a tall man turned the corner and strolled past her Crown Victoria. She glanced at the photograph on the dust cover of the book beside her and compared it to the man as he passed under a streetlight.

Costello was out of the car and hustling to catch up to Jonathan before he reached the door to his building. "Mr. Scanlan."

Jon turned to see a short dark-haired woman in a heavy coat standing at the bottom of his stairs. She was holding something in her hand but was too far away for him to make out what it was. "Special Agent Costello with the FBI." Costello studied Jonathan's face for his reaction but noticed only mild interest.

"Is this about my phone call to the police?"

"They kicked it over to us. Can we go inside?"

"Sure." Jon unlocked the exterior door and led the FBI agent to his unit on the second floor. Costello glanced around the living room and kitchen. The only thing that caught her eye was the volume of books stacked in uneven piles on the floor.

"Big reader?"

"Part business, part pleasure. I teach contemporary English lit. at San Francisco State."

Costello took off her coat and draped it over a chair. "May I use your bathroom?"

"Of course." Jon pointed toward a short hallway. "Second door on the left." He wondered if this was the result of a real need or another way of examining his habits. As he watched the agent make her way to the bathroom, he was surprised by how petite she was. He thought she would have fallen short of whatever the Bureau set as a minimum height requirement.

When she came back into the room, Jonathan was seated in one of the living room chairs. She waved him back as he began to stand. Jon noticed that Agent Costello was attractive in an offbeat tomboy way. "Please, don't get up. Mr. Scanlan, what do you make of the connection between your book and the murders?"

"I don't have a clue. It can't be a coincidence, I mean how could it be? Three people killed in the same sequence that they appear in *Culprits*. What would be the odds?"

The agent stared at Jon for a moment before responding, "Yes, what would be the odds?" Jon felt uncomfortable with Costello's intense expression. "How well is your book selling?"

A few dominos fell into place. "Not well. Are you suggesting I ran around the country murdering prominent liberals to push the sales of my book?"

Costello shrugged, "I'm not suggesting anything. But just out of curiosity, where were you during the period of the killings?"

Jonathan felt a rush of anger, "This is bullshit. Remember, I called you, well . . . the police anyway. Why would I do that if I had any connection to these murders?"

"I've found people do all types of strange things, but you haven't answered my question. Where were you?"

Jon's first impulse was to throw the petite agent out of his apartment. Common sense prevailed as he realized he was being deliberately provoked. "I was trout fishing in the Trinity Alps."

"You have someone who can back this up?"

Jonathan's anger shifted to concern. "I don't know. I was by myself. I do this every year during spring break. I might have some receipts from a store up there."

Costello's eyes gave nothing away. Jon could not tell if she was seriously considering him as a suspect or simply fishing. "You must be desperate if you're looking at me. I'll tell you where you should be spending your time."

The agent did not bother to respond. "Watching Judge Joseph Carlson."

The conversational diversion caused a break in Carmen Costello's focus. Jonathan felt an immature sense of satisfaction at her blank expression. "Why should I be watching Judge Carlson?"

"Because he's chapter four."

CHAPTER 7

The sound of her footsteps echoed down the corridor as Carmen Costello walked toward her cubicle in the nearly deserted Federal Building. It was late, she was tired, and she wanted to be home in bed, but she could not ignore Scanlan's comment. The San Francisco police had passed the call over to the FBI when multiple murders in three different states were mentioned. Costello was the most junior agent in the San Francisco office; therefore, she was given the task of running down what was believed to be a low-quality lead. None of the bookstores she called in the city had a copy of *Culprits of the American Culture*. She finally found one at Book Passages in Corte Madera, which had meant another hour in the car driving to Marin County and back. She had skimmed the chapters devoted to Fredberg, La Blanc, and Wellstone before her meeting with Scanlan but had not had time to think through the connection.

She sat at her workstation and tried to think through what she had to do. *Culprits* was such an obscure book no one in law enforcement had seen it to connect it to the killings. Until now, the three murders were being handled as individual cases by the police in New York, Washington, and San Francisco. Linking the killings shifted the case to the Bureau, and the nature of who had been murdered would elevate the investigation to the director level. Her momentary flush of pride over her role in tying the assassinations to the book was quickly extinguished at the thought of what would happen to her career if Judge Carlson was killed while she was sitting on the information. She quickly dialed Ross Del Monica's emergency number. Del Monica was the station chief of the Bureau's San Francisco office, and in Carmen's opinion, a real asshole.

He answered on the second ring. Carmen could hear a television in the background. "This is Carmen Costello. I'm sorry to disturb you, but something important has come up."

"What is it Agent Costello?" A hint of irritation in his voice.

"I've come across something that links the murders of Bernie Fredberg, Winnie La Blanc and Marc Wellstone."

There was a pause. "Who's Bernie Fredberg?"

"A left-wing radio talk show guy who was killed in New York about two weeks ago."

"Why do you believe there's a connection?" Carmen could hear the doubt in Del Monica's voice.

"A San Francisco author named Jonathan Scanlan recently published a book titled *Culprits of the American Culture*. The first three chapters were about Fredberg, La Blanc, and Wellstone."

"This was worth the emergency call?"

"Fredberg, the first victim, was chapter one, La Blanc the second victim, chapter two, and Wellstone chapter three. The crimes occurred in a time span of less than two weeks, and all three weren't just killed, they were assassinated with no pretense at robbery or assault."

"What do we know about this author?" More interest now.

"Not much. He teaches English literature at San Francisco State. I met with him tonight."

"Could he be the doer?"

"He doesn't have a good alibi, trout fishing in the woods alone when Fredberg and La Blanc got it and home alone in his apartment when Wellstone was killed, but I don't think so."

"Based on your vast range of experience?" Del Monica made no attempt to mask the sarcasm.

Costello bit back her anger, "No. He just seems too squared away. I agree we need to look at him, but he wasn't rattled when I showed up. His reactions were normal when I pushed him."

"We'll see. Give me his address."

"1906 Green Street, apartment 2B. I'm worried about the safety of the other people discussed in the book. Chapter four is devoted to Judge Joseph Carlson of the Ninth District Court of Appeals."

Another pause, "Right. I'll make some calls and line up protection for the judge."

"What do you want me to do?"

"Make a list of the other people that are in this book and leave it on my desk. If these killings are connected this is going to be huge." Carmen could hear the wheels turning in Del Monica's head as her boss considered how he might take credit for the discovery.

———

The man sat on a folding chair in the back of the Econoline van positioned across the street from Judge Carlson's home. Magnetic signs on the van's doors indicated it was owned by R. Johnson Plumbing of Oakland, and the windows were heavily tinted making it virtually impossible to see inside the vehicle. He was pleased that the judge was as predictable as most people. Every morning at 7:00 Carlson went outside in his robe to pick up his newspaper and to allow his Cocker Spaniel to relieve himself on the front lawn. At 8:30 the garage door opened, and the judge backed his Volvo sedan out onto the street and turned north toward an access road to Highway 80 and the Bay Bridge.

Mary Carlson's habits were less routine. The judge's wife frequently spent the entire day inside the Spanish style stucco home. When she did leave home, she did so at different times and drove away in different directions. The man in coveralls sitting patiently in the van had no interest in Mary Carlson other than to know when she tended to be in her house in the Berkeley hills and which vehicle each member of the family drove. The man closed his notebook and shifted to the front of the van. He was satisfied that the information he had collected over several days was adequate. He had considered tapping the judge's phone and installing listening devices within the home but had rejected the additional steps as unnecessary.

As he drove down the sedate tree line street, a plan began to form in his mind.

CHAPTER 8

The last stragglers had to stand in the crowded briefing room. Del Monica tapped the rostrum impatiently to end the buzz of conversations. While it was too early to bring the press into the investigation, he knew he would be briefing the regional director later in the morning via teleconference and had selected a gray pinstriped suit and muted burgundy tie for the occasion. He had made a note in his planner to order a new suit from Brooks Brothers if the case reached the director level.

"Alright, settle down. We have discovered what appears to be a connection between the assassinations of three prominent people." He had decided to use the term assassination at every opportunity, believing it had greater impact than killing or murder. He glanced down at his notes to be sure he had the correct names. "On April 28th, Bernard Fredberg was shot to death in Manhattan. On May 8th, Winnie La Blanc was stabbed to death in Washington D.C., and as I'm sure you are aware, Marc Wellstone was garroted three days ago at the Pacific Union Club. The apparent connection is to a book titled *Culprits of the American Culture*, it was written by a San Francisco author name . . ." Del Monica again glanced at his notes. "Jonathan Scanlan. The first chapter talked about Fredberg, the second La Blanc, and the third Wellstone." The agent paused to let the point sink in. "Another linkage is that all three victims are nationally known figures and very active in what might be called the political left. I want Stone, Lawrence, Kitashima, and Bassillio to focus on Marc Wellstone's murder. Lee, Aylworth, Rubin, and Marsh dig into this author. Rocha, pull together a team to provide protection to others mentioned in this book that reside within our jurisdiction. Start with Judge Joseph Carlson who is the subject of chapter four."

Del Monica held up his hand as several agents started to collect their coffee mugs and notes, "I'll be speaking with the regional director in a few hours, and I would hope we'll be given the lead on this. This could become the largest case this office has ever handled, so I want your very best."

Agent Costello remained standing against the wall as the room emptied. It was not lost on her that not only was her contribution in establishing the connection not mentioned, but Del Monica had not bothered to assign her to the investigation. She made no secret of the fact that she considered Del Monica to be an empty suit, a man more consumed with his own ambition and appearance than achieving meaningful results. Carmen had toyed with the thought of requesting a transfer to another office, but such a move was considered career limiting particularly for a new agent. By the time she reached her workstation and checked her inner office messages, she found she had been assigned to Judge Carlson on the midnight to eight shift.

———

Jonathan stretched out on the sofa with a beer and surveyed the condominium. Everywhere he looked, he saw sports paraphernalia. Framed Joe Montana and Steve Young jerseys were in positions of prominence, as were two of Jerry Rice; one from his days with the Niners and one from the Raiders. Signed programs from Barry Bonds, Jason Schmidt, and Steve Finley were wedged between signed baseballs and football helmets resting on Plexiglas stands. A basketball signed by the 1975 championship Warrior team rested on a stand at the center of the coffee table. While most of the collectables related to the local teams, a fair amount was tied to sports figures from beyond the Bay

Area. Signed score cards from Palmer, Player, and Nicklaus sat where one would expect to see family photos. Baseballs that had played prominent roles in World Series games rested in holders in the bookcase. It was a sports nut's Disneyland.

Unlike his former college roommate and close friend, Jon found no interest in sports collectables. Scanlan and Cal Hulse were polar opposites. Hulse was a brilliant programmer, a rock star in tech circles, and Jon could not figure out the basic features of his cell phone. While Cal spent a significant amount of his discretionary income on his paraphernalia collection and knew the batting average of every member of the 1962 Yankees, he could not throw a baseball across the driveway. In contrast Jonathan was a gifted athlete. In high school, he had been a star outfielder on the baseball team and a scratch golfer. He turned down several baseball scholarships to concentrate on his first love, golf. He collected shelves of trophies through high school and college, but his dreams of making the tour ended when he twice failed to make the cut at Q school. Scanlan was a lean six foot two while his friend was a pliable five foot nine. As different as they were in appearance and skills, a mutual bond of trust and respect had emerged during their time in college that remained intact in the years that followed.

The weather had been pleasant, and Jon had walked from his apartment to Cal's place on Pacific. He had arrived early to tell his friend about his visit from Special Agent Costello and the connection between the killings and *Culprits* before the other poker players filtered in. Hulse remained uncharacteristically silent as he listened to Jon's story. Unlike Jonathan, Cal was not a reader and had done no more than skim his friend's book.

"Were you able to find any receipts from your fishing trip?"

Jon shook his head. "No, but I used my credit card a few times when I bought gas and at a market in Weaverville."

"Did you mention this to this FBI person?"

"No, I didn't think of it at the time. When she started asking me to come up with an alibi, I lost it. It's not fun to sit there and be accused of being some type of a mass murderer."

Cal waved off the explanation, "I wouldn't worry about it. I'm sure they're putting you under a microscope right now. They'd have to be totally incompetent if they didn't check out your credit card history."

The doorbell sounded announcing the first of the arriving players. Hulse glanced back at Jon as he went to buzz in his guests. "This is serious shit, but I can't see them staying with you beyond an initial look."

Neither Jon nor Cal mentioned Scanlan's situation once their friends arrived. The game was always nickel, dime, quarter with no one winning or losing more than thirty dollars in an evening. The group was a collection of Cal's friends, which meant it resembled a Mensa meeting. In addition to Cal and Jon, the group included a physicist named Carlos, a research biologist from Genentech named Greg, and two electronic engineers who designed advanced weapons systems at Lockheed. With the exception of Jon, the group was incredibly homogenous. Without exception, they possessed stratospheric intelligence, were horrible poker players, and dressed like Polish refugees. Carlos Hermosillo applied a decision theory formula to every hand while Greg Stokes alternated between folding before he saw the other players cards and running a bluff against solid hands. Cal tended to remain in the game too long and Alan from Lockheed tended to become agitated when he had winning cards. Harold, the other Lockheed player, was unreasonably committed to an obscure probability theory. Jon was normally assured of walking away the winner, but this evening his thoughts were far from the game and he left with a lighter wallet.

CHAPTER 9

Two agents sat in a Suburban parked in front of the Carlson home. Ross Del Monica had come up against a stone wall when he tried to talk the judge into inside and outside protection teams. Joseph Roth Carlson was the most liberal judge on the most liberal federal court in the land. The Ninth District Circuit Court of Appeals set records as the court with the most overturned decisions in the United States and Judge Carlson considered it an honor to have rendered more of those decisions than any of his colleagues. Carlson publicly acknowledged his commitment to shift the mores of the country to the left through judicial activism. His progressive agenda did not embrace the functions performed by America's military services, the CIA, NSA, and certainly not the FBI. In his view, the military and law enforcement agencies were tools of the fascist administration. There was no way on God's green earth he was about to allow two FBI agents access to his home without a court order.

Mary Carlson did not share her husband's skepticism, but neither she nor the station chief could effect a change in the judge's inflexible position. He also rejected the proposal that he be driven to and from his office by agents. Carlson reluctantly agreed to alter his schedule and the route he took on his commute to appease his wife. When Del Monica pressed for greater cooperation, the rail thin judge became livid. "Your job is to go out and catch whoever is committing these crimes, not to invade my privacy with these Gestapo tactics. How dense can you be? Any idiot could tell you it has to be some right-wing nut! What about this author? He does a hatchet job on progressives, and right after this obscure book is released the people he writes about start getting killed. Apparently, no one at the FBI can figure out that this just might boost the sale of the book?" When Del Monica tried to reply Carlson waved him off, "Get out of here and do your job, FBI agent." With that the tall gangly judge spun on the heel of his tasseled loafer and marched out of his living room.

The nightmare continued for the Bureau the following morning. Carlson gave no hint of what he had in mind as he allowed his escorts to trail him from home to the US Court of Appeals for the Ninth Circuit on Seventh Street. He parked in the underground garage, but instead of proceeding to his office, he made his way to the courthouse steps and the collection of waiting reporters and television cameras. He ignored the shouted questions as he glanced at the group with their shoulder held cameras and microphones. He blinked into the sunlight and held up his hand for silence.

"The lackeys of the administration have kept silent regarding a radical right-wing plot to systematically eliminate progressive leaders from the political landscape. The assassinations of Bernard Fredberg, Winnie La Blanc, and Marc Wellstone were the first stages of a plot to weaken the movement that is rescuing our country from the tyranny of the far right. This act of genocide is designed to quell the most strident voices of the liberal establishment. Well . . . . I will not be silenced. I understand I am possibly the next target of these murderers. Are we to allow death squads to roam our nation eliminating political dissent? You might also ask why this plot has not been made public. Why has the FBI kept this secret from the media? Could the genesis of this conspiracy rest within our government? I stand before you to demand public hearings to uncover the truth and to expose the involvement of those behind this murderous campaign. I urge Congress to investigate the handling of this investigation by the FBI and to provide oversight to insure the Bureau does its job."

A dozen questions were shouted at the judge. The reporter closest to Carlson shoved her microphone inches from his face and was able to gain his attention. "You called these killings a right-wing plot. Do you have proof that they were connected?"

The judge held up his clenched hand and extended a finger to emphasize each point. "One, they were all assassinated, not killed in a robbery or domestic dispute. Two, the three murders occurred within a brief span of time. Three, the victims were all leaders in the progressive movement. And four, they were all featured in a right-wing hate piece titled *Culprits of the American Culture.*"

The reporter's confused expression was mirrored by her colleagues. "What type of hate piece? Was this a magazine article?"

Carlson shook his head. "A book of lies and misrepresentations."

The judge found no reason to mention that he had not read the book and had no interest in doing so. "You asked for a connection? Mr. Fredberg was chapter one, Ms. La Blanc chapter two, and Mr. Wellstone chapter three. The exact sequence of the assassinations. I am the subject of chapter four."

A black reporter from Channel 7 pushed into the dialogue, "Who wrote this book and are they considered a suspect in these killings?"

The judge shrugged. "The author is a man named Scanlan, I don't remember his first name. You'll have to ask the FBI about his involvement. Perhaps they'll be more forthcoming with you than they are with me."

A print reporter from the Chronicle shouted into the void that followed the judge's response, "Judge Carlson, aren't you concerned about your own safety? What is being done to protect you?"

Carlson offered a tight smile and an expression of righteous indignation. "We can't be intimidated by these cowards. The far right has always been the refuge of the country's immoral bullies. They see the shift in the attitude of the American people, and they're frightened. We have an obligation to standup for what is right even if it puts us at risk." While he had no intention of mentioning it to the reporters, the judge had organized the courthouse press conference to remove himself from the assassins list. He reasoned the killers would realize he was now under federal protection, and that his every move would be chronicled by the media. If they wished to continue their mad plan there had to be easier targets to attack.

The FBI agents shadowing the judge watched the press conference with distaste. They knew their jobs would be made more difficult with the involvement of the press, and they, as well as Carlson, would now be operating in a public fishbowl.

CHAPTER 10

The first casualty of the Carlson press conference was Jon. He had just stepped into his classroom when he was waylaid by Constance Naify, the administrative assistant to the president of the college. As a part time untenured teacher, Jon had never met the woman and for that matter had never had a private conversation with her boss, Irene Woods. Naify was a pleasant woman, but uncomfortable in adversarial situations. When Jon told her, he had a classroom full of waiting students, Connie blushed as she shook her head. "President Woods insisted you meet with her immediately."

Sensing the futility of arguing, Jon shrugged and followed the assistant to the Administration Building. He could tell he was not being summarily summoned to be complimented on his stellar work, but no reason for a tongue lashing came to mind. And why the college president? If he had violated some minor rule, it would be the department head's responsibility to dole out the criticism.

His stomach tightened when he was led into the conference room adjacent to the president's office. Four people were seated at one end of the table, and Jon could tell the meeting had been underway well before his arrival. Connie Naify acted like she had just dropped the prisoner off at the torture chamber as she turned without a word and beat a hasty retreat. Jon recognized Woods, Jeffrey Livingston his department head, and Rosa Ortega from Human Resources. He had never before seen the fourth person at the table. Scanlan heard Connie close the door behind him as he waited for someone to tell him what was happening.

No one bothered to stand up to greet the latest arrival, another not very good sign. Finally, Irene Woods broke the silence. "Mr. Scanlan, please sit down. I believe you know Jeffrey and Rosa. This is William Fisher." The middle-aged man in a dark suit nodded but made no other effort to acknowledge his new acquaintance. "We are here to discuss what action to take as a result of your involvement in the investigation of these . . . these political killings."

Jon could not believe this was happening, "I have no involvement."

Fisher leaned forward in his chair as if to add emphasis to his words. "That's not what Judge Joseph Carlson said in his news conference today. I believe he said the FBI considered you as a suspect."

A surge of anger replaced Jon's initial feeling of disorientation. "I don't care what Carlson said. My only connection to the crimes is my book, *Culprits of the American Culture*. Three of the people profiled in the book have been killed, that's it."

Woods stepped back into the conversation, "That may be so, but we have to protect the university's reputation."

"What about my reputation? I haven't been charged with any crime. I assume the topic of the moment is firing me. What are the grounds for terminating me?"

Irene Woods motioned toward the man in the dark suit, "That is why we have asked Mr. Fisher to join us. His specialty is labor law." William Fisher smiled at the introduction as he continued to study Jonathan.

Fisher was about to speak when Rosa Ortega interjected herself into the discussion, "You are not being terminated. While the matter is under review, you will be placed on paid leave of absence."

"Will I be allowed to participate in this review?"

Woods provided the answer, "We'll let you know. That will be all. Please give Ms. Ortega your parking pass and faculty ID."

No one in the room spoke as Jonathan stood, placed his identification badge and electronic entry card for the faculty parking lot on the table, and walked out of the conference room.

The drive back to his apartment went by in a blur. Jon replayed the dialogue of the meeting and his exchanges with Irene Woods and the attorney in his mind as he drove home. He knew the college would act to protect itself and that their decision regarding his future had been determined before he ever entered the conference room. What he did not know was what he could do to salvage his future.

CHAPTER 11

There was no reason to join the motorcade, he knew where the judge was going. The man and woman stood and listened to Carlson's statement and his exchange with the press. The assassin was dressed in a conservative gray suit, white shirt, and muted tie. His appearance blended well with the lawyers, witnesses, and federal employees entering and leaving the building. The woman wore an unremarkable blouse and skirt and no jewelry to be noticed and remembered. His hair, now dyed a light blond, was longer that his usual military cut, and the Oakley sunglasses obscured part of his face. She also wore sunglasses, the large round lenses and heavy frames that were popular a few years ago. The makeup she wore was designed to disguise her beauty and her clothes to hide her figure. They stood in the cluster of onlookers beyond the reporters and cameramen, positioned opposite the judge and away from any of the cameras recording the event. They neither spoke nor showed any emotion as they observed the news conference. The man did take note of the positions of Carlson's protective detail.

———

Richard Owens was watching a CNN feature on famine in the Sudan when the network cut away to a breaking story. He recorded the segment and began scribbling notes as he watched Judge Joseph Roth Carlson's hastily organized press conference. Owens played back the brief recording several times until he was confident his notes were accurate. He ignored the comments of the CNN reporter on site as he dialed the chief of staff.

The call was fielded by Marge Carrol, Eugene Baronian's assistant. Owens accepted the screening process as necessary, but it was never pleasant. Marge screened all of Baronian's calls and used her judgment to determine which callers were worthy of the chief of staff's attention just as Baronian filtered out most of the requests for contact with the president. While the speech writers on West Wing might have unfettered access to Martin Sheen, no such open-door policy existed in President Prescott's White House.

"Marge, I need to see Gene immediately."

"What's it about?"

"A federal judge in San Francisco just held a press conference. He claims there's a plot underway to kill the leaders of the left, and that the FBI is taking it seriously. I don't think we want to be blindsided by this at the next press briefing."

There was a pause as Carrol considered whether it was sufficiently important to interrupt Eugene Baronian's schedule. "Ok, I can give you twenty minutes. Be here at two forty."

"You better ask Don MacMillan to join us." MacMillan was the official White House spokesman.

Owens spent the next hour and a half surfing the web for stories related to Judge Carlson's statements, the Fredberg La Blanc and Wellstone murders, and *Culprits of the American Culture*. The killings were well documented, but he could not find a single reference to the book. When he Googled the name Scanlan, he found too many references to sift through in the time he had available.

The speech writer arrived ten minutes early for his meeting with the president's chief of staff. In addition to his notes, he brought a DVD recording of the portion of the new conference that had appeared on

CNN. He was joined by Don MacMillan moments before Marge Carrol waved them into her boss's office. Eugene Baronian was a man of considerable bulk. Most people found him to be an outgoing, jovial man and, unlike several former chiefs of staff, he was generally well liked by the White House staff. Owens had never had a problem with Baronian, but he sensed a hardness beneath the good guy exterior.

The chief of staff motioned toward the visitor's chairs as he wound up a conversation on the phone. "Marge said this was something about a plot to kill the lefties?"

"Why don't we watch this recording first?" Owens stood up the shoved the DVD into the player in the bookcase. He turned to MacMillan as Baronian used the remote to start the recording. "Have you heard about this?"

The spokesman shook his head, "I've been tied up in staff meetings all day."

The three men watched the screen as Judge Carlson held sway with the media. When the recording ended, Baronian turned to Owens, "Not what I'd call a fair and balanced gentleman. You think there might be substance to what this man says?"

The speech writer shrugged, "Maybe, maybe not. I called a couple of local bookstores, and they don't have a copy of this book he mentions. It'll probably take me a day or so to get it. If what this judge says is correct and Bernard Fredberg, Winnie La Blanc, and Marc Wellstone were murdered in the same sequence as they appear in the book, it seems like a hell of a coincidence. I think we need to find out where the Bureau is on this thing. I didn't want Don standing up there like a deer in the headlights when the press pounce on this."

Baronian nodded, "Good catch. I'll make a call to the Bureau. Find some copies of the book, and Don, if they ask you what the president knows about this tell them the truth. He knows nothing beyond what's appeared on the news."

CHAPTER 12

With the top down, it was uncomfortably cool until Jonathan and Gale Kerrigan were over the Golden Gate and passing Sausalito. Jon had been growing increasingly restless in his apartment and jumped at Gale's suggestion for lunch in Napa. Gale had insisted on taking the BMW and he had not cared enough to argue. Their relationship was uncluttered by commitment, a situation that seemed to work for both. Gale was twenty-six, very attractive, intelligent, and normally in a good mood. The fact that she was the only child of an incredibly wealthy family and therefore had more money than God did not enter the like-ability equation. In fact, Jon liked her in spite of the bucks.

Judge Carlson's fifteen minutes of fame had eventually brought the media to Jonathan's door which was another reason he wanted to get out of the city. His refusal to provide a statement or give an interview had not dampened their enthusiastic pursuit of a story. He had finally disconnected his phone, and when he left his apartment to meet Gale it was like running a gauntlet. Jon hoped their interest would wane as the story aged.

"So, you don't look too perky," Gale smiled as she kept her eyes on the road, her perfectly coiffed blond hair barely buffeted by the wind.

"I've had better weeks."

"What's the story at State?"

Jonathan shrugged, "Right now I'm on a paid leave of absence while they figure out what to do. It's pretty obvious they want to fire me, but they're afraid of a lawsuit."

"Have you talked to a lawyer?"

"Not yet. I guess I'll have to at some point." Jon swiveled around to watch the cars behind them as Gale turned off 101 and onto highway 37. "I have to believe one of the SUVs back there is filled with my friends from the FBI."

"A little paranoia going on?" A brilliant smile accompanied the question.

Jon shook his head, "Hardly. They're not very subtle about it. I don't get it. They must have pulled my credit card records and have seen the charges when I was fishing. I couldn't have been running around the country whacking these people as the same time I was charging gas in the Trinity Alps."

"Maybe they don't have anything better to do."

Jonathan thought about it for a moment. "You're probably right. The book leads them to me, and so far that's the only connection to the crimes. Not a very comforting thought."

Gale smiled, her teeth a testament to early orthodontic care and serious whitening. "Come on, lighten up. We'll have a nice lunch, drink a little wine, and enjoy the day."

Jon returned her smile. "Ok. It's a deal."

He tried to focus on the moment and push his problems from his mind. When they reached Napa, Gale crossed the valley at Trancas and turned north on the Silverado Trail. The weather was perfect with a cloudless sky and temperatures in the eighties. Jonathan began to relax as they drove past the valley's wineries and vineyards. They had just passed the turnoff that led to Lake Hennessy and Chiles Valley when Gale turned up a winding road that laced up the eastern hillside. A driveway dipped down into a parking area leading to the entrance of the hotel and restaurant.

"Have you been to Auberge?"

Jonathan shook his head, "I've heard of it, but I've never been here."

"Best view of the valley and the food's wonderful." A valet opened Gale's door and took her car keys. "And this is my treat. The poor boy needs cheering up." Jonathan noticed Gale's statuesque figure and outstanding legs garnered the attention of the young men as they paused in their car parking activities.

The hostess led them through the dining room and out onto the deck. Their table was by the railing and offered an unobstructed view of the valley. Jon wondered what strings Gale had pulled to secure one of the restaurant's better tables on short notice. The menus presented an array of appealing, expensive choices. Jon's usual beverage of choice was beer, but today he went with the flow and joined Gale with a glass of Frank Family Chardonnay.

"Mother called last night. She thinks I should stop seeing you." The comment was offered without inflection or emotion.

Jon glanced away from Gale for a moment before replying. He suddenly wondered if the elaborate lunch was designed to reduce the sting of a kiss off. He looked back at Gale but could read nothing in her expression. "Guilt by association?"

A slight smile, "Something like that. Mom and Dad are into appearances. It's socially awkward to explain to your friends at the country club why your daughter is dating someone connected to these murders."

"Perhaps your mother's right."

"No. She's not right. We both know you're not involved other than through *Culprits*." Gale reached across the table and took Jon's hands in hers, "I'm not going to abandon a friend because it might allow my parents to avoid an awkward conversation. The only reason I'm telling you this is we probably won't be having dinner with them next week."

Jon had agreed to accompany Gale to a dinner party celebrating her father's fifty-fifth birthday. The loss of an evening of painful conversation with a room full of the Kerrigan's friends did not come as a major body blow. Jon felt a surge of warmth toward the woman seated across the table. They had been friends for two years and neither expected the relationship to move to another level. It would have been very easy for Gale to eliminate the controversy by stepping away from him. Some of Jon's friends viewed Gale as a woman of little consequence, an attractive trust fund baby who did not have to work. He had always known there was greater substance than appeared at first glance.

"I can live with that."

Now a full-blown smile, "I knew you could. Say, let's order. I'm thinking of having the Ahi."

They stretched the lunch until well after 2:00, enjoying the sun, the view, the food, and the company. Jonathan found Gale physically attractive, but for reasons he could not define he felt no reason to advance the relationship beyond its comfortable limits. None of these thoughts intruded into the luncheon as they worked their way through their entrees and another round of Chardonnay. Not even the presence of the black SUV that pulled off the shoulder to take position behind them on the Silverado Trail could dampen their spirits as they left the restaurant. Jon had assumed they were going to drive straight back to the city. When Gale took a left off Trancas and headed toward Napa's downtown area, he turned to his driver.

"A little detour. I want to pick up some wine."

They parked in the lot next to an old two-story stone building on the corner of Main and Clinton. Gale led the way up the front stairs and into the business. "It's called Vintner's Collective. I came across it about a year ago. It's a tasting room that specializes in high end wines from small wineries."

The interior was surprisingly small but tastefully decorated. The young man behind the counter greeted Gale like a long lost relative. Gale introduced Jon to Andrew who immediately insisted they try the new release from Showket. Jon politely waved off the offer and glanced around the room while Gale went through the sniff and taste ritual. A wine rack and display stand against the wall presented the wines sold by the Collective. Even though he normally preferred beer, Jon believed he was somewhat familiar with Napa Valley wines. He did not recognize one of the labels on display.

Gale had moved on to Mi Sueno, Phelan, and Longfellow when Jon realized it was time to call it a day. While not drunk he could tell Gale did not need another glass. Jon figured the two cases of wine Andrew loaded into the BMW's trunk cost about the same as his take home pay for a week.

Jon drove home through the East Bay with the black SUV in tow. Gale was asleep before they passed through Berkeley.

———

The asking price for the two-story Mediterranean two blocks from Judge Carlson's home was two million six hundred thousand. Not an extravagant price for the neighborhood but costly enough to eliminate the tire kickers. The online virtual tour presented a high ceiling entry with tile floors, a spacious living room dominated by a large fireplace, a formal dining room, and a kitchen/family room separated by a huge island topped with granite. The second floor presented an enormous master bedroom with an appropriately large master bath and his and her dressing rooms. Three smaller bedrooms, each with its own bathroom, completed the upstairs. The home sat on a quarter acre lot on the south side of the street. The virtual tour showed the magnificent view of San Francisco and the bay, but it did not display the grounds below the house which sloped down to the street below.

The man walking up to the side door off the garage did not care about the view of the bay, the height of the ceiling in the living room, or the Wolf range in the kitchen. There were only three features he found interesting. The owners were no longer living in the home, access to the street below through the backyard, and a seldom used balcony off the master bedroom. He was dressed in realtor casual; slacks, sport coat, dress shirt, and loafers. As this was Berkeley, he did not wear a tie. He rested the large case he was carrying on the driveway as he worked on the lock. Unlike other realtors, he did not bother with the lockbox on the front door. Within moments he was inside.

CHAPTER 13

The television trucks were no longer positioned outside his house when the judge pulled out of his garage. Two weeks had passed, and nothing had happened. In breaking news stories, two weeks was a lifetime. He paused for a moment to find his sunglasses before turning north onto his street. His protective detail placed their coffee mugs in the Suburban's cup holders and pulled out behind Carlson's Volvo.

A cool morning breeze blew across the Berkeley hills from the bay and the cloudless sky held the promise of another warm spring day. The judge turned on the car's radio to catch the traffic report and to listen to the call-in program that followed the news, traffic, and weather segment. He preferred Ronn Owens on KGO, feeling comfortable with the commentator's progressive slant.

The man on the balcony of the Mediterranean style home took off his sport coat, rolled it to create a pad and placed it on the decorative railing. With practiced skill, he opened his case and removed the components of his rifle. It was his third morning on the balcony. Judge Carlson has turned south and away from the $2.6 million-dollar home the prior two mornings. He knelt, keeping his head below the top of the railing as he assembled the weapon, slammed the clip into place and worked a shell into the chamber. The surgical latex gloves he wore did not impair his dexterity. Periodically, he was forced to raise his head to peer around the corner of the house. He knew the exposure created risk. An observant neighbor might wonder what he was doing on the balcony of the empty home at eight fifteen in the morning. Unfortunately, it was the only way he could see the approaching Volvo.

Like most professionals he tried to remove as many variables as possible. The distance between the balcony and the killing zone had been carefully measured, both with a laser device sold to golfers and by actually pacing it off as a double check. The TTR-700 tactical sniper rifle had been sighted in for exactly the measured distance, two hundred and forty yards, not a challenging shot for the man crouched behind the railing. The moving automobile, the wind, and the distance between Carlson's vehicle and the trailing protective detail created the most interesting variables.

He heard the approaching car before he saw it. A quick glance confirmed that it was the judge's Volvo. As it passed his position, he could see Carlson at the wheel. The black Suburban followed approximately twenty yards behind. He released the weapon's safety as he lifted the rifle to the railing, resting his forearm on his coat. He could see the back of the judge's head and the shape of the headrest as he sighted on the rear window. The assassin controlled his breathing as he gradually took up the slack on the trigger. At just over two hundred yards the Volvo began to slow as it approached an intersection. The street sloped up separating the vision of the car from the trailing SUV. The moment it crested the slight hill and leveled off in the intersection the man released the trigger. He saw the Volvo's rear window explode as he fired two more shots into the vehicle. The car swerved violently to the right and slammed into a Honda parked on the street. The assassin knew the first shot had hit its mark. The two shots that followed were unnecessary insurance. He ducked below the balcony wall, pulling his sport coat and rifle out of sight. Remaining below the railing he swept up his casings, dismantled the weapon and stowed it inside his case.

The agents from the Suburban were standing in the street trying to pinpoint the location of the shooter as the man made his way through the backyard and out to the street below. A waiting sedan pulled away from the curb and paused only long enough for the assassin to throw his case on the floor of the back seat and slide into the vehicle. They were on the freeway inching toward the Bay Bridge before the police and emergency vehicles arrived.

———

Station Chief Ross Del Monica was taking his first sip of coffee when the call came in. He slammed the mug down with such force a plume of steaming coffee sprayed across his desk. "How did this happen?"

Tim Rocha tried to keep his voice in check, "It happened because he wouldn't let us drive him to work. Refused to let us close enough to protect him."

"Jesus Christ." The station chief's thoughts were less focused on the unfortunate Judge Carlson and more on the assassination's impact on his upward crawl through the Bureau's hierarchy. Having the man you are assigned to protect blown away did little to enhance your reputation. "This is bad, really bad."

This was information Agent Rocha already knew. Del Monica could see his career disintegrating before his eyes. "How did they do it?"

"We think the shots came from the balcony of a house a few blocks from Judge Carlson's. It's for sale and vacant. We have a forensic team on the way, but when we went in it was clean. It had to be a pro. A moving target at about two hundred and fifty yards."

The station chief hung up and called Carl Lee, the lead agent investigating Scanlan. "Judge Carlson was just murdered. Where was Scanlan?"

"He spent the night at his girlfriend's place. As far as we can tell he's still there."

"As far as you can tell. Could he have slipped out? Find out. Now!" Del Monica slammed the receiver onto its cradle in frustration. With his thoughts still focused on self-preservation, he began dialing the regional director's number.

CHAPTER 14

Ross Del Monica tried to control the panic in his voice as he asked to be connected to the western regional director. Helen Hanavan's assistant explained that her boss was in a budget meeting. The edge of desperation came through undisguised, "I have to speak to Helen. Please break in on the meeting."

A moment later, Hanavan's clipped New England accent was on the line, "What is it Ross?" The regional director knew Del Monica would never interrupt her in a meeting unless it was an emergency.

"Judge Joseph Carlson was just assassinated."

There was a long pause before Hanavan spoke. "I understood he was well protected. How did it happen?"

Del Monica sighed, "The judge imposed limitations on our protective efforts. We weren't allowed in his home for example. He wouldn't let us drive him to work and back. Seclusion was out of the question." The rationalizations sounded weak, even to his own ear.

A moment passed before Hanavan responded, "We can go into that later. How was he killed?"

"The crime scene people are just arriving at the site, but I was told it was a long-range shot. He was in his car on the way to work. They think the shot came from a vacant house near where Carlson lived. Forensics will go over every inch, but it doesn't look promising."

"Where was the author of this book?" While the regional director's voice remained calm and controlled Del Monica could sense her underlying anger.

"We've had him under surveillance. He was at his girlfriend's apartment at the time of the killing."

"Which does not mean he wasn't involved." The statement did not seem to warrant a reply. "Send me everything you have on this. I don't want anyone in your office speaking to the press. We'll handle that from our side."

The second she was off the line with Del Monica, the regional director began dialing her boss. She swore as she listened to his voice mail recording. Helen Hanavan had grown up in a family of cops. Her father had put thirty years on the force in Portland Maine, and her brother had just passed the detective exam in Boston. Helen believed politicians were at the bottom of the social order and reporters only one rung above. Carlson's craving for the limelight insured both would soon be crawling up the Bureau's ass. She hung up without leaving a message and dialed a second number, one restricted to the director's direct reports, his counterpart at the CIA, the secretary of Homeland Security, and the president. William Palacin answered on the first ring.

With Palacin small talk was frowned upon, "Judge Joseph Carlson was just shot and killed."

Palacin swore, "I thought Del Monica's people had him under wraps."

"Carlson wouldn't cooperate. All he allowed them to do was sit outside his house and follow him around."

"Goddamned idiot. The last I heard we didn't have a strong candidate."

"No. We've been watching the author, Jonathan Scanlan, but I don't see it. We know he didn't do Carlson. When Wellstone was killed we had a few crazies confess, you know, the ones that hear voices and come out of the woodwork every time there's a high-profile murder, but nothing believable." Hanavan paused for a moment. "Bill, it's early days, but I think we're dealing with a pro."

"Because of how Carlson was hit?"

"A long distance shot at the driver of a moving vehicle? Not a lot of people at the Bureau could have pulled it off, and think of the others. One thrust of a knife into La Blanc's heart and how many amateurs would use a garrote?"

The director thought for a moment. "The Fredberg killing didn't seem that professional."

"If you think about it, it could. Trying for a head shot in a dark room with a pistol isn't a high percentage deal, but one in the chest to put him down and the second to finish him off is. Using the cushion to muffle the shot kept things quiet. Every kill was well planned and clean. We can't tell if it's a man or a woman."

"So, you think someone hired a professional killer to whack these people?"

Hanavan could not tell if Palacin was buying her theory. "I'm just saying it's a possibility. It's also possible that an accomplished killer is doing this on his own." The regional director leaned toward the hired assassin alternative but knew it was too early to close any doors.

The regional director could hear her boss's mind working. William Palacin had grown up through the ranks and was one of the most pragmatic men Hanavan had ever met. "You could be right. I'm going to call in the profilers and create a task force. Give me six of your best people. We'll draw about the same amount from the other regions and coop the local offices when we need them. This isn't going to be the president's favorite day in office. I don't need to tell you this is going to be a circus. Who's in the next chapter?"

Hanavan had to think for a minute. "Lawrence Clarke, the actor."

"Southern California?"

"Topanga Canyon in the hills."

"Put him under a blanket, and this time don't take no for an answer."

Palacin's next call was to his assistant, "Alice, call Baronian, I need to meet with the president. Tell him there's been another *Culprits* assassination."

———

Gale was in the shower when the doorbell rang. Jonathan had slept restlessly and slipped out of bed at first light. He never slept well in a strange bed, not that he was a complete stranger to Gale's bed. He thought it might be the ambiance. Maybe the frilly pillow covers and stuffed animals made him feel like he was sleeping in an adolescent girl's room. He sat at the breakfast table in his underwear, drinking coffee and wishing he was in his own apartment. Jon would have left an hour earlier, but he had not wanted to wake his friend when he retrieved his clothes.

At first, he ignored the doorbell. It was not his place and he was not about to open the door in his boxer shorts. The problem was the caller did not go away. For a moment the bell stopped ringing, only to be replaced by serious pounding on the door. Definitely not a neighbor asking to borrow a cup of sugar. Jonathan stood by the door and shouted, "Just a minute, I have to get dressed."

The pounding stopped while he went into the bedroom and slipped into his pants. He opened the door to find two men in dark suits. They flashed credentials and tried to push their way into the unit. Jonathan blocked the doorway and when the larger man put his hand on his chest Jon knocked the hand away. The bigger man gave Jon a hard look and was reaching for his handcuffs when his companion stepped between them. He raised his hands and smiled. "Alright, alright. Calm down. Jonathan Scanlan, right?"

Jon glared at the smiling agent, "You know who I am. You've been following me for over a week."

The attitude had no effect on the man. "True. Say, why don't you let us in? I'm sure Ms. Kerrigan wouldn't want her neighbors in on our conversation."

Jonathan could hear Gale coming in from the bedroom. "A conversation is when you talk to me, and I talk to you. That's not going to happen." When Jon stepped back to close the door the larger agent blocked it with his foot.

"Do you have a warrant, and how did you get in the entrance?" Gale's voice came from behind Jon and temporarily stopped the two men.

"Are you a lawyer?" a heavy portion of sarcasm in the man's voice.

Gale's voice was calm, "No, but you're going to need one if you force your way in here without a warrant."

The two men shared a glance. The smaller agent stepped to the side and looked past Jon as he directed his question to Gale. "Was Mr. Scanlan with you all morning?"

"Why?"

"Because someone killed Judge Carlson."

There was a long pause before Gale responded. While Jonathan's innocence was not in doubt the magnitude of the moment flooded in like an oncoming wave. Much of the confidence was gone from her voice, "Yes, Jon was here with me."

CHAPTER 15

The man watched the woman sleep and tried to decide if he could kill her. It was not a simple question. He knew if he was ever caught it would be because of her. She was sloppy in her tradecraft and imprecise when following instructions. She was a worrier, and this caused her mind to stray from the objective. He kept her role to a minimum, but in his line of work even the most modest task could be the thread that caused the ball of twine to unravel. She had been late picking him up outside the Pacific Union Club, which could have spelled disaster. It had only been a minute explained by traffic congestion, but in his business such a lapse was unforgivable.

He thought he might love her, but that too was not a question easily answered. Love was to him as vague and undefined as a prostitute's promise. His mind strayed to a dog he had once had as a child. A mixed breed female named Cassy. He remembered how he had felt when she had strayed to the nearby road and had been hit and killed by a passing car. He had been nine and it had been the last time he had cried. Certainly, he had not loved his parents. They were mean spirited Bible thumpers, seeing only evil in the world and in their child. God's will was dispensed with a heavy hand, and as the focus of their reconciliation with the Lord, he recognized the pleasure they gained from their cleansing. At fifteen he left home, lied about his age, and joined the army. He never returned. Years later, when he heard his parents had died, he felt nothing. As he watched her chest rise and fall with her steady breathing, he tried to visualize life without her, but no picture came to mind.

They had flown out of Sacramento rather than the more obvious San Francisco and Oakland alternatives. After wiping down the Honda, he left it parked near the bus station with its keys in the ignition, confident it would be stolen within the hour. The car, like the white van, had served its limited purpose. Both had been purchased for cash and had experienced several license plate changes during their brief exposure to the man currently calling himself Andrew Gasparini.

The Fredberg killing had been ridiculously easy. Big Winnie was only slightly more difficult for the sole reason it involved public streets in daylight. The first real challenge had been the billionaire, Marc Philip Wellstone. That hit had not been easy. There was a long list of contract killers that could have sent the talk show host and the champion of the minorities to their maker. Wellstone was well protected by a professional staff and rarely exposed himself. The assassin viewed the bogus invitation as a work of art and Wellstone's subsequent execution a creative achievement. The judge had simplified his own death by keeping the FBI at arm's length. Until now, the degree of difficulty had been unrelated to his compensation, one hundred thousand per killing.

Lawrence Clarke would be another matter. Unless the actor was a complete moron, he would accept every recommendation made by the Bureau. The assassin had no doubt he could succeed. There was always a window of opportunity, however narrow. He had recommended the selection of a different target, someone discussed in *Culprits* but not in a sequential chapter, but his employer had been insistent. No explanation had been given, the fifth target had to be the subject of chapter five. The assassin accepted the challenge, but not at the current price. He slipped out of bed without waking the woman, picked up the throwaway cell phone he would use for the call and went out on the porch that wrapped around the farmhouse. The night air was heavy with the first hint of humidity and he could hear the croaking of frogs in the stream at the edge of the property. He dialed the number he had been given and spoke without preamble when he heard the mechanically distorted voice.

"The next chapter is going to be extremely difficult. The price has to increase." He did not believe their conversation could be intercepted or that his employer would be foolish enough to record the call, but there was no reason to tempt the fates.

The demand was not unexpected. His employer was surprised that renegotiation had not been required for Judge Carlson. "What do you want?"

"Five hundred."

"Ridiculous."

"Then find someone else."

"We can go to two."

"Not good enough. The risk is too great. Five, or find another contractor." He ended the call, confident their conversation would be continued.

He listened to the sounds of the night while he waited. A full moon cast its light over the meadow and the line of trees bracketing the creek. While not one given to reading, he had located a copy of *Culprits* when he was visiting Bernie Fredberg in New York. The book contained thirty-five chapters and he wondered how deep into the text his employer wanted to go.

He answered the cell on the first ring. He thought he detected tension in the distorted voice. "We can go to three, that's it."

He had known before the call that five hundred thousand was out of the question. He considered countering with four but discarded the thought. He believed he was at the upper limit. "Alright. I'll start the process when one fifty is received by my bank."

"It will be there tomorrow."

The contract killer was not a curious man. He had never met his current employer and would have refused such a meeting had it been requested. None of the people who had utilized his services knew him beyond a voice and an email address. He was not known to the law enforcement community in the United States or in Canada, the only countries in which he operated. As he closed the phone and walked back to bed, he thought about retiring when his present obligation was concluded. His needs were simple, and he had enough money to walk away and live comfortably. He smiled at the idea of living quietly on the small farm. While there were moments when the conversion to a sedate rural life seemed appealing, he doubted it would ever happen. The thrill of the hunt was too strong, a narcotic he did not believe he could kick. He slipped into bed, turned on the bedside lamp, and began reading chapter five.

———

Palacin had arrived early as was his habit. He was escorted into the Oval Office where he sat and gathered his thoughts. He knew an avalanche of criticism was about to descend upon the Bureau and most of it would be landing on him. Eugene Baronian and President Robert Prescott came into the room at precisely 1:00. The FBI director barely had time to stand when the president's long strides carried him across the room. He gave Palacin a firm handshake and a pat on the arm. His chief of staff was less effusive, offering only a nod as he settled into one of the chairs.

Prescott looked ten years younger than his sixty-three years of age. He worked out regularly and could still run an eight-minute mile. Palacin wondered if Prescott would still have his youthful appearance when he left the White House. The job had a way of aging a man.

"Gene said there's been another killing linked to this book."

"That's correct, Mr. President. The subject of the fourth chapter was Judge Joseph Carlson from the Ninth District. He was killed with a long range shot to the head this morning."

Prescott shook his head. Baronian lost his composure, "Jesus Christ, we're going to be gang raped by the media. Didn't you have this guy under protection?"

Palacin remained controlled, "The judge refused to cooperate. Maybe we could have handled it differently, but he refused to allow us in his home or to let us escort him to work and back."

"Maybe?" The chief of staff was nearly shouting as he visualized the political fallout.

The director was not about to criticize Ross Del Monica's performance in front of the president. That was an issue that would be handled internally. He met Baronian's glare without blinking. "We gave him round the clock protection to the degree he would work with us."

The president raised his hand as his chief of staff started to reply, "This isn't getting us anywhere. Do you have any idea who's killing these people?"

"We believe the four victims were all killed by the same person and that the killer is a professional. We've had the usual number of wackos coming out of the woodwork to take credit for each of the murders, but none of them are viable suspects."

Baronian could not contain himself, "You don't know who the killer is, or who hired him."

It had not been presented as a question, but Palacin answered anyway. "No, we don't. We've organized a task force to push the investigation, but at this time there's nothing I can tell you."

"What's the story on the author?"

"So far as we can tell, he's not involved. We had him under observation when Judge Carlson was shot. We'll keep looking at him, but I don't think it'll take us anywhere."

Prescott shook his head. "It doesn't make any sense. Why would someone kill these people and why do it in the order that they appear in this obscure book?"

When no one responded, Palacin promised to keep them informed. After the director left, the chief of staff turned to the president. "We could deflect some of the heat by firing him."

"It's not his fault."

"The public expects to see something happen. The media is going to lay this at our door and what do we say? We're forming a task force? Not exactly a grabber."

"I'm not going to fire Palacin to make the *New York Times* happy," The president paused as his thoughts took another turn. "Find me a copy of this book. Who is talked about in the next chapter?"

"Lawrence Clarke."

"The actor? Is he still around?"

"He hasn't had a show for a while, but he's still around. Every so often he gets booked on one of those game shows for over the hill actors, but mostly he's chaining himself to the gates at Northrup or hanging out with Castro."

Prescott had to smile. "You watch the game shows?"

The big man's face flushed a bright pink. "No, no. I Googled him when I knew he was going to be the next guy on the list."

CHAPTER 16

J udge Carlson's death could not have received more coverage had he been the president. Every news service that owned a helicopter had it flying over the Carlson home and the murder scene. Sound trucks blocked the narrow streets of the Berkeley hills, and for the first time in everyone's memory the Claremont Hotel had to turn away requests for rooms as media personalities flooded into town.

Editorials and television commentators followed predictable patterns. Those favoring the Right offered sympathy to the judge's family and analysis of the crime, including criticism of the protective measures provided by the FBI. The liberal voices in the media felt no such restraint. Editorials in the *New York Times* and the *Los Angeles Times* lauded Carlson's virtues, declaring him to have been the brightest legal mind on the bench and a champion of the disenfranchised. When all available platitudes were exhausted the focus was shifted to the Bureau's ineptness and how that incompetence was directly connected to a lack of leadership in the White House. A few Far-Left commentators began beating the drums of a right-wing conspiracy.

The Democratic leadership in the Senate and House jumped on the bandwagon. The DNC's talking points stressed the president's failure to support gun control legislation, his lack of commitment to find a right-wing killer that obviously shared his political views and his lack of leadership which manifested itself in the Bureau's performance. The most vocal of the senators pounded his fist on the rostrum and shouted demands for a full senate investigation. His face flushed with self-righteous anger as he laid claim to knowledge of a White House cover up and a possible criminal conspiracy that precluded a legitimate investigation by the FBI. He concluded his fiery speech with the statement, "One does not send the fox to investigate the killing of chickens in the henhouse." The media loved the line and shared it with the nation on every newscast carried by the major networks.

The Chronicle and the local San Francisco television and radio stations could not give the story enough coverage. With few facts to discuss, the commentators and print journalists ran rampant with speculation. One editorial described the murders as products of a right-wing death squad while another hinted at complicity within the FBI. When *Culprits* and Jon were mentioned, the book was trashed as a Far Right hit piece and Jonathan as a "person of interest" in the killings. While Cal and Gale were unbending in their support, Jon noticed other friends distancing themselves. Two of his golfing buddies found their schedules too loaded to sneak in a game and people Jon thought he had been close to at San Francisco State no longer returned his calls. Representatives from several radio and television shows had called with offers to appear on their programs. They all promised Jonathan an opportunity to voice his side of the story, but he knew the media personalities involved and was sure the interview would be a journalistic ambush. He continued to toy with an offer from Fox News.

With nothing better to do, Jon was thinking about trying to get on as a single at the Presidio golf course when the phone rang. He glanced at the digital display and recognized his agent's number.

"Hi Harvey."

"Hello Jonathan. I just received a call from Tri City Publishing." Jon waited for the punch line. He assumed his pompous literary agent was about to tell him Tri Cities was pulling *Culprits* from circulation, "They're going back to press for a second printing."

Jon was mildly surprised. When the book was accepted for publication he had hoped for a larger print run. "How many copies?"

"Two hundred thousand."

The number took Jonathan's breath away, "Paperback?"

"No, hardcover. Their resources are somewhat limited. They're negotiating an extended bank line and if it's approved they plan to immediately go into a third printing. There's a chance it might make the Best Sellers List."

Jon was staggered by the news. When he was off the line he sat down and tried to absorb the impact of the book's success on his life. He never expected to make serious money with *Culprits*. The book had been written as a vehicle to express his thoughts and as a challenge to his literary skills. Jon's greatest love was fiction and for years he struggled to create something he could point to with pride. Each of his ventures into fiction fizzled into frustration by the fifth chapter. *Culprits*, on the other hand, seemed to write itself. He tried to inject humor and style into the project, and on the whole, was pleased with the result. Even without a third printing, the revenue from the book was more than Jon could make in ten years of teaching. He tried to think of what he wanted to do with his newfound wealth and nothing came to mind, nothing except crawling out from under the accusations that he was involved in the murders.

He suddenly felt he needed to share the news with someone. Gale was at Tahoe with her girlfriends for the week, so he decided to try Cal. Jon's call was bounced into voicemail, which he knew meant nothing. Hulse never answered his phone. He would listen to the recordings and decide which calls to return and which to ignore. Jon kept it brief. "Cal, I've come into some money. Call me back and I'll spring for dinner."

Thirty minutes later his friend was on the line. "How much money? Are we talking McDonalds or Fleur D'Lys?"

Jonathan laughed, "How about something in the middle? What time works for you?"

"I'm finishing up a project that's going to take a little time. How about around eight o'clock?"

"I'll call you back."

Jon lined up dinner reservations and left a message for his friend. He spent the balance of the afternoon making notes for a second book. Bringing *Culprits* to market had not been an easy task. Jon could fill a suitcase with rejection letters from literary agents uninterested in the project. He had not signed up with Harvey Balkin because he liked the man. Balkin Literary Associates had been selected as it was the only agency willing to take on the book. The agent's attitude had reflected a lack of enthusiasm for *Culprits,* and Jon had been surprised that Balkin had been able to secure a publisher, even for a ten thousand print run. Jonathan knew *Culprit's* phenomenal success was the result of its inexplicable association with the murders, but he believed it could still pave the way for a successful second project. It was after seven o'clock when Jon looked up from his notes and realized he had to hustle to meet Cal.

Jon had picked Boulevard and was surprised to be able to obtain a reservation on such short notice. In a city known for its restaurants, Nancy Oakes eatery was consistently one of the most popular in town. He was a few minutes late and was immediately escorted to a table by the windows. Cal Hulse was already seated sipping a pink drink in a martini glass.

Jon ordered a beer and pointed at his friend's glass, "What is that?"

"A cosmopolitan."

"Are guys allowed to drink those things?"

Cal choked back a laugh. "I'm getting in touch with my feminine side. What are we celebrating?"

"*Culprits* is selling like crazy. They're doing a huge second printing, and my agent said it could make the *New York Times* best seller list."

Hulse tipped his glass toward his friend, "Congratulations. I didn't know there were that many FBI agents."

"Very funny." The thought crossed Jon's mind that Cal might not be completely off base. "Give me a hard time and I'll make you drink another one of those."

The conversation drifted to sports and the NFL draft. Neither was encouraged over the prospects for the Forty Niners. They were waiting for the check when Jon's expression turned serious, "The money from the sale of the book is great, but it's coming at a hefty price. If they don't catch whoever is doing this, people are always going to wonder if I was involved. From what I've read I don't think the FBI has a clue."

"Maybe they're making progress, and we just don't know about it."

"Have you seen what's going on in Congress? They're laying into Prescott every day. They might not get into specifics, but I think the FBI or the White House would say something positive about the investigation if they could."

Cal Hulse disconnected from his friend and gazed sightlessly toward the window and into the evening. Jonathan had seen the look before when Cal's mind turned to a difficult programming problem. Jon was checking his watch and wondering how long his friend would remain lost in thought when Cal turned his attention back to his companion. "Why don't we figure it out?"

It was the first time in Jon's memory his friend had said something so completely ridiculous. His expression mirrored his thoughts as Cal shook his head. "Why not?"

"Because we don't have any experience in solving crimes. Because we don't have access to the physical evidence from the crime scenes. Because . . ."

Cal waved him off as Jon struggled to come up with additional reasons. "Let's examine the problem. You said you don't believe the FBI has any idea who's killing these people or why they're being murdered. Let's accept that as being true. What that tells us is all their experience is not helping them solve the crimes. The same argument applies to physical evidence. You don't think they're making progress. If you're right, whatever they have isn't helping them. Perhaps someone looking at this from a completely different perspective might see something the FBI missed."

Jon realized where his friend's mind was traveling. This was just another problem, no different than a vexing programming issue. He shook his head, "Cal, I appreciate your wanting to help, but I think the idea of playing Miss Marple is a little naive."

Hulse met Jon's skepticism without wavering, "Jon, do you think they have anyone in the FBI more intelligent than our friends?"

Jon did not know what Cal was talking about, "What friends?"

"Carlos, Harold, Alan, and Greg."

"Your poker gang? What do they have to do with this?"

"Jon, I have an IQ that's off the charts, and I couldn't carry water for Carlos. Greg and Harold are on par, and Alan is world famous in a field overrun with geniuses. There's more brainpower in the room when we play poker than you can find in all the combined government agencies, and trust me, I know. I've consulted with most of them."

"A physicist, a biologist, a programmer, and two weapons designers? I grant you all you guys are brilliant, but what do any of us know about how to find a killer? And beyond that, what makes you think they'd want to get involved in something like this?"

Jon's questions brought a smile. "One reason is they like you. I know you think of them as my friends, but that's not the only reason they like to come over and lose money, usually to you. They like both of us. But the biggest reason is they're problem solvers. That's how we all excel. Our fields are different, but we all make our living solving problems, and that's what this is, a problem to be solved."

Jonathan shrugged. He remained unconvinced that pure intelligence would overcome the obstacles that seemed to be stopping the trained professionals. On the other hand, he could see no downside to involving the poker group and he knew Cal wanted to help. "Alright, let's do it."

Cal was invigorated by the challenge. He literally jogged out of the restaurant in his enthusiasm to launch the project.

CHAPTER 17

He had never played a leading man. He was not the type. Lawrence Clarke had a long and profitable career as a character actor. At first, he tended to play the friend of the hero, the one that was usually killed so the lead could seek justice and revenge. As he aged, he moved to other roles, the veteran cop riding herd over the young and reckless protagonist and as a hard-nosed editor trying to offer sage advice to an aggressive investigative reporter. For several years he played the part of a fair and fearless district attorney in a long running television series. Clarke acted for money. He really did not care if he played the role of a kind and decent man or a deranged killer. The one exception was his district attorney character. The combination of power, respect, and judicial brilliance was hard to leave on the set when the day's shooting was over.

In his younger years, he had not found interest in politics. Perhaps the struggle to stay employed in Hollywood was too consuming. Only when he reached the status of a fixture within the acting community did he hear the siren call of political activism. Lawrence had never been touched by the horrors of war and held no religious beliefs but, nevertheless, he could not find any excuse for the United States to engage in armed conflict. Clarke held banners in peace marches and spoke of the evils of war at rallies. As he grew older, the acting roles diminished and his political activity increased. While the antiwar movement remained his primary focus, Lawrence also became an advocate for normalizing relations with Cuba. He considered Castro to be a champion of his people and a victim of American tyranny. Once a year he joined a group that made a pilgrimage to Cuba to show solidarity with the beleaguered leader.

The actor also found it incredibly *in* to be on the Far Left in Hollywood. At sixty-three he no longer chased women as he had in his younger years, but he also had not completely withdrawn from the hunt. His antiwar posture and disdain for the administration opened nearly every door in town. Lawrence had more dinner and cocktail party invitations than he could possibly accept, and not infrequently, they led to an attractive woman in his bed. He knew some of his colleagues did not share his affinity for Fidel, at least not publicly, but his position certainly did not hurt his social standing in the film community.

When Clarke first heard about *Culprits of the American Culture* and the series of killings, he could not connect himself to the Fredberg, La Blanc, and Wellstone deaths. He had met Marc Wellstone at Los Angeles fundraisers and had heard of Winnie La Blanc, but he could not accept the concept that he was a target as the result of a book he had never heard of. His initial reaction to the Bureau's attempts to provide protection was much the same as Judge Carlson's. Lawrence's unabashed hatred of the country's military extended to the CIA and FBI, and he viewed the Bureau's efforts at best as an intrusion into his privacy and at worst an extension of the government's domestic spying program. Clarke's posture shifted dramatically when the judge became the late Joseph Carlson. His righteous indignation evaporated at the sight of crime scene photos from the Berkeley killing. Clarke allowed the agents free access to his home and would have agreed to sleep with them had they asked.

The first two weeks under federal protection passed without incident. Clarke remained in his home with the exception of one trip into Los Angeles to meet with his agent and the producer of a television series scheduled for a fall release. On his one outing, three vehicles were utilized to drive the actor to and from the meeting. Lawrence made the trip in a Suburban driven by heavily armed agents with more Bureau personnel in lead and chase vehicles. The string of black Chevy Suburbans resembled a small funeral procession.

His home remained in perpetual twilight with the drapes drawn and blinds closed. The rear of Clarke's residence hung over the canyon; in normal times, he enjoyed sitting on his deck in the evening and watching the sunset and the onset of evening. Now two agents watched the back of the structure from the deck, and Lawrence was told to stay inside and away from the windows. Not surprisingly, the federal agents did not share Clarke's political views, nor were they interested in his experiences as an actor. They were charged with his safety but felt no need to become his friend or even to engage in conversation with the man. By the third week, all the resentment that had been buried beneath a veneer of fear came bubbling back to the surface. Lawrence found the agents presence oppressive and made his feelings known at every opportunity. With each day his mood became increasingly sour and his behavior more petulant.

The catalyst that set off the confrontation was an invitation to the screening of *The Last Woman* starring Susanne Davis and Richard Metcalf. The Samuel Goldwyn Theater had been booked for the evening and everyone who was anyone would be in attendance. Lawrence pushed the invitation across the breakfast table toward Lynn Cameron, the senior agent on the 6:00 to 3:00 shift, "I'm going."

Cameron ignored Clarke's confrontational tone, read the invitation and shrugged, "It's in three weeks. This could all be over by then, but if it's not, an event like this offers too much exposure."

"Maybe you didn't hear me. I'm going." Lawrence's body language said it all. He sat rigidly in his chair with both arms crossed at his chest.

Lynn Cameron knew her job was to protect Clarke and not to argue with the belligerent little man. Thankfully that task would fall to her superior, the Los Angeles office agent in charge. She slid the invitation across the table and left the room without responding.

———

The man previously known as Andrew Gasparini closed the motel room door and dropped the bag of sandwiches on the bed. The woman glanced away from the television for a moment before turning her attention back to the soap opera.

"Egg salad on wheat."

She nodded and pulled the deli sandwich from the bag without looking away from the program. A distinguished man with a British accent was telling a beautiful blond woman that the child could not possibly be his. The contract killer, now calling himself Jack Robles, could not understand how anyone could watch such drivel. While he found her choice of entertainment mind numbing, it filled her day leaving him free to study his next target. So far Lawrence Clarke was proving to be every bit as difficult as he had imagined.

The actor's home was isolated. His nearest Topanga Canyon neighbor was at least fifty yards away and on the other side of a curve in the road restricting his view of the actor's residence. The contract killer had driven by and had been able to see the garage, front door from the street, and the Bureau car in the driveway. His best point of observation was from a nature trail on the other side of the canyon. The trail curled up the hill, and at one point he had an unobstructed view of the house. He could see two men standing on the deck scanning the area with binoculars. He was not worried about being seen. It was a Saturday, and the weather was perfect. He was just another hiker on the well-traveled path. He wore shorts, a tee shirt, and running shoes to fit in with the local hikers. The baseball cap pulled low over his forehead and sunglasses would leave little to identify if the agents on the deck decided to snap a picture. He pretended to stop to drink from a water bottle while he studied the home and surrounding cover. He was not surprised to see drapes and blinds covering the windows. The protective detail seemed to know what they were doing, and while he believed there was enough cover for a nighttime approach he doubted Clarke was stupid enough to step out on the deck. He also knew the brush and rough terrain that would offer cover would also restrict his escape.

He knew the ruses that would normally give him access to the home would not work in the Bureau's presence. A man reading the gas or water meter would be cleared with the utility company. Packages would be carefully inspected and the Fed Ex or UPS driver screened. These obstacles did not discourage the man, they just confirmed his insistence on requiring a higher price for the hit. The one element that he knew he had in his favor was time. No deadline had been placed on the assignment, and sooner or later the situation would change. The Bureau could not afford to maintain this level of protection forever, and he was sure the actor would eventually chafe at the restrictions on his life. He just had to wait.

CHAPTER 18

They held their first meeting at Cal's condo following the tradition of the poker game. Jonathan did not know what to expect, but he believed the evening was probably going to be a huge waste of time. He was buzzed into the unit and found Carlos arguing with Hulse in the kitchen. Hermosillo was waving his arms and pointing to something on a huge whiteboard that now dominated the dining room. Cal's face was flushed, and he was about to rebut the physicist's theory when he noticed the new arrival.

"Jon, there's beer and water in the fridge."

"Great, what's going on?"

Both men glanced away, embarrassed as misbehaving children at the playground. Cal pointed to a mathematical formula scribbled on the whiteboard. "Carlos has the idea that the killings can be interrupted through a series of equations. I think the approach is crazy."

Jonathan studied the symbols and numbers and found them incomprehensible. For all he could tell they could be mathematical gibberish or the secret formula for Coca Cola. "Ok, I'm open to anything, but how can a formula help us figure out who's killing liberals?"

Carlos Hermosillo shrugged his shoulders. His native Spanish accent was barely evident when be turned to Jon, "Values are assigned to each element of each crime: time, place, methodology, and so on. Understand, what I've developed so far is just a generic model. As we learn more about the person committing the murders, we add that information into the equations."

Jon could not see how the symbols on the board could help identify the killer, but since he barely passed algebra his frame of reference was limited. He also did not want to discourage his friend.

Carlos' eyes radiated the intensity he felt over the project and Jonathan knew a rejection of the approach would be a blow to the physicist. "If you think this can lead us somewhere, go for it."

The doorbell rang before Carlos could launch into a mind-numbing explanation of each component of his mathematical model. Harry Kurtovich and Alan Thielen, the two advanced weapons designers, joined the party and began presenting a timeline for each of the killings and a master timeline for the overall string of murders. Jonathan sat back and listened to the four men in the room as they argued over details of the crimes. He was amazed at the amount of time and effort they had devoted to the analysis.

When Greg Stokes arrived, he was no less prepared. The research biologist had created a matrix that encompassed the entire population of people capable of performing the killings, segmented by prior vocation, necessary physical characteristics, psychological profile, and intellectual capacity. Within prior vocation, there were subcategories such as United States military experience, foreign military experience, and domestic law enforcement experience. The group began enthusiastically expanding the breakdowns with suggestions such as prior criminal experience.

It was after ten when they began to run out of steam. They agreed to meet the following week, and to continue working on their assignments whenever they could during the seven days. Jon was on his way to his car when his thoughts were interrupted by his cell phone. He could tell something was wrong when he heard Gale's voice.

"Hi Jon, can you come over?"

He glanced at his watch, "I guess so. What's wrong?"

"I'll tell you when you get here."

He started to press her when he realized she was off the line. Gale lived in a six unit apartment building owned by her parents. The building was perched on the steepest part of Telegraph Hill on Jones Street. Jon had seen underpowered cars fail to make it up the hill. Finding a parking place in the neighborhood after everyone was home from work was as difficult as finding an honest politician. After circling the block for fifteen minutes, he was able to grab a spot vacated by a Miata. The Jeep was a little big for the space, but Jon did not think it would draw a ticket. He pulled up the collar of his jacket against the chill wind blowing off the bay. Jon had barely touched the button by Gale's name when the buzzer released the locks on the entry door. Gale had the pick of the apartments when the building was purchased and had selected the unit on the north side of the third floor. The tradeoff was a magnificent view against two flights of stairs. Jonathan realized he was starting to slide out of shape when he finished the climb. The door opened the instant he knocked revealing the tear streaked face of his friend. Jonathan's mind raced with the possibilities.

Without a word, she turned and walked into the living room. Jon followed, took a seat in one of the chairs and waited. Gale paced the room for a moment before turning to her friend. Her voice broke as she tried to speak, "Remember what I said when we were in Napa? I think it went something like, you're my friend and I know you didn't have anything to do with these murders and I don't care if it makes my mom and dad uptight. Remember?"

Jon did not bother to answer. Gale paused as she pressed a tissue to her eyes. "Well, I know you didn't have anything to do with the murders, but I have to stop seeing you."

Jon remained silent, waiting for the other shoe to drop. "The FBI went to my parents' house and questioned them about my possible involvement in all this." She made a vague sweeping motion with her hand. "I guess they could handle a few comments at the Bohemian Club or the country club but being questioned by federal agents was the last straw. They've hired an attorney on my behalf, a criminal attorney, and have forbidden me to see you again." She could not make eye contact with Jon as she waited for him to say something. When he did not, Gale broke through the heavy silence, "I know I'm an adult, and I could tell them to go to hell, but I can't, I just can't. My father told me if I refused, I would be on my own; no more free apartment, no more Beemer, no more trips to Europe unless I paid for them myself. Jon . . . I don't make enough to take a vacation to San Jose."

Jonathan held up his hands, "Gale, it's alright. I understand. I would never ask you to make a choice between your parents and me. Look, you'll always be my friend. Maybe when all this is over they'll feel differently about me, and we can be together." As he said it he knew things would never be the same.

He stood and held her as she cried in his arms. When her tears were spent, he left the apartment without another word.

CHAPTER 19

The political drums began as a slow steady beat, gradually increasing in tempo until the sound became deafening. It began with fiery speeches on the Senate floor. Each blue state senator praised the accomplishments of each of the murder victims to the point they were not recognizable to immediate family members. Bernie Fredberg was a tireless fighter against the tyranny of the administration. Winnie La Blanc was lauded as a champion of the voiceless, and Marc Wellstone was regarded as a man of principal who recognized the injustices in the United States and dedicated himself to correcting those inequities. Judge Joseph Carlson was described as a legal scholar and a man brave enough to see beyond legal precedence when the interests of the disenfranchised were at stake. When the senior senator from New Jersey finished his eulogy for the fallen, he accused the administration of gross negligence and hinted that the president had no interest in finding the extreme right-wing perpetrators.

The junior senator from California stepped it up a notch when she demanded a bipartisan committee be established to review the performance of the Federal Bureau of Investigation, and what, if any, direction they were receiving from the White House. The best was saved for last when the senior senator from Massachusetts pointed toward the White House and declared he had information from confidential sources within the administration that they had no interest in halting the systematic program of genocide. The demeanor within the House of Representatives was no less raucous. The democratic controlled House took the lead. Three days after the floor debate, a vote was taken to establish an investigative House committee with full subpoena powers. It passed on a straight party line vote.

The following day the committee chairman, New York Representative Anthony Cadenasso, issued subpoenas to FBI Director William Palacin, the director of homeland security, and the president's national security advisor. Not very veiled threats were made that both the president and the vice president would be called if the committee felt their testimony was needed.

The evening following the vote to create the special investigative committee, President Prescott called a meeting of all the individuals that were in the committee's line of fire. Each invited individual was told to bring along any staff they thought might be helpful in dealing with the situation. The size of the group warranted the use of the Situation Room.

The president glanced at his notes while everyone was jockeying for seats at the conference table. He waited a moment for the inconsequential conversations to subside. "You all know why you're here. The loyal opposition has pounced on these crimes as an avenue to attack our administration and derail the programs we've set in motion. I don't wish to denigrate the motives of Representative Cadenasso or other members of the committee, but clearly this is all about politics. Midterm elections are coming up and our friends on the other side of the aisle believe they can use this issue to sway uncommitted voters to their candidates." The president turned to Palacin. "All this goes away if we can arrest or at least identify the people behind these crimes. Where are we in the investigation?"

Bill Palacin shook his head, "I can't give you much good news. Our forensic team picked up some fibers from what may have been the shooter's coat at the Carlson crime scene. We also have a few strands of hair that might have come from the killer. Unfortunately, these items aren't very helpful as we don't have a suspect for comparison. We believe the killer is a professional and probably not acting alone."

"What about the other crime scenes?"

"By the time we were brought into the investigation the crime scenes had been released so all we have to go on is coming from the local police in each jurisdiction, and that's not much. We have our forensic team looking at everything the locals collected. Frankly Mr. President, this whole investigative committee thing is bullshit. The Bureau is being criticized for not solving the Fredberg, La Blanc, and Wellstone crimes and for not protecting these people. Our involvement started after Wellstone was killed. I admit we don't get a gold star in our efforts to protect Carlson, but the task was made more difficult when he wouldn't cooperate."

Maurice Spencer, the national security advisor, broke into the discussion. "So, what you're saying is you don't have a clue who's murdering these people."

Palacin glared at the man seated across the table. Spencer was ex Pentagon and a firm believer in the superiority of the military services over domestic law enforcement agencies. The director knew Spencer was baiting him in the never-ending campaign to move closer in the president's inner circle. "I believe I've made myself clear."

Prescott moved to bring the meeting back on track, "Have you been able to figure out how this book is tied into the killings?"

"No. We've thoroughly investigated the author, Jonathan Scanlan, and can't see how he would be connected to the murders."

The national security advisor could not resist tossing another barb at the Bureau, "Scanlan's book is highly critical of each of the victims. He referred to Winnie La Blanc as a huckster and Marc Wellstone as a spoiled rich boy dedicated to turning the country into a socialistic society. He's obviously way off the scale on the Right. How could you so blithely dismiss him as a suspect?"

Before he could respond, Marshall Griggs, the director of Homeland Security stepped into the argument. "I don't want to speak ill of the dead Maurice, but Winnie La Blanc was a huckster and Wellstone did want to move the United States toward socialism. I've read *Culprits of the*

American Culture, and I don't consider it way out there. Frankly, I liked it and thought it was thoughtful and well written."

Helen Hanavan had never before attended a meeting of this stature. She had listened to the NSA director's comments and recognized them as political posturing. She was not naïve in recognizing the potential damage an inappropriate statement could make to her career, but Maurice Spencer's implied accusations rose like bile in her throat.

"Mr. President, we've had Jonathan Scanlan under surveillance since this came to our attention. We've monitored his communications and we've talked to nearly everyone close to the man. His mother, Jane Elizabeth Scanlan, is a fifty-seven-year-old former grammar school teacher. His father, Richard Stephen Scanlan, is a retired sixty-two-year-old vice president of finance from Lathrop Trucking, a regional trucking firm that serves the western states. When Richard Scanlan retired, they sold their home in Burlingame California and moved to Scottsdale Arizona. Jonathan Scanlan has a BA in English literature from UC Berkeley, a MS from San Jose State and a PhD in contemporary literature from Berkeley. He was teaching contemporary English literature courses at San Francisco State University until the school placed him on a paid leave of absence as a result of his book's linkage to the crimes. Based on an analysis of *Culprits* and the views stated to his friends and others close to Scanlan, our behavioral science personnel have categorized the man as a sane, reasonably well balanced, moderate Republican with no violent tendencies. He has no affiliations with Far-Right organizations, and many of his friends are definitely liberal. He's thirty-one years old, single, heterosexual, and dating a woman named Gale Kerrigan. Scanlan went through undergraduate school on a full ride athletic scholarship for golf. When he finished his Bachelor degree, he tried to get through the PGA Qualifying School but missed the cut. That's when he went back to college and extended his academic career. *Culprits* is his first published work, and, as Director Palacin stated, we see no connection between Mr. Scanlan and the crimes."

Hanavan was surprised she had been allowed to present her monologue without interruption. She first glanced at the director before leveling her stare at Maurice Spencer, "We can confirm he was with his girlfriend at the time of the Carlson shooting."

An uncomfortable silence followed, and Hanavan wondered if she had overstepped. The national security advisor realized he might have overplayed his hand. "I'm sure the Bureau has been thorough. I'm just saying Scanlan's possible involvement can't be completely dismissed. If we assume this was the work of a professional, someone had to pay the bill." Spencer tried to read the president's reaction.

William Palacin recognized he was not as skilled at navigating the political waters as his predecessor. He normally kept his views to himself and avoided contact with the denizens of Capital Hill at every opportunity. As he responded to Maurice Spencer, he silently wished he could be back on the job and out of this meeting. "We're continuing to keep Mr. Scanlan under close observation. His financial records, however, don't indicate any form of payment of the magnitude that would be needed to pay for a contract killing, much less four. He's received substantial revenues from the sale of his book, but that money came to him well after the Carlson killing, and so far, it's still sitting untouched in his bank account."

Prescott turned to his chief of staff. "Gene, get Owens started on a response. I want to express sympathy for the victims, but I also want it to be clear the Bureau is vigorously pursuing every lead. Let's not come right out and say it, but I also want the message to get across that this committee is grandstanding. And there's absolutely no basis in fact for the charges being thrown around. I think we should mention that if Senator Mallory has information that we're not trying to solve these killings he should be asked to reveal his source. Bill, please keep us informed of any developments."

As they filed out of the Situation Room, the FBI director wondered how long he had before someone started calling for his head.

―――――

The man dressed in browns and blacks lay motionless in the brush on the hillside. The two-foot-long arm of the directional microphone extended through the thicket and toward the window of Lawrence Clarke's home. The drawn drapes of the family room muffled the sounds reflecting off the window but did not entirely eliminate them. His task was made more difficult by the television set that seemed to always be on. After nearly an hour of listening to CNN, he shifted the microphone to a kitchen window. The first voices he heard were from two of the agents talking about basketball. One appeared to be a big Lakers fan and thought Kobe Bryant was a class act. The other, a Timberwolves follower, thought Kobe should be doing time in Colorado. The man on the hill had no expectation of an immediate revelation that would offer an opportunity to reach Clarke. He barely glanced to his right as a family of quail made their way past only yards from his position. His training and experience allowed him to remain motionless for hours, invisible to the people he was hunting.

CHAPTER 20

He decided the most promising concept for his next book was the origin of political correctness and its impact on America. Satisfied that he had a theme he could work with, Jonathan began roughing out an outline. One idea seemed to spring from the next as he scribbled page after page of notes. His only breaks were to make more coffee and a midday sandwich. It was after six when he pushed back from his breakfast table and realized he had been absorbed by the project for nearly eight hours. Jon stretched his back and shoulders, stiff from hours of immobility. A glance into his refrigerator confirmed he had nothing in the apartment for dinner. Jonathan was on his way down the steps leading to the street when he looked at the Crown Victoria parked in front of his building. The agent who had initially questioned him was watching him from the driver's seat. It took a moment for her name to come to him.

Jonathan walked up to the car and bent down by the passenger's window. He made a motion with his hand and the window receded, "Hi Agent Costello. I'm on my way out to dinner. Want to join me?"

Carmen Costello stared at him for a moment before responding, "What are you talking about? As you no doubt know my job is to keep you under surveillance."

"You can watch me from across a table, can't you? Look, I have to eat, you have to eat. Besides, you'll never find a parking space on Union so you're going to have to stand outside the restaurant while I have dinner. How much sense does that make?"

Costello thought about it for a moment. She could not remember anything in her training that prohibited having dinner with the subject of an agent's surveillance, but the concept seemed a little strange. "I'll get a separate table."

Jon smiled at the idea, "Fine. Want to walk down with me or do you have to follow at a discreet distance?"

Carmen tried to hold back a smile and failed, "I think I'm allowed to walk next to you." She locked the car and joined Jon on the short walk to Union Street. It was Thursday evening, and the street was crowded with pedestrians. Union ran through a district known as Cow Hollow; for the six blocks between Gough and Steiner its restaurants, bars, and small shops were a magnet for the bay area's singles and young couples. Balmy Indian summer weather was helping to bring out the young professionals in search of a good time and perhaps companionship. They passed a few small groups of young women, and Carmen noticed several were giving Jonathan a serious appraisal.

Jonathan pointed to Luisa's, a popular Italian restaurant sandwiched between an interior decorator and a tanning salon. Carmen shrugged her consent, and they elbowed their way through the bar to the hostess. Jonathan had been in several times, and while not a regular, was recognized by the attractive young woman tending the station, "Hi Mary. How long a wait?"

The hostess glanced at her list. When she looked up she offered Jon a smile that seemed beyond professional courtesy to Carmen, "About thirty minutes. Jonathan isn't it?"

When Mary bent down to write Jon's name of the list, Carmen was certain the hostess was intentionally providing Jonathan with an extensive view of cleavage. The idea bothered Costello, but she was not sure why. As they moved into the bar, Jonathan smiled at the petite agent. "I'm going to have a beer. Can I get you anything?"

Carmen bristled at the suggestion. "No, you can't get me anything.

Maybe you forgot why I'm here. This isn't a date, and I thought we were going to get separate tables."

Jonathan smiled and pointed around the room. "Agent Costello, the place is packed. No one is going to get a table by themselves. They'll tell you to eat at the bar, and as you can see there aren't any openings."

"Then we need to go someplace else."

Jon shook his head. "It's Thursday night and anywhere you go will be the same thing. I'm going to eat here. The food's good, the service is friendly, and the prices are reasonable."

Carmen bit back a remark about the friendly service as Jonathan wedged his way between two people at the bar and ordered a draft. When he turned back to Costello he extended a glass of water. The agent stared at the water for a moment. "Look, it's free. It's not like I'm bribing you with a glass of water."

Carmen accepted the glass as she wondered how she had placed herself in her present predicament. She could imagine what Ross Del Monica would say if he learned she was with her surveillance subject in a bar waiting to have dinner together. She ignored the obvious glances from several men in the crowded room. As they waited in silence Carmen became more and more convinced that sharing a table with Jonathan Scanlan was not a wise move. The decision to leave and wait outside was mitigated by the fantastic odors drifting into the bar from the dining area and the fact that all she had eaten that day was fruit and toast at breakfast. When the smiling hostess appeared to lead them to a table her rumbling stomach won the debate.

The place settings were positioned next to each other at the small table and Carmen made a point to take the chair across from Jon to reinforce the image they were not a couple. Jonathan ordered another beer, and Carmen told the waiter she would stick with water. Neither spoke as they studied the menu and avoided eye contact. The silence became awkward as they waited for the waiter to return to take their order. Jonathan was the first to break. "Where are you from?"

"Look, this isn't a first date," her response was unnecessarily harsh to her own ears. "Sorry, but let's keep this in context."

Jonathan shrugged, "Just trying to make conversation. I know you can't say anything about the investigation."

Carmen felt foolish in the silence that followed, "I grew up in Southern California, near Glendale."

Jon was about to try to extend the conversation when the waiter arrived. Carmen ordered a salad and linguini with clams. Jonathan decided on the fried calamari appetizer and osso buco, which was one of the evening's specials. As the waiter retreated with their orders, Jon glanced at the FBI agent seated across the table. He realized she was more attractive than his initial impression. Her features were delicate, dominated by eyes that reminded him of Audrey Hepburn, a slightly upturned nose straddled by high cheekbones. Her dark hair was cut short in a pageboy, which flattered her small face.

When the salad and calamari arrived, Jon offered to share his appetizer. Carmen eyed the large platter as she shook her head. It looked delicious compared to her tossed salad and she was starving. After a moment's hesitation, she reconsidered, "Alright, if you let me pay for part of it." Carmen's fork pounced on a large piece before Jonathan could agree.

Carmen began working on her salad when Jon's appetizer was a memory, "What led you to become an FBI agent?"

She shrugged, "I have an uncle who just retired from the force in L.A. I always admired him and thought law enforcement was something I wanted to do. How about you? What made you want to write a book?"

Jonathan wondered if the question stemmed from curiosity or a more professional interest. "Like you said, it's something I always wanted to do. I tried to write fiction, but I couldn't put it together. I don't know how many times I'd start a story and then . . . I guess it's like they say, those that can, do, and those that can't, teach. So, I tried nonfiction, and here we are."

The honesty of his words threw Carmen off stride. She took a few more bites of what was left of her salad before responding. "I thought *Culprits of the American Culture* was well written." For some reason she found herself blushing.

The arrival of their entrees allowed Carmen time to mentally regroup. As she twirled her pasta around her fork, she tried to analyze her reaction. She did feel like they were on a first date, which she knew was totally ridiculous. While the Bureau had ratcheted down their level of interest in Scanlan as a suspect in the killings, they had not dismissed his possible involvement. The problem was she found she liked the man, and that feeling was coloring her judgment.

"Now that you're not teaching, what do you do during the day?" She told herself to at least ask questions that bordered on the investigation.

Jonathan did not have to ask how his dinner companion knew he was on a leave of absence. "I've started another book. I should say I'm working on the outline. I haven't actually started writing."

She looked up from her pasta twirling, "What's it about? Can you tell me?"

"Why not? Like *Culprits*, it's nonfiction. It's about political correctness, how it arrived, why it seems to be exclusively available to the liberal side of American society."

Carmen paused for a moment. She was not about to be drawn into a discussion about the country's politics. "Do you think the new book can be a successful as *Culprits?*"

Jonathan laughed, "No. I was lucky to get *Culprits* into print. No one wanted it. My agent finally found a small publisher in the Midwest that needed to fill a slot on his nonfiction list. The print run was ten thousand, and I doubt half of them were sold. The murders sold the book, not me. I'm just hoping some of that success will carry over to my next project."

She could not believe this guy. Carmen knew about the revenue Jonathan had received from *Culprits* and that the killings were the driving force behind the book sales. It was another matter for him to come right out and describe a perfectly logical motive for the murders. She looked down at her dwindling pile of linguini. She almost felt guilty questioning someone this honest.

"Why are the people you discuss in *Culprits* in the particular sequence? You know, Bernard Fredberg first, Winnie La Blanc second?"

Jonathan shrugged, "No significant reason. I tried to put the people that I consider the biggest offenders at the back of the book and the less important in front to keep the reader going. Beyond that it was entirely subjective." He paused for a moment as he thought about her question. "Carmen, if you're asking if I was involved in the killings the answer is no, not in any way, shape, or form. I have no idea why someone would use my book as a serial killing guide. I'm willing to take a lie detector test or whatever you people use nowadays to prove what I'm saying."

The offer took Carmen aback. She wondered how Del Monica or whoever above him making the decision would react. She also noticed that she was now Carmen and not Agent Costello. She started to remind Jonathan that their relationship was one of special agent and the subject of surveillance when something made her stop. She told herself that part of any interrogation was gaining trust, and one step in that process was having the subject identify personally with the interrogator. While she would not admit it, she also liked the feeling of being called Carmen by this man.

"I'll relay the offer to my superiors. If you'll excuse me for a moment, I have to use the restroom." In truth, she needed a break to collect her thoughts. She realized as soon as Jonathan made the offer she would have to explain how she had come into direct contact with the man.

She washed her hands to have something to do as she thought through the problem. She also forced herself to consider her feelings. She had to admit she was attracted to Jonathan, and the feeling was frightening. The last man she had been involved with had been in Southern California before she joined the Bureau and was shipped off to Quantico. There had been a few casual dates since then, but nothing more serious. The last thing she needed was a relationship with someone the Bureau still considered a "person of interest".

When she returned to the table she could see the leather sleeve containing the check. Jonathan waved in the check's direction. "You're sure I can't pick this up?"

Carmen looked at the bill, "Not if I want to keep working for the Bureau."

When the waiter came by she told him how much to put on her credit card. After the man left Carman turned to Jonathan. "I want to ask you for a favor. I never should have come down here with you. My job is to simply watch you and record your movements. I can't tell my boss you offered to take a polygraph test over linguini and osso buco. If I tell him you came over to my car and talked to me while I was in front of your house, will you back me up?" Carmen was nervous as she waited for Jon's response. If he refused, she knew she would have given Del Monica all the ammunition he needed.

"Of course," the words brought a wave of relief to the special agent.

The walk back to Jonathan's apartment went by far too quickly. Their parting seemed surreal to Carmen as he turned toward his entry and she to her car. She paused and looked back over to top of the Crown Victoria, "Goodnight Jonathan."

He smiled at the small woman by the car, "Goodnight Carmen."

CHAPTER 21

It was the man's sixth day behind the directional microphone listening to snatches of conversations. He parked below the hill and walked the nature trail at first light each day. The last two hundred yards were made on his knees and elbows, keeping his profile below the tops of the scattered brush. He never left until the lights in the house were dimmed and he was certain the actor had gone to bed.

Compared to his experiences in the military the assignment was a walk in the park. The problem was mental, not physical. Keeping alert eighteen hours, much of it lying in the sun, took every ounce of his concentration. In a brief moment of self-reflection, he wondered if ten years ago he would have found the same challenge to remain focused. The microphone recorded onto a cassette, but he wanted to hear what was said when it occurred. The problem was, nothing of consequence was being said. Once in a while, he could hear Clarke insulting the agents guarding him; occasionally he caught someone on the protective team complaining about the actor, but none of that was helpful.

He was beginning to consider demanding more money when Clarke's voice broke into his thoughts, "I told you I was going to accept the invitation."

"We've been through this before Mr. Clarke. Nothing's changed."

"Get this through your bureaucratic head. This isn't something we're debating, it's something I'm doing," the actor's voice was petulant.

A few minutes later the man on the hill could hear the agent's side of the conversation, as she talked to her station chief. "That's right." And then later, "I told him, but he said that's our problem." Another pause followed by, "All right, I'll tell him."

A man with less patience might become agitated by the lack of specificity in the snippets of conversations he had been able to retrieve from his listening device. He had no idea what event the actor was demanding to attend, but one thing was certain, a window was about to open.

———

After a brief debate, they agreed to call themselves the Pacific Avenue Irregulars. Alan Thielen was a Sir Arthur Conan Doyle disciple with the dedication of a Grateful Dead fan. He had read the Sherlock Holmes series several times and was inspired by the Baker Street Irregulars. Jon felt like he was back in high school. Carlos was the first at the whiteboard, presenting a complex mathematical formula that Jonathan found totally incomprehensible. He was surprised to find Cal and Greg Stokes even bothering to argue with some of the more obscure elements of an equation. Carlos was a small, trim man of indeterminate age. His defining elements were his mind-boggling intelligence, the intensity he brought to his theories, and his total devotion to his wife and children. It was difficult to joke around with Carlos.

Alan and Harold were the next at bat. They laid out the timeline of all known events related to the killings. Their approach was thorough and clinical. While on par with anything the law enforcement agencies had on their blackboards, it offered nothing that might advance the investigation. Stokes, the research biologist, drew a rough pie chart on the board. He segmented it into slices of potential killers, assigning a probability factor to each piece of the pie. The highest probability was assigned to the segment titled "prior domestic military."

Jonathan studied the pie chart for a moment before asking the obvious question, "Alright Greg, why do you think someone with prior domestic military experience is killing these people?"

Greg Stokes blinked several times as he turned away from the board. Greg was not a people person. His recognized brilliance was in research, not in the sale of the breakthrough concepts he developed at Genentech. They had MBAs for that. When someone questioned his conclusions the tall, angular biologist tended to stutter.

"It's . . . it's apparent," he stopped for a moment to collect himself. "We could be mistaken, but the probability points to one killer for all four events. This means we're talking about one man or woman who is skilled at killing with a pistol, knife, garrote, and rifle. The most telling are the garrote and rifle. The common criminal might be fine with a pistol or a knife, but it's unlikely they would also be skilled with the last two murder weapons. Judge Carlson was in a moving vehicle nearly three hundred yards from the point of fire. It's also important to consider the killings appear to be totally devoid of clues."

When Jon offered a questioning expression Greg smiled, "Cal was able to access the New York, D.C., San Francisco, and Berkeley police systems. He said it wasn't difficult." Another small smile, "I believe the assassin was trained by a sophisticated military service, and there are not too many organizations capable of producing someone of this caliber. Israel, Russia, the UK, and it may surprise you to know France, are candidates, but the leading odds-on winner is a home-grown US killer."

Cal jumped in while Jon was absorbing Greg's reasoning, "Why?"

"Two reasons. First, the crimes have all occurred in the United States. If you need an assassin, it would seem obvious you would hire someone familiar with the language, customs, and geography. Why bring in someone who has to figure out where to go and how to get there? Reason number two, we produce more skilled killers than any other five nations on the world. Between the Seals, Rangers, Special Forces, and Delta Force there are thousands of potential candidates out there."

No one in the room spoke for a moment as they absorbed Greg's analysis. Each realized that, while helpful, the theory did not point to any particular person. However, if accepted, it did narrow the scope of the search. Jon was the first to respond. "Greg, I believe this is significant. How can we pursue this line of reasoning? Can we create a list of the former members of these specialized forces?"

Greg pointed at Cal. Their host thought about the question for several moments. "I don't think so. The files on these special ops types would be more classified than Microsoft's source code. If I even tried to probe into this level of the Department of Defense database, all the bells at the Pentagon would go off. I don't mind a little roaming through the records of the unenlightened, but these boys employ folks every bit as bright as yours truly, and we're talking serious time in a federal facility if they trace it back to us."

Jonathan nodded, "We're not going to do something stupid. I'm a complete believer in Greg's analysis. Are we all together on this?" Cal, Carlos, Harold, and Alan nodded agreement. "Ok, so maybe this is as far as we can take this line of reasoning for the moment, but now we have at least one box we can check off. Let's look at other parts of the puzzle. Let's consider every possible motivation for killing these people and why *Culprits* was used as a game plan."

Most members of the Pacific Avenue Irregulars had mixed feelings over the progress of their investigation as they made their way home. Perhaps because he expected so little from the group, Jonathan was encouraged by the limited conclusion they had reached and optimistic that they were capable of reaching further into the puzzle.

———

Jonathan was early for his lie detector test. When they were ready he was escorted into a small windowless room and asked to sit at a table beside a middle aged humorless man wearing a bright green tie with a light blue shirt. Jon wondered if the man, who never bothered to introduce himself, was colorblind. After sensors were attached, the man began with a series of test questions. Jonathan answered yes or no as the man read from a list of prepared questions.

He tried not to look at the needle as it bounced along a rolling sheet of paper, recording his reactions. Questions about the killings were interspersed between those asking about his profession and age. Jon could feel sweat trickling down inside his shirt as the man's monotone voice droned on. When they finished, Jonathan asked the man how he had fared. The slightly built, balding technician shook his head and left the room.

After Jonathan had been escorted out of the federal building, Ross Del Monica motioned for the polygraph technician to follow him into his office. Without preamble he pointed to one of the visitor's chairs, "So, how did Mr. Scanlan do?"

The man with the green tie shrugged, "I'd have to say he passed."

"What does that mean, 'I'd have to say'?"

"Some of his answers were marginally acceptable, but that's normal. Everyone who takes the test is nervous."

"So, he didn't have clean answers to every question?"

"No one does."

"And people can beat the test? Isn't that right?"

"It's happened."

"Listen to me, De Souto. You'll write this up as an inclusive analysis. Are we clear on this?"

"Yes sir."

CHAPTER 22

Russell Brinkley had a splitting headache, and the source of his discomfort was nestled in the deep folds of the man's silk covered, down filled sofa. The aging actor's arms were crossed in the classic posture of rejection, his face distorted with belligerence. Brinkley was certain Clarke was barely listening to the Bureau's Los Angeles station chief's arguments and accepting none. Lynn Cameron watched the process with a mixture of amusement and distaste.

"Mr. Clarke, I'm going to be brutally honest with you. Whoever killed Bernard Feldberg, Winnie La Blanc, Marc Wellstone, and Judge Joseph Carlson is very good at what they do. They've left virtually nothing at any of the crime scenes that would allow us to determine who they are. The killer could be short or tall, white or black, man or woman. How do you expect us to protect you if we have no idea who's out there?"

"You're saying I can't attend the event because of your incompetence. Bullshit. I told your flunky two weeks ago I was going to the screening. Your organization has had ample time to put things in place to protect me."

Brinkley bowed his head for a moment as he fought to control his temper, "Mr. Clarke, the studio has refused to allow us adequate access.

Do you know why Judge Carlson is dead?" The station chief paused to give the actor an opportunity to answer. "He refused to listen to us. Carlson would be alive today if he allowed us to protect him."

"How about, he'd be alive today if you and the people you work with weren't idiots. Do you have any idea how much I pay in taxes each year? I pay more to the government than everyone in this room and all their relatives and friends combined. And what do I get for my money? I get a president who's a moron, an administration that never saw a war they didn't want to fight, and I get a keystone cop operation that can't protect me in downtown Los Angeles."

"Carlson was killed by a head shot at over two hundred and fifty yards, and he was in a moving vehicle at the time. The shooter is very, very good. Would you like me to show you what the judge's head looked like again?"

The memory of the graphic images forced Lawrence to look away. When he answered the station chief, some of the truculence had faded from his voice. "No, I don't want to see your goddamned photos. I'll agree to reasonable conditions, but make no mistake, I'm going."

Brinkley shook his head in frustration as he left the actor's home. He knew the aspirin in his pocket were useless in combating his headache.

———

The television had been off and the man on the hill had been able to hear enough of the conversation. He assumed the screening would be a major event and, as such, mentioned somewhere in the local papers. As much as he wanted to be off the hillside researching the upcoming opportunity, he knew he had to remain hidden until nightfall.

The afternoon dragged on without incident. The television was back on, obscuring any conversation that took place in that portion of the house. He listened to the agents on the deck, but nothing of interest was said. It was after seven when he was able to crawl away from his listening post. The woman was out when he reached the motel and an empty wine bottle sat in the wastebasket. She occasionally drank more than she should, and her potential lack of discretion made him uneasy.

He paged through the day's copy of the Los Angeles Times looking for a reference to an upcoming screening but found it difficult to concentrate.

He was rereading the entertainment section when he heard someone at the door. The nine-millimeter Glock he had acquired only weeks before was in his hand as the key turned in the lock. When he saw it was the woman, he slid the weapon back into his daypack. He tried to keep his voice level as she crossed the room and placed a shopping bag on the dresser. "Where have you been?"

"I went to the store. I had to walk, remember?"

He had only acquired one car, a nondescript Honda Accord, since returning to the West Coast. He could easily have purchased a second vehicle rather than leaving her stranded each day, but he did not want to be distracted by thoughts of the types of problems she could unwittingly create. "Sure honey, I hate keeping you penned up like this, but it shouldn't be much longer. Say, why don't we go somewhere nice for dinner?"

When she turned and smiled, the small room seemed to grow brighter, "That would be fun. Give me a few minutes to freshen up."

He changed into slacks and a polo shirt and spent the remaining time studying the paper. There was no mention of an upcoming screening. When she came out of the bathroom, he felt the usual rush. She was extraordinarily beautiful. This evening she wore her light brown hair up, emphasizing her high cheekbones and large almond eyes. The simple dress she wore looked like it had been designed for her figure. When he saw her like this, he was reminded of pictures he had seen of Sophia Loren in her youth. In heels she was two inches taller than his five ten and the contrast between the two went well beyond simply height.

He was not an unattractive man but not someone one expected to see on the arm of such a beauty. The stamp of the military was unmistakable. Men that had shared the training and combat in the elite forces shared a look that could not be erased with time. It appeared in the hard lines of his face, the intensity in his eyes and with every move of his muscular body. When they were together, he always thought of *Beauty and the Beast.*

The man had selected a restaurant in downtown Los Angeles, not far from the Westin Bonaventure. Anywhere they went the woman would be remembered, even in an area absorbed with physical beauty. He reasoned that the constant turnover of visiting businessmen and tourists from the hotel would make it less likely the memory would last. Traffic was predictably slow. He smiled as he glanced at her, "I'm having difficulty finding out about a screening that's supposed to happen in about two weeks."

It was offered as a casual remark with no expectation of useful information. He was surprised by her response, "Have you tried the trades?"

"The what?"

"The trade magazines. That's all they talk about. Who's appearing in what, how the movies are doing at the box office, that kind of thing. If it's a low budget film, it might not be mentioned. Is it a major movie?"

"I'm sure it is, or Clarke wouldn't be making such a big deal about attending."

The woman was silent for a moment, "Are you planning on doing it at this screening?" Her tone was neither accusatory nor supportive. She had long ago accepted what he did for a living.

"I don't know. I'll have to study the physical layout when I find out where it's being held and what kind of protection he's going to have."

Each held their thoughts as they moved toward the center of town.

CHAPTER 23

Brinkley's first phone call was to the Global World Studio's administrative office. Global's CEO and executive VP were not surprisingly unavailable. Equally not surprisingly, the studio's in house legal counsel was available.

"Mr. Brinkley, Martha Holbrook here. How can I help you?"

"Good afternoon, Ms. Holbrook. I'm sure you're aware of the current situation regarding Mr. Lawrence Clarke. He's considered a potential target in a string of murders. Your studio offered him an invitation to the screening of *The Last Woman*. The Bureau would appreciate a cancellation of that invitation."

"I'm sure Lawrence Clarke would never expose himself to the type of risk you're suggesting if he believed he would be in danger."

"Counselor, I believe I'm in a better position to offer an objective appraisal of the risks involved than Mr. Clarke."

"Agent Brinkley, Lawrence has discussed this matter with us directly and has assured us his security is not in question. Lawrence is an old and dear friend of Suzanne Davis. I believed they worked together in *Lies*, *The Protectors*, and *The Art of Love*. If Mr. Clarke says he's not concerned, we see no reason for him not to attend the screening."

Russell Brinkley's first reaction was to tell the studio's representative that he was not an agent but the head of the Los Angeles Bureau office.

However, sensing this might be an unprofitable correction, he refrained. Hollywood's traditional liberal bias was coming through unspoken and extremely loud, "Ms. Holbrook, our objective is to keep Mr. Clarke alive. We would appreciate the studio's cooperation. Should it be resolved that Mr. Clarke will be attending the event we need to secure his safety while he's at the theater."

"Adequate security will be provided by Global."

"You mean rent-a-cops? Judge Joseph Carlson was killed because he rejected our recommendations."

"Really, Agent Brinkley? I understood Joseph Carlson was murdered because of gross incompetence on the part of your organization."

"Pleasant chatting with you counselor," Brinkley hung up before the studio's attorney could respond. His next call was to Helen Hanavan.

He described his efforts to dissuade the actor from attending the event and the studio's position. Hanavan's response pleased Russell no end, "Tell this little twit we're going public. Tell her the director of the FBI will be issuing a press release tomorrow explaining how Ms. Holbrook and the management of Global World Studios are refusing to cooperate with the Bureau and, in doing so, placing Lawrence Clarke's life at risk."

The chief of station redialed the studio's main number and asked to be connected with the public relations department. The man who came on the line introduced himself as Jerry Tessandori. "Mr. Tessandori, my name is Russell Brinkley. I'm the chief of station of the FBI office in Los Angeles. You may be aware of the recent series of killings linked to a book titled *Culprits of the American Culture*. The first four people featured in the book have been murdered in the sequence in which they appeared in the book. The fifth chapter is devoted to Lawrence Clarke. Your studio has invited Mr. Clarke to attend the screening of *The Last Woman*, and he's accepted that invitation. We would like to have Mr. Clarke's invitation withdrawn. Should that not be possible, we need to have a team of our people at the screening to insure Mr. Clarke's protection."

"I don't think I'm the right person to be talking to. Let me transfer you to our administrative office."

"Jerry, your administrative office referred me to your legal counsel who informed me the studio would not be cooperating with the FBI."

Tessandori had no idea why this man on the phone was discussing his problem with him. "If that's what the studio's attorney said, then I guess that's it."

"No Jerry, that's not it. There's an excellent chance that if we go along with your legal counsel, Mr. Clarke will be murdered at the screening and, should that occur, it's a sure thing the Bureau will be blamed for his death. Call it cover your ass if you will, but tomorrow the Director of the FBI will issue a press release sighting your studio's lack of cooperation. He will make it quite clear we are being denied access to the screening, and he will quote your attorney when she said, 'adequate security will be provided by Global'. So, you see, Jerry, I really am talking to the right department."

The public relations man did not reply for a moment as he absorbed everything Brinkley had said. The chief of station could hear the concern in Tessandori's voice, "Alright, I think I have it. Give me a number where you can be reached." The station chief gave Jerry his office and cell numbers. "Ok, this is going to take a little time. I'm not exactly high in the pecking order here."

"I don't know when the director will be issuing his press release, but remember he's three hours ahead of the west coast."

Brinkley smiled as he visualized the hurriedly called meeting and the expression on Martha Holbrook's face when Jerry dropped the bomb.

CHAPTER 24

Film industry trade magazines littered the bed as the assassin skimmed through their contents. He had no interest in movies, and as a result, found the combination of hype, gossip, and facts only a film buff could appreciate painfully boring. He recognized few of the names of the actors, actresses, producers, and directors mentioned and could care less about how their careers were faring. His research yielded a list of seven films scheduled for immediate release. It appeared four were going to be introduced with little fanfare, and one was scheduled to debut at a small film festival in New York. It seemed unlikely Clarke was planning on flying to New York to attend the festival and see the movie titled, *The Soldier's Daughter*, but there was little of the film industry the man found comprehensible. He handed the article to the woman who was watching a made for television movie.

"Do you think the screening they talked about might be this movie being released in New York?"

She glanced through the article and shook her head, "This isn't what they refer to as a screening. A screening is a private showing of the film, usually inviting all the people who had anything to do with it and all the celebrities the studio can round up."

"What about these two?" he handed her another trade magazine with two dog-eared pages.

She read both articles and nodded. One was a film titled *Light of Dawn* and the other *The Last Woman*. "It could be either one. They're both big budget films from large studios."

He studied the articles hoping to find something that would point to the screening Clarke was planning to attend. Both events were in Beverly Hills and separated by only five days. The film from New Republic Studios was being presented at the Cecchi Gori Fine Arts Theater and *The Last Woman* from Global was scheduled to be shown at the Samuel Goldwyn Theater. Nothing additional in the articles proved helpful. He sighed as he began putting together his gear for another trip up the Topanga Canyon hillside.

———

The call from Global Studios came as Russell Brinkley was leaving his office for the evening, "Mr. Brinkley, my name is Jim Peoples. I'm head of security over here at Global."

"Good evening Jim. What course of action has the studio decided to take?"

Brinkley could hear the man chuckle before he answered the chief of station. "You don't have to be the Great Swami to get this one right. I've been instructed to cooperate fully, or at least, almost fully."

"What does the almost involve?"

"They're not going to rescind Clarke's invitation. Apparently, he's tight with the leading lady in the flick, and Ms. Holbrook's concerned you plan to flood the place with a SWAT team."

"Gee, we hadn't thought of that. Thank her for the suggestion."

Peoples laughed, "I know, she makes all the lawyer jokes seem real. How many people do you think you need inside?"

"I won't know until I see the facility. Any chance I can meet you there tomorrow?"

"Sure, how about ten? I'll bring along one of the coordinators who planned the event."

When they finished their conversation, Brinkley made calls lining up three of his agents for a trip to the theater.

Jon spent much of the week refining the outline for his new book. When he needed a break, he grabbed his bag and headed out to one of the local golf courses. Usually, he was able to walk on as a single without much of a wait. After failing to make the cut at the PGA's Qualifying School, Jon no longer worked on his game and his scores reflected his fading commitment. His once picture-perfect swing felt ragged and his timing was off. The one aspect that remained was his enjoyment of the game and the ability to block out life's distractions as he worked his way around the course.

He was on his way back from a round at Harding when a thought popped into his mind. He called Hulse from his cell and asked his friend to see if he could organize an impromptu meeting of the Irregulars. Cal called back to say Alan and Greg could not make it, but the rest of the crew would be at his place at seven. Jonathan asked his friend to be patient when Cal pressed him to know what his friend had in mind. Jon stopped at a corner market for beer and chips for the team before heading over to Cal's condo.

There was a minimum of the small talk and joking around that usually preceded their gatherings as Cal, Harold, and Carlos waited for Jon to provide a reason for the meeting. He smiled at the skeptical expressions, "Show me the money."

Jonathan's small audience was singularly unimpressed. Carlos was the first to voice his cynicism. "Great line from a movie, but what are you talking about? You want us to try to trace the money paid to a professional killer?"

Jon shook his head, "I want to know who was buying my book." When there was no reaction he smiled. "Think about it. When the first murder occurred, I doubt five thousand copies of *Culprits* were sold. We know the book is the template for the series of killings, so we know the people who orchestrated these murders purchased one or more copies well before Fredberg was shot," he waited for the logic to sink in.

Carlos was the first to extend the thought, "Alright, but how can we figure out who bought your book?"

Cal stood up, excited by the challenge, "If they used a credit card I might be able to trace the purchases. I can't get into the credit card company's database, but I'm sure I can access your publisher's records and find out which bookstores ordered the book. Then I can access their databases and pick up the credit card transactions. We have to hope they were careless and used a credit card. If they paid cash, there'll be no record."

"It's worth a try," this from Harold, "But what happens when we have a list of several thousand names? How can we pick the bad guys out of the pile of good guys?"

Jonathan held up his hand, "I think I have a way, but let's first see if we can collect the information. Think about it. We started off with nothing. Having a chance at put the people behind this on a list takes us a lot further down the road. How long do you think it will take to put the list together?"

Hulse thought for a moment, "Maybe three days."

"Ok, let's tentatively plan on meeting Thursday. If you need more time push it out."

Jonathan smiled and waved to the agent double parked outside Cal's condo as he made his way home. It was not a breakthrough, but it was progress.

CHAPTER 25

A weather system had moved in from Hawaii carrying strong winds and heavy rain. The man working his way up the nature trail was oblivious to any discomfort brought by the storm. What he did care about was the lack of hikers on the path. The agents watching from Clarke's deck would certainly question why a man would be climbing the hillside trail in this type of weather. This understanding forced him to find good cover before the actor's home came into view. He low crawled the last two hundred yards to his listening position.

It was after two when he picked up the sounds of the chief of station's arrival. Thankfully, the man turned off the television. The assassin adjusted his earphones and listened intently. The noise of the rain was obscuring the conversation in the living room. He swore to himself, and he decided he had to move closer to the house. As quickly as he could, he broke down the listening device and crawled thirty yards closer. He set up again, pointing at the room's large picture window. The voices were still muffled, but he could understand most of what was being said.

"The studio agreed to allow our people into the theater."

"Swell, I hope they enjoy the film," the actor's sarcasm belied his comment.

"They won't be there for the movie, Mr. Clarke. They'll be there to try to keep you alive. I'd hoped you might have reconsidered attending the event."

"Screw you."

"Also, Special Agent Lynn Cameron will be your companion at the screening."

The actor exploded, "If you think I'm going with that cow, you're out of your fucking mind!"

Russell Brinkley leaned close to Clarke as the older man sat in his customary spot on the sofa, "Listen you ungrateful little piece of shit. I'm a heartbeat away from putting you in protective custody and locking you up in a safe house. I'm not going to allow the Bureau to be blamed when you get blown away."

Most of Brinkley's remarks were lost to the man on the hillside. He was growing increasingly frustrated by the lack of specificity. The information he had heard was useful, but he still had no idea which screening Clarke was going to attend.

"You can't talk to me like that." The two agents inside the house smiled for the first time in weeks.

"Grow up Mr. Clarke. Ever since we arrived you've treated my people like dirt. We're here to save a life, namely yours, and you behave like you're on some higher moral plane. You're an actor for God's sake, not a Nobel Prize winner. You'll follow our instructions to the letter or the screening's off."

Lawrence's voice was hoarse with rage, "You can't stop me. I know my rights. You and your government thugs hate me because of my political activism."

Brinkley laughed, "We could care less about your politics. To us you're just another assignment. Do you want us to leave? I can have a consent form here within the hour and we're gone. Perhaps your friends at Global can keep you from ending up like Fredberg, La Blanc, Wellstone, and Carlson." The chief of station threw out the challenge hoping Lawrence's distrust of the Bureau would allow him to find the offer believable. In truth, he had no authority to abandon the actor.

The little man on the sofa threw up his hands, "Alright, alright. I'll take your agent with me and follow your instructions. Just leave me alone."

The man lying on the rain drenched hillside smiled. Finally, the first piece of the puzzle fell into place.

He broke down the directional microphone and began the slow crawl away from the house confident he had just completed his last trip to the hillside.

CHAPTER 26

He dropped his muddy clothes in a pile on the motel room floor on his way to the shower. The contract killer's mind was racing with alternatives as he let the hot water cascade over his body. He attributed much of his success to his skill at planning and attention to detail. There were thousands of men trained to kill efficiently, some better with a long rifle or pistol. Few, of course, carried the skills they developed in their elite branches of the military into their civilian lives. He recognized that their concept of morality guided them to less violent career paths. While he accepted the mentality that allowed men to kill in the name of their country but to find the termination of a civilian target a moral barrier they could not cross, he considered it a blessing he shared no such limitation.

His concern over the current assignment was the limited time available to adequately plan the kill. The actor's termination was not the challenge, but his ability to do so and escape without leaving trace evidence presented serious difficulties. He toweled off and quickly dressed in chinos and a sport shirt. The woman was thumbing through the trade magazines as a soap played on the television.

"Let's go to the movies."

She looked up in surprise. They had never attended a film together, "What's playing?"

"It doesn't matter. Wear one of the plain-Jane outfits and the glasses."

They drove into Beverly Hills and found parking two blocks from the theater. The heavy rains had abated, tapering off into an unpleasant drizzle. They stopped at a Starbucks on Wilshire, a block from the Samuel Goldwyn Theater. He wanted to be early, but not so early that they were the only patrons waiting for the next showing. Neither spoke as they watched the parade of people walking past on Wilshire Boulevard. He had been in the area twice before and each time he found the locals to be a confusing blend of pretension and shallowness.

At forty minutes before the showing, they left the coffee house and walked toward the historic theater. The Samuel Goldwyn Theater is best known as the home the Oscar presentations and headquarters of the Academy of Motion Picture Arts and Sciences. He left the woman near the ticket booth and walked past the theater, studying the adjacent buildings and the structures across the street. When he returned, the man purchased two tickets to *Paranoia,* and they made their way into the lobby.

Forty or fifty people were already in the lobby, many in line to purchase food and soft drinks. He crossed the open area, pacing off distances. He assumed the food concession area would be removed for the screening and Champaign and hors d'oeuvres would be served by a catering organization. He left the woman in the lobby and went in the men's room. The layout was conventional, but the facility was much larger than he expected. He washed his hands and returned to the woman in the lobby. Before they went in to take their seats, he again walked the perimeter of the area looking for additional potential exits. There were none.

The configuration of the theater was traditional, sloping from back to front. He memorized the positions of the exit doors on the ground level and from the balconies. The single screen facility was larger than he had imagined, with over a thousand seats. They sat near the rear on the end of the aisle. Several times they had to stand to allow patrons to make their way past to seats closer to the center. The theater was slightly over half full when the house lights dimmed. A moment later the curtain lights were extinguished followed by the lights on the walls, leaving only the spotlights playing on the two nine-foot Oscar statues flanking the screen. When they went out and the film began, the man and woman slipped out of the aisle and out of the theater.

As they walked back to their car, the woman tried to hide her disappointment, "Couldn't we have stayed and watched the movie?"

When he did not bother to answer, she asked, "Did you find what you needed?"

He shrugged and turned up the collar of his jacket against the light rain. "I don't know. I have to think about it."

She did not bother to interrupt his thoughts on the drive back to the motel.

———

Special Agent Costello was parked in her usual spot when Jon walked out of his building. He was smiling as he approached the passenger side of her car. He tapped on the window, which she reluctantly rolled down. "Thanks, but I've already eaten."

"Hi Carmen, how are you this evening?"

"I'm fine, Mr. Scanlan. What do you want?" Thoughts of their dinner together had bothered Carmen all week. She felt she had been manipulated into an uncomfortable and potentially career shattering situation. She also had to admit she enjoyed being with Jonathan.

"Please, it's Jon. I have something to show you."

"Well, what is it?"

"It's in my apartment."

"What is this, a line? You have something to show me bring it down here."

Jonathan shook his head, "It's about two hundred pages of computer printout. What do you want to do, spread it out in the front seat of your car?"

"Come on Jonathan, what's this all about?"

He shook his head, "I'll explain everything to you upstairs, not through your car's window on the street. Let me ask you two questions.

Do you believe I'm behind all these killings?" Jon watched her as she weighed the consequences of answering his question. She again felt she was being drawn into something beyond the boundaries of her role within the Bureau.

"Unofficially and personally, no. But my personal opinions have no bearing on the conduct of the investigation."

"Well said. My second question is, would you like to be the agent that cracks the case?"

Carmen simply stared at him for a moment. When she did respond her voice sounded foreign, as if coming from someone else, "Do you know who is murdering these people?"

"If you want to know what I have come upstairs." Jonathan turned away from the window and walked up his entry stairs. He stood waiting at the door.

A dozen voices were speaking within her head. The prudent ones were telling Carmen to follow her assignment and stay in her car. She could report their conversation to those above her and let them deal with Jon and his printout. The louder voices reminded her of the lack of recognition she received when she made the connection between *Culprits* and the killings. They also told her that the connection had come from Jonathan. Carmen slipped out of the car and walked toward the entry to the apartment house.

He unlocked the outer door and led her to his unit. Not much had changed since her prior visit. Books still littered the floor, and the furnishings were the same. It did not appear any of the money from *Culprits* went into the apartment. He motioned her to a seat in one of the armchairs.

"Ok, a little background. I guess you know about my poker group. I'm sure the Bureau has checked them all out and found them to be upstanding citizens. Your research may have also told you that they're all serious brains, I mean beyond anything you've previously encountered. Well, the group decided to apply that boatload of intelligence to the crimes."

Carmen sat up in the chair, "Whoa, hold on. The investigation of these killings isn't amateur hour. If they've interfere . . ."

Jonathan held up his hand, "They haven't interfered with anything. No one has visited a crime scene or talked to anyone. Correct me if I'm wrong, but there really isn't much to interfere with. The reason they still have you sitting outside my apartment is they don't have a clue who's behind the murders." Carmen settled back in her chair, her expression giving away nothing.

"Our first conclusion was the killings were performed by a professional killer." When Jon saw a reaction he again held up his hand. "I know, the FBI already figured that out. We also concluded the killer had extensive military training, probably in this country and with one of the elite forces, Seals, Delta, something like that. Has the Bureau reached that conclusion?"

The question caught Carmen off guard. She thought for a moment before she answered. "I don't know. They may have. I'm a rookie field agent, and they don't share everything. I know they brought in the behavioral people. What led to this conclusion?"

"The methods used in the killings, the expertise in each instance. Where does one learn to use a pistol, knife, garrote, and rifle, all with perfect proficiency? The US turns out more men and women skilled in the art of killing than any other five countries combined. Another factor we considered was that all the assassinations occurred in this country. A professional could have been brought in from Europe or Israel, but why? They would be more easily noticed and remembered."

"Can we get to this printout thing?" Carmen tried to appear impatient to mask her curiosity.

"Alright. Before Fredberg was killed my book was a nonstarter. The initial print run was ten thousand, and less than five thousand were distributed to bookstores prior to his murder. Less than half of that amount was sold to consumers by those outlets. It's common sense the people behind these killings purchased *Culprits* well before Fredberg was shot. So, we tracked the bookstores and Internet providers that received shipments and then we tracked the credit card purchases of the people who bought the book through those outlets. Of course, we have no idea who might have purchased the book for cash."

"By track, you mean hack?" While Carmen felt the need to present the righteous image of the Bureau's moral authority she felt herself being drawn into Jonathan's logic.

"Let's not split legal hairs. I wanted to show you this at one of our meetings, but well, several of the guys have high level security clearances, and I'm the one who's on the line. If this becomes an issue, I'll say I accessed the information and none of the Irregulars had anything to do with it."

"The Irregulars?"

Jon blushed, "One of the guys is a big Sherlock Holmes fan. Holmes used a gang of street urchins he called the Baker Street Irregulars."

"Sweet Jesus, save me," she could not stifle a smile.

Jonathan became deathly serious, "Can the Bureau produce a list of two thousand names that might include the identity of the person behind the murders and possibly the killer?" When Carmen did not reply he turned away. "I'm going to have a beer. Can I get you anything, a glass of water?"

"How about coffee?"

Jonathan knew the Irregulars now numbered seven.

CHAPTER 27

He had to get away. The inane television program intruded on the thoughts. He grabbed his jacket and left without explanation. He drove the city streets without direction, absorbed in the complexities of the problem. The rain had ended, but the streets still glistened with reflections of the city's lights. He lowered his window and let the scent of the wet asphalt reach him.

He had never worked with the Bureau, but he believed he understood their priorities and processes. He also respected their abilities and dedication. The actor's exposure began with the drive from his home to the theater. He would ride in the backseat of a Bureau vehicle, probably a Suburban, with at least four agents. If they did it right, there would also be a lead and a chase vehicle loaded with agents. His arrival offered another opportunity. They might try to shield the man, but he guessed the cameras and fans lining the walkway would draw Clarke away from his cover.

Once inside, it was a completely different ballgame. Clarke and his FBI chaperone would be mixing with the collection of celebrates, film critics, and hangers on. Agents would be manning the exits and watching their adopted child from strategic positions. Once the actor moved from the lobby to the seating area, he was unreachable. There was no way to know where he would be seated. When the event was over, the door of opportunity opened again. Clarke would leave beside his Bureau escort and surrounded by his fellow theatergoers. Other Bureau personnel would probably close in if they could reach him. The exit would be a repeat of the arrival.

He knew he could easily gain access to the event. The most direct method would be to kill one of the service people and use their identity card, perhaps someone from the catering organization. Even the largest catering companies used part time people and the turnover was enormous. But what to do when he arrived? A thrust of a knife and Clarke was dead, but this was not a suicide mission. Avoiding the woman with the actor would not be difficult in the crowd, but assuming he was not shot by one of the watchers, how could he exit the building? A question without an answer. That left the arrival and the departure.

He concluded the only realistic chance at both his prey and a clean escape was a long range shot from one of the buildings near the theater. He needed a special weapon and he needed access to the roof of a building facing the front of the Samuel Goldwyn Theater.

On the drive back to the motel, he used his throwaway cell phone to call a man he had dealt with once before. He gave the man his specifications and did not argue over the price. He offered a thousand-dollar bonus if the weapon was available within twenty-four hours. Tomorrow would be devoted to a study of the buildings surrounding the theater.

His thoughts drifted back to the woman waiting at the motel. When they met, she was working at a diner in Phoenix. He was passing through after an easy assignment in Santa Barbara. The kill had gone down as an accident and he had decided to keep the Dodge Ram he had been using and to take a few days to work his way home. Like every man who stopped at Herb's Diner, he was immediately taken by her beauty. Unlike the others, he recognized she was totally lost. It took two weeks. At first, he was kind and considerate. He was there three times a day. On day three, he coaxed her to a low budget dinner at one of the franchise restaurants in town. He knew a big-time splurge that soon would have frightened her off. The fourth day was drinks after work and dinner at a more upscale place in Scottsdale. He listened to her and the rationalizations that had led to the job at the diner. When each evening was over, he drove her to the trailer she rented in a sprawling low-end park and left without the expectation of a kiss.

On the third date, after her third drink, Carol Morrison became more introspective and more honest about the circumstances that led to her life in Phoenix. The man she knew as John Lesser listened without judgment. Her father had died when she was eleven. Six years later her mother married a man Carol could not stand. Months after the wedding bells ceased to chime she found her mother bent over the kitchen counter in pain. Barbara Morrison said she hurt herself slipping in the shower. Two weeks later, a theoretical fall in the bedroom sent Carol's mother to the hospital. Dislike grew to hate as she watched her stepfather systematically abuse her mother. She was seventeen when she left with nothing more than a suitcase filled with her clothes. A high school degree and no recognizable skills led to low wage jobs in fast food franchises and eventually to the diner.

He offered understanding without condescension and when the accumulation of cocktails and wine made her vulnerable he drove her home and tucked her into bed. She was surprised to find him at his usual position at the counter the next morning.

He offered his slightly off-center smile and pushed his coffee mug toward Carol. "I think we both need more of this. Pick you up at seven?"

Carol had never met a man like John. Unlike the others, he was solid. Perhaps not as attractive as the men she had known and somewhat older, but how many of them had taken her home without the expectation of time in her bed. After the next dinner, he moved into her trailer. One night he asked her if she would wish that her stepfather would disappear.

She turned and studied him with the almond eyes he knew he could never leave behind. Her voice was barely a whisper, "Yes."

He said nothing. Two days later Barbara Morrison reported her husband missing, and her daughter left Phoenix in the Dodge Ram.

———

They had divided the printout in half. Carmen pulled the coffee table in front of her chair and began a methodical review of the list. Each entry noted the buyer's name, credit card number, and the location of the purchase. If a corporate card had been used, the name of the organization was shown. Whenever an entry caught her attention, she used a highlighter to record her interest. Jon followed the same process at the breakfast table. They found it easier to find purchasers they could eliminate rather than those that peaked their interest. A purchase by Wendy Koch in Topeka Kansas could go into the low probability category, but how could a purchase by Douglas Wood in New York be assessed? It was nearing midnight when they finished the first pass. The list of those requiring further evaluation had been whittled down to just over a thousand.

Carmen jumped up when she glanced at her watch, "I have to go. My replacement is due in a few minutes."

"We need to talk about what to do next."

"I know, but not now. I'll call you tomorrow."

Carmen raced out of the apartment and into her Crown Vic just before Todd Siders, her late shift replacement, pulled alongside her car. She gave the agent a nervous wave as she pulled away. She tried to sort out her mismatched feelings as she drove across town to her apartment. The attraction she felt toward Jonathan frightened her. It was not as if he was the first man in her life to ignite an interest. At twenty-four, Carmen had experienced a number of infatuations, some she had even considered to be love at the time. In Jonathan's case, she questioned the genesis of her attraction. She had seen the polygraph test results and credit card receipts from his fishing trip that pointed to the man's innocence. Could her feelings be tempered by seeing Jon as a victim? The bird with the broken wing to be taken home and nurtured? She shook her head at the thought. Whatever the source of the magnetic pull, it was not prompted by pity.

The defining term of her adolescent years had been competition. As the only female in a family blessed with three older brothers, Carmen had recognized she could not compete with her siblings in tests of speed or strength. Her battlefield became one of academia. While her brothers set Cresenta Valley Senior High rushing titles on the football field and won regional competitions in the local swimming pools, Carman established herself as the leader of the debating team and as class valedictorian. The focus and purpose that allowed her to define herself within her family carried Carmen into a scholarship at UCLA and into her position at the Bureau. She knew her parents would never admit that, while they boasted of their daughter's posting at the FBI, they would really prefer to see her married and settled down with a growing family in a tract home near theirs.

CHAPTER 28

He stood in front of the theater and tried to visualize the arrival process and how the celebrities might leave the event. His exposure to the film industry was limited to a fleeting memory of actors and actresses arriving at the Academy Awards ceremony. He had a mental image of handsome men in tuxedos and beautiful women in revealing gowns as they walked down a red carpet. A wall of photographers and fans lined the path to the theater. But this was not Oscar night. Would they use the red carpet? Would a corridor of fans and camera flashing photographers be around? He looked across Wilshire and studied the buildings across the street. They were all commercial proprieties with retail businesses on the ground floor and the upper levels dedicated to office space. Most of the buildings had that nineteen fifties or sixties look and none went higher than four stories.

The man wore a Southern Cal Edison outfit complete with utility belt and the appropriate tools shoved into what appeared to be the appropriate holders. He wore glasses with tinted lenses and carried a clipboard to complete the masquerade. The assassin walked to the corner and crossed Wilshire when the signal changed. He worked his way down the street until he was standing opposite the theater. Without pausing, he walked into the building's small lobby and took the stairs to the third floor. He had hoped they would lead him to the roof. When he opened the door from the stairwell, he found himself staring down a carpeted corridor. Doors to small businesses were spaced at intervals on both sides of the hallway. At the rear of the building, he found the restrooms which were locked and another door he assumed gave access to the stairs leading to the roof. The names of each of the businesses occupying space appeared on small plaques next to the entrance to each enterprise. He wrote down the names of the three firms that occupied spaces on the side of the building facing Wilshire.

As he finished noting the name of the third business, a middle-aged woman stepped out of one of the offices on the south side of the building. A key on a chain dangled from her hand. She paused on her way to the restroom, "Can I help you?"

"Is there a Wilcox Financial in the building?"

She thought for a moment, "I don't think so. Didn't you check the directory in the lobby?"

"It's a new business. I wasn't sure they'd have it on the directory."

The woman paused for a second, as if sensing something out of place. The last thing he needed was a complication at this stage of the plan. "Well . . . good luck," she turned and began walking toward the restrooms.

He found the encounter mildly unsettling. As he left the building, he wondered what element of his clothing or behavior had raised the woman's antenna. When he was standing in front of the theater, he used his range finder to measure the exact distance to the front of the building across the street.

———

The FBI regional director read the analysis for the third time. She wished the behavioral science people would refrain from injecting their psychological jargon into every profile; psychometrics, psychobiology, dissociative psychosis, and psychotic episodes were terms that laced their reports. Boiled down to its essence, the in-house shrinks believed the shooter to be a white male in the twenty-five to thirty-five age range, a loner by disposition, and a sociopath by nature. They surmised he had experienced a difficult childhood and had possibly been abused. The profile concluded with the assessment that the killer was of above average intelligence, highly organized, and had spent time in the military service, quite possibly leaving with a less than an honorable discharge.

Hanavan shook her head and threw the report across her desk. It had taken the behavioral science people three weeks to prepare this totally useless profile. She had not hoped for much, but the lack of specificity was breathtaking. The only assessment that might prove helpful was the subject's possible history with the military. Hanavan wondered if she would ever see an analysis that described the person they sought in useful terms. The killer is a six foot ten, eighty-two-year-old philatelist living in Portland Maine. Not likely.

The phone rang as she was scrolling through the morning's emails. "Regional Director Hanavan, it's Delia Hill in communications. We just received a message you may want to see. The sender seems to be taking credit for the killings tied to that book."

"Any reason to believe it's not another crank?"

"I wouldn't know ma'am, but it is different."

"How did it come in?"

"An email to the general gov.org box."

Normally a communication such as this would be routed to a local field office and assigned to the agent at the bottom of the pecking order, but nothing was normal about this case, "Send it on Delia."

The forwarded email appeared on her screen before she was off the phone.

Bernard Fredberg
I will make thee a terror, and thou shalt be no more; though
> *thou be*
sought for, yet shalt thou never be found again, saith the
> *lord God.*
Winnie La Blanc
That at the name of Jesus every knee shall bow, of things in
> *heaven,*

and things in Earth, and things under the earth
Marc Philip Wellstone
For Christ also suffered once for sins, the just for the unjust
that He might bring us to God, being put to death in the
*   flesh*
but made alive by the Spirit
Judge Joseph Roth Carlson
Also, the angels who kept not their first estate, but left their
*   proper*
habitation, he has reserved to everlasting chains, under
*   darkness,*
to the judgment of the great day. Likewise, Sodom and
*   Gomorrah,*
and the cities around them, which, after their example, had
*   habitually*
committed uncleanness, and gone after other flesh, are set
*   forth an*
example, suffering the punishment of an eternal fire.
The Hand of God

Helen Hanavan read the message several times, searching for a connection between the biblical quotations and the killings. She knew Winnie La Blanc had dropped to her knees before collapsing to the city street, but the linkage was tenuous at best. The involvement of the religious Right was one of the possibilities considered by the Bureau, but until now there had been no tangible connection beyond their imbedded dislike for the murder victims. It would not be the first time a fringe group of extremists from the far right resorted to violence. The bombing of abortion clinics came to mind. The regional director thought The Hand of God also had a familiar ring.

She also knew the source of the email could very well be the work of an unconnected nut, a prank, or a religious zealot making the case that each of the lefties deserved to die. She added a cover note and forwarded the message to the director, the behavioral science group at Quantico, and the leaders of the investigative teams in each region.

CHAPTER 29

It was the first meeting of the Irregulars held at Jonathan's apartment. Alan and Harold eyed Carmen with undisguised distrust. Their desire to help Jon was balanced in equal measure by the potential risk to their security clearances. It had taken a week to talk them into coming.

In contrast, Cal was fascinated by the inclusion of an FBI agent and Carlos viewed Carmen's involvement as a stamp of quasi legitimacy on their efforts. Following a round of handshakes the Lockheed engineers sat on one side of the room and appeared committed to remain in an observational role. Jon had never had this many people in the apartment at one time and realized his living room/breakfast area was a little tight for seven people.

Jon dropped the edited printout on the coffee table, "Alright, we've gone through this thing a number of times and the list is down to six hundred people."

"What criteria did you use to cross purchasers off?" Cal already knew the answer but asked the question to draw others into the discussion.

Jonathan shrugged, "We made a few assumptions. The killings were well planned which, we believe meant whoever is behind this purchased the book well before Fredberg was murdered. We dropped off the libraries. After that, it was completely subjective. A female purchaser in a rural location was given less weight than a male living in a major city."

Carlos shook his head, "While we may agree the assassin is a male we can't make that distinction regarding the person behind the killings and for all we know they live in the boonies."

Jonathan turned to Carmen, "Carlos is right. The person writing the checks could be a woman and she could live anywhere. It's also possible they paid cash and won't be on the list or they had someone else buy it for them. We were trying to whittle the list down to a manageable number and we don't have much to work with."

Harold Kurtovich raised his hand, feeling like he was in the fifth grade as he did so, "We might have more than you think. Correct me if I'm wrong, but maybe we should step back and see if we can develop criteria we can work with." When no one responded Harold continued, "Ok, I think we can agree on eliminating the libraries. From what you said, Jon, there weren't that many copies of the book purchased before the first killing." When Jonathan nodded agreement, Harold pushed on, "Alright. What was the date of the first murder?"

"April 28th."

"And when did the first book sale occur?"

Cal picked up the printout and began paging through it, "I can do a sort by purchase date, but it looks like mid-February."

Kurtovich turned to Carmen, "How long would it take someone to set up a well-planned killing?"

She shrugged. "The shooter had to observe Fredberg long enough to know his daily pattern. If I had to guess, about a week. The building had a doorman and Fredberg had a security system so, adding in a little time to develop an entry plan, let's say a minimum of a week."

Harold nodded, "Alright, but you're talking about the killer. If we're looking for the person who hired the assassin, we can assume the book was purchased sometime before the killer began studying the first victim."

Carmen began to see where Harold was going. "Right. So, we can back up the timeline."

The weapons design engineer offered a shy smile. "Let's say you wanted to kill a number of liberals and for some reason you felt like following a sequence, such as the chapters in *Culprits*. You'd probably buy several books before you selected Jon's. Do you think you'd have the assassin lined up, waiting to be told about his target, or would you figure out the target first, then hire the killer?"

Alan Thielen broke into the discussion, "I would think the target comes first. Otherwise how could you agree on a price? I'm sure the amount that a killer charges depends on the assignment's degree of difficulty."

Jonathan could sense the growing enthusiasm within the group. Harold pushed on, "Right. So how much time would it take between when Jon's book is purchased and the assassin is hired?"

Carlos jumped into the building scenario. "One day's too short, two weeks maybe too long. We have to assume the person behind this already had someone in mind for the job."

Cal nodded. "So, let's say four days minimum." When no one objected he flipped over one of the sections of the printout and began writing on the back. "Ok, I'll run the list through a sort by date of purchase. If Carlos is right, the purchase occurred between March 31st and April 10th."

Jonathan had another thought, "I think we may have another criterion." He turned to Carmen. "How much would it cost to hire a professional assassin?"

Costello shrugged, "I have no idea."

"But a lot, right?"

"I guess. We've agreed the killer is very good at what he does, and the victims are all high profile. Fredberg and La Blanc probably weren't a big challenge, but Wellstone had very heavy security and the Bureau was watching Carlson."

"Fifty thousand?"

"At least. I'd guess more for Wellstone and Carlson."

"Let's stay on the conservative side. If we assume fifty thousand each for Fredberg and La Blanc and seventy-five for Wellstone and Carlson, someone paid the killer at least two hundred and fifty thousand dollars. Not many people have that type of money lying around."

The concept brought silence to the room. Jon continued his thought. "So, we have a modified list based on our timeline. How do we figure out the net worth of the people on the new list?"

"A credit report?"

Greg Stokes shook his head. "Not enough useful information. You can have a wonderful credit rating without having much money. I just had an idea. Can you get a home address on the people on the list?"

Cal thought for a moment. "Sure. We know the city or town of purchase, so I can run a merge with the directories. Of course, this only works if they live near where they bought the book. I already have an address if they purchased on Amazon or one of the other major online outfits."

Stokes smiled, "There's a new information system called Zillow.com. You enter the address of a property and it'll give you an estimated value based on comparables. If we assume this person has a great deal of money it seems logical they'd own an expensive home. We have to keep in mind values in the area. A high-end home in San Francisco is worth a lot more than one in Dayton Ohio."

Cal gave Jonathan a pensive glance, "The sort by purchase date will only take a few minutes. I can merge the directories in one or two hours. I have no idea how I can integrate this Zillow information. I might be able to access their system. If not, we have to access each address as a separate entry, which will take a great deal of time."

"Time is a function of money, Cal. If you can't crack their database, I'll pay to have a team of data entry people take this on. At least I can put some of the *Culprits* money to good use."

Carlos turned to Carmen and asked the question that had been on several minds. "Agent Costello, why are we doing this? The Federal Bureau of Investigation has almost unlimited resources and tens of thousands of talented personnel. Why are you sitting here with a room full of volunteers trying to solve these crimes rather than working with a team of your trained experts?"

Costello remained silent for a moment as she sat in one of

Jonathan's overstuffed chairs. She was so small her feet barely touched the floor. When she spoke, her voice was hardly above a whisper, "Mr. Hermosillo, I love my job with the Bureau, and I believe our agency is honestly dedicated to protecting our country. I'm a rookie agent, and I don't have a very good working relationship with my boss, the head of our San Francisco office. If I brought this to his attention, several things would happen, none of them good from your perspective. While he would grab any breakthrough, you've made as his own personal achievement, he would legally crucify each and every one of you for violations of the privacy statutes. This would ruin your lives while what you've developed would be a stepping-stone to his next rung on the Bureau's ladder. I also believe your friend, Jonathan, has been savaged in the press and the Bureau has sat back, knowing he had no involvement in the killings. Your little band of volunteers has made more headway than anything I know about at the Bureau, which is pretty exciting for a rookie agent."

"But at some point, this has to be turned over. Assuming we come up with a short list of high probability candidates the FBI has to come into the picture."

Carmen nodded, "I know. I'm trying to figure out a way to transfer the information without screwing up my career or your lives." She turned to Cal. "Can your computer work be traced back to you?"

Cal thought for a moment, "They employ talented people and have some awesome hardware, so I have to believe they could work it out."

The mood in the room had shifted from almost giddy to an unsettling countenance. Jonathan tried to lighten the collective malaise. "Look, it's just another problem to solve. If we're bright enough to figure out who's behind the killings we can certainly develop a plan to transfer the information without leaving our fingerprints on the cookie jar."

After the meeting, Jon walked Carmen back to her Bureau car. "How long do you think they'll keep me under surveillance?"

Carmen shrugged, "No one seems very interested in our reports. It's hard to say, but probably not much longer."

"You know, when it started it really pissed me off. Now I sort of look forward to it, at least the evening shift."

"Good night Jon." Carmen held back her smile as she slid into her Crown Victoria.

CHAPTER 30

The assassin stared at the headline for a moment before he shoved his quarters into the news rack and pulled out the paper. The bold type banner read:

BREAKTHROUGH IN CULPRITS MURDERS.

He was not a man easily frightened, but the thought of an inadvertent error that could lead to his door sent a chill down his spine. He quickly scanned the lead article, which shifted his alarm to confusion. The biblical quotes associated with each victim had been received by the *New York Times* and *Los Angeles Times* from an anonymous source. The writer of the article provided comments from several legal experts and former law enforcement officers, some suggesting the killer was taunting the investigators. The inference that an unbalanced far right religious fanatic was systematically murdering the country's secular progressives was laced through the article.

The killer's initial reaction to the article was one of relief. Not only was the so-called breakthrough unrelated to him, it would divert the attention of the FBI down an unproductive path. His second thought was less comforting. What if the message had been sent by his current employer? He knew nothing beyond the voice at the other end of a telephone connection. The motivation of his employers did not concern him. He viewed himself as a mechanic, performing a service for those willing to pay the appropriate price. But what if his current employer was a religious crazy? Someone like that would be careless, they would make mistakes which the investigators would exploit. He needed to think, and the motel with the woman's inane television programs made that impossible.

He crossed Sepulveda and walked two blocks to a diner. The morning crowd was thinning, and he had no trouble finding a stool at the end of the counter. He ordered coffee and reread the article. The quotations made no more sense to him on the second reading. He considered his connection to his employer and the probability of being identified if things went wrong. He believed the payments were untraceable. Each payment was bounced from numbered account to numbered account in offshore banks famous for their confidentiality. Their initial contact had followed the usual protocol; first a message sent to an untraceable email address, then telephone conversations using a series of disposable cell phones.

He never identified himself to any of his employers and used a different alias in every city. He knew his greatest exposure was the woman, but he did not want to think about that at the moment. He wanted to call and ask his employer if he or she had sent the email to the press, but that would have to wait until after he terminated Lawrence Clarke. At the conclusion of his assignment, he would receive an email providing the number of the next disposable cell phone. Prior to that, he had no way to make contact. As he walked back to the motel, he decided he was safe for the moment.

The undecipherable communication stirred the fires of controversy in the media and on Capitol Hill. *The New York Times* editorial section blossomed with a new round of attacks against the administration, citing everything from incompetence to a cover up. Several columnists demanded the head of the FBI and the usual ultraliberal senators and congressmen made inflammatory speeches and demanded hearings. One congresswoman made a statement at a Black Caucus meeting that the president knew who was committing the murders but would not reveal their identity as they were wealthy conservative donors. The political cable shows trotted out their experts who argued over the meaning of the biblical quotations and the effectiveness of the criminal investigation. The email saved a slow news day.

The Bureau traced the communication to an Internet café in Chicago. The user paid cash and was unremarkable enough to not be remembered by the staff.

———

With the screening only a few days off, Lawrence Clarke was in a jubilant mood. His hair stylist and tailor had both been to his home to prepare him for the event. He spent hours on the phone networking with friends who would also be in attendance. He was even civil to his protective team. While most of the actor's telephone calls were made in the presence of the agents in the house, one required more finesse. Clarke locked his bathroom door and used his cell to call a close friend. Claudia Kirkland had slept with most of Hollywood and was beyond easy. She was simply available and that fulfilled Lawrence's set of requirements.

"Claudia darling, it's Lawrence." When there was a momentary silence, the actor realized there could be more than one Lawrence in Ms. Kirkland's past, "Lawrence Clarke."

"Of course, Lawrence. I've been thinking about you and that awful book," Claudia affected a southern accent ever since she played Blanche DuBois in *A Streetcar Named Desire* on off Broadway.

"Yes, the last two months haven't been easy. How have you been?" Lawrence had no real interest in how Claudia was faring, but a little conversational foreplay was necessary.

"Marvelous. I just got back from cruising with Brett and Julia in the Caribbean. They have the most wonderful yacht they keep in Antigua."

Clarke's mind wandered as he considered which of the Barlows

Claudia had been servicing. He concluded the answer was probably both, "That sounds fantastic. Will I be seeing you at *The Last Woman*?"

Claudia could not hide the disappointment in her voice, "No, I'm afraid not."

Lawrence's heart beat a little faster, "That's a shame, it should be a splendid event. Say . . . you know Susanne Davis and I have always been close. I'm sure I can arrange another ticket if you'd like to go."

"I'd love to," no hesitation there.

"I have a little problem with the FBI protective team they have guarding me. Would it be a terrible imposition to ask you to meet me at the theater?" Clarke held his breath while he waited for her answer.

"No, of course not."

"Wonderful, I'll have the studio deliver your ticket no later than tomorrow. I'll meet you in the lobby."

The aging actor did a little dance in the bathroom before he walked back into the company of his protectors.

CHAPTER 31

Carmen sat next to Jonathan as they waited for the rest of the Irregulars to arrive. The double life she was leading was taking its emotional toll. She was not sleeping well and having difficulty concentrating. Earlier in the day, she had been called into a team meeting and watched Ross Del Monica preen before his dedicated audience. The man reminded her of a defensive back celebrating after tackling a running back who had just ripped off a twenty-yard run. Somewhere along the line priorities had been lost.

Cal came in carrying his briefcase. Absent was the usual joking and idle comments that had seemed an indelible part of the poker group. As the others arrived, each glanced at the black briefcase which had become the eight-hundred-pound gorilla in the room. Everyone knew they were nearing the end of their journey and each wondered if the trip would end successfully.

Hulse stood while the others remained seated, "There were just over three hundred copies of *Culprits* sold in the defined time frame. A few went to libraries, which I eliminated. I was able to develop addresses on all but thirty of the remaining purchasers. When I used Zillow to determine values, most of the buyers were, as you'd expect, of modest means. Many were in apartments, which pushed them off the list. We ended up with fifteen that would probably qualify as wealthy. I don't think we can arbitrarily eliminate the thirty without addresses. Most used corporate cards which could indicate money and position."

No one spoke for several moments. Jonathan stood and shook his friend's hand, "I know we all hoped one name would be left, but that's not how it works. We started with everyone as a potential suspect and now we have about forty-five. That's incredible. The question is, what do we do next?" Jon turned to Carmen, "What if I went to the Bureau with our thinking, not our results? If I told them they could narrow the search through the timeline and then shrink it further by isolating the people, who could pay for a professional?"

Carmen smiled, "Two problems. First, you have less than no credibility with the Bureau. For God's sake, you're their only suspect. They might concede you may not be the killer or the money behind the hits when they stand around the water cooler, but keep in mind, you're all they have. Second, our local hero is a peacock, an empty suit filled only with his own ambition. He's not going to pursue a line of reasoning he can't claim as his own, and when you give a recorded statement that wouldn't be possible."

"What about going over his head?"

Carmen shook her head, "I can't help you, but it might work. I've heard Helen Hanavan is a reasonable lady, but realistically, I think no one would listen."

Carlos spoke into the growing silence, "So, that means we go further. How can we examine these forty-five people? I understand in today's age of data bases and information services there are few secrets." He looked at Cal for a response.

The programmer offered a vague smile, "You're right about that. Everyone says your records are secure and then sells their database to the next telemarketer. Insurance, health, even tax records are available if you know where to go."

"And you know where to go," from Carlos it was a statement, not a question.

Cal hesitated, then nodded. Jonathan glanced around the room; no more than two months ago these men were Cal Hulse's friends and fellow poker players. Now he felt close to each of the men. "Alright, but Cal, any digging you do has to come back to me. If someone was as talented as you and could trace back the source of these inquiries, how could they make the connection?"

"Anytime you access a system you leave an electronic fingerprint. If you're good the print is difficult to trace. You can bounce it around the world, use electronic cutouts and other tricks, but if they're really talented, they can bring it back to you."

Jonathan smiled, "Let's make it easy. Use my computer as the source. Think about it, I'm looking for my salvation. Why wouldn't I be trying to find out who's responsible for the killings? So, what if I step over the line while I'm trying to clear my name. If anything, it gives me a platform to present our theories and what we've come up with. How could they know I can't figure out how to turn the damned thing on?"

The fifth meeting of the Pacific Avenue Irregulars ended on a note of optimism.

———

The timing left a great deal to be desired. The theater doors opened at seven thirty and the businesses in the building ended their workday at either five or five thirty. In theory, the two-hour gap allowed more than enough time to access the building and set up shop in one of the third-floor offices. Unfortunately, several of the office dwellers worked late and time had not allowed him to develop a record of the work habits of each employee. He had watched the building for several evenings and had not been surprised by the erratic pattern of departures by the office personnel. If someone were still there when he broke in, he would have no choice but to kill the late working employee. He took no gratification in terminating the life of someone who was simply in the way, but such collateral damage was not unknown. The office lights appeared to be on timers, offering no assurance of the unit's occupancy.

He wore coveralls of the same color used by the janitorial firm under contract with the building knowing the subterfuge was of modest value. The cleaning crew arrived at twelve thirty each night, and he hoped to be long gone by then. The assassin stood across the street, four buildings down from the theater as he watched the trickle of departing workers begin at four thirty. A small surge occurred just after five thirty, and a man and a woman left just after six. There was no further activity during the next thirty minutes, and at six thirty he walked back to his parked car and retrieved the stainless-steel case containing his weapon.

It was a clear evening with a mild wind from the west, not strong enough to affect the trajectory. The lobby was empty as he entered the building, bright in the glow of the overhead florescence lighting. The man, now showing medium length black hair and a neatly trimmed Van Dyke beard, walked past the elevator to the stairs. He took them two at a time to the third-floor landing where he paused. He placed the case on the floor and eased the door open with latex gloved hands. The brightly lit hallway was empty.

Without hesitation, he walked to the last office on the floor. Any of the three facing Wilshire would have served his purpose, but the third, which housed a small CPA firm, was closest to the theater entrance. The door was predictably locked which only delayed his entrance a minute. He opened the door slowly, scanning the room as it became visible. The office was bathed in florescence light, but no one was in sight. He slipped inside and walked across the space to the windows facing the street. The assassin placed his case on the ground and extracted a glass-cutter from one of his coverall pockets. He shifted a table and pushed a desk back to the windows. After using a tape measure to ensure the proper height above the desk he attached the glass-cutter's suction cup to the window and carved a circular cut with its diamond edge. The round piece of glass popped out cleanly.

He was on his knees opening the stainless-steel case when he heard the office door swing open. A man in his fifties walked in with the key to the restroom dangling from his hand. The middle-aged man had the end of day look, rumpled shirt and slacks, his tie askew, and the burden of the day etched in the lines on his face. He was half way across the office before he noticed the man in coveralls. He stopped, a confused expression on his face.

"I thought . . ." in one smooth motion the assassin raised his silenced pistol and fired. The nine-millimeter slug caught the man squarely in the chest, ending his inquiry. The assassin walked over to the dying man's body and shot him once more in the temple. The black-haired man returned his pistol to his pocket, knelt at his case and resumed assembling his rifle. After snapping the scope in place, inserting the clip and chambering a round he carefully rested the weapon on the floor. With the office lights burning brightly, he was visible to the gathering crowd in from of the theater. The last thing he wanted was someone on the street to spot a man with a gun. He pushed one of the executive chairs away from the window and waited for the timer to extinguish the office lights.

———

The four-agent protective team had been expanded to ten for the evening. The first argument of the evening came when Clarke realized they were planning on delivering him to the screening in a Suburban. "Are you out of your mind! Even the grips will arrive in limos."

Lynn Cameron let the tuxedo clad actor rant for a few minutes. When he began to run out of steam, she pointed out the terms of the deal. He had agreed to go along with the Bureau's security measures and using their vehicles was definitely one of the conditions. "Think of it this way, Mr. Clarke, everyone has a limo, but you'll be arriving surrounded by ten armed bodyguards. I bet even the stars of the film won't have that."

The thought mollified Lawrence, as did Agent Cameron's appearance. As his evening's escort she was wearing the best and only gown from her closet, a simple black form fitting dress and high heels. Her gold band necklace with matching earrings would, without question, be the most modest display of jewelry at the screening, but she looked good. Clarke was surprised by the transformation and wondered why he had considered her unappealing during the prior weeks. When they were bundled into the Suburban's back seat, Lawrence was able to catch a decent view of the federal agent's well-shaped thigh. He gave a passing thought to placing his hand on her leg before rejecting the idea as unwise.

The actor's SUV was sandwiched between a lead and a chase vehicle. Lawrence spent the drive visualizing how he would lose the agents and connect with Claudia.

CHAPTER 32

When the lights went off, the assassin placed his weapon's tripod on the desk. Three days earlier he had driven into the desert between Los Angeles and Palm Springs and sighted in the Belgium made rifle. The distance was so minimal he could easily place a round within a two-inch circle with open sights. With the Leopold scope, the variable would be less than an eighth of an inch.

His original thought was to shoot from the roof. The height would offer a cleaner angle when the target appeared in a crowded environment, but practicality won the day. A conclusion the dead CPA on the floor might not share. The building's floor plan forced the use of the third floor rather than the roof. The position of the stairway meant traversing the length of the building before he could reach the main stairwell. The additional time offset the marginally better firing position.

While he waited for the arriving celebrities and fringe players, he thought about taking Carol away after the kill. He knew sitting in a low-end motel for weeks had placed a strain on the relationship and the idea of a brief vacation appealed to him. He had never been to Yosemite. Years ago, he had read about the Tenaya Lodge, but then there was Hawaii. Not Honolulu, maybe the big island or Lanai. He was still thinking about the islands when the first limousines began to arrive.

He placed the cross hairs on each of the guests as they stepped out of their impossibly long limos. It was a scene out of *Ground Hog Day*. Each ridiculous vehicle disgorged a handsome man in a tuxedo and a gorgeous young woman in a sparkling gown cut to her navel. He began to wonder if they had another entrance for the unattractive people.

At seven forty-five, a black Suburban inched its way to the entrance. A mass of men and women screened the rear passenger door from his view. He clicked off the safety and waited for a clear shot. He had a momentary glimpse Clarke's balding head as he slid out of the vehicle. Not enough of an opening for a clear shot. His angle on the third floor was offset by the difference in height between the short actor and the taller men and women surrounding him. The man's escort had to be eight inches taller than Clarke. His cross hairs followed the entourage as they forced the actor to shuffle into the building.

The assassin clicked on the safety and sat back. Round one had passed, and Lawrence Clarke did not have a scratch on him, but there was still round two. He had learned years ago to never press, never take the excessive risk. If Clarke left the way he arrived, the only one to lose tonight was the man on the floor.

———

Jonathan watched his friend's fingers dance across the keyboard. It was like watching a Chinese opera. Every so often Cal would make little noises as he burrowed into the private lives of the people on the list. Jon could neither tell from his friend's expression or sounds if things were being uncovered or if the man's efforts were proving worthless. At six, when she came on shift, Carmen joined him on the sofa. The incongruity of having the federal agent assigned to his surveillance sitting next to him as his best friend hacked into a variety of secure databases no longer seemed relevant.

What did seem relevant was the presence of the attractive woman beside him. Tonight, she was wearing a tailored suit with a skirt short enough to reveal her well-shaped legs. Jonathan felt his throat tighten as he turned to Carmen, "Hungry?"

Cal glanced away from the screen, "Sure, you have something here?"

"No, but we can bring something back," he looked at Carmen, nervously waiting for a response.

She tried to contain a smile, "If you're going out I have to come along. The government's paying good money for me to keep an eye on you."

Cal did not look away from the screen as he pushed his way into another restricted file. "Remember, no cilantro."

They turned the collars of their coats up against the chill wind blowing off the bay as they walked down to Union. The usually busy street was surprisingly quiet. They paused and studied the menus of several eateries before moving further down the street. Jonathan turned to Carmen as they glanced at the posted menu outside The Blue Light, "What do you feel like?"

She shrugged, "I don't know, some of these places are kind of expensive."

As they reached the corner at Webster, a smile came across Jon's face, "I have an idea. Let's see if we can get in without a reservation."

"Where?"

"It's a surprise."

Carmen began to press for an answer but relented when she saw Jonathan's enthusiasm. He took the small woman's arm and led her to Fillmore where he steered her toward the bay. Without pausing, he started to walk into Plump Jack. Carmen stopped at the entrance.

"Come on Jon, I can't afford this."

"It's my treat."

"You know I'm not allowed to do that," the memory of her uncomfortable feelings after their dinner at Luisa's came to mind.

"Carmen, think about it. How much worse is it to let me buy dinner than to work with us on the investigation?" Before she could answer, he slipped into the restaurant. A moment later, he popped back out, his engaging smile in place, "We're in luck. They can seat us right away."

"Jonathan . . ."

"Come on, in for a penny, in for a pound. Aren't federal agents allowed to date?"

He had trouble reading her expression, "Is that what this is, a date?"

"I hope so," he extended his hand, waiting for Carmen to reach a decision. His smile remained in place, belying the tension that gripped his body. He was not optimistic as he tried to gauge her reaction. He felt a surge of relief as Carmen smiled and took his hand.

Jonathan had been in the small restaurant before, but somehow the room seemed brighter as he sat next to Carmen. He turned to her as he paged through the wine list. "What do you like? Chardonnay, Pinot, Cabs?"

"Jon, I'm working, I can't have anything to drink."

Jonathan was about to respond when Carmen's cell phone began ringing. She pushed away from the table and quickly walked across the restaurant. She answered the second she reached the sidewalk. It was Ross Del Monica's administrative assistant, a woman named Elena Goodhue.

"Ross has called a team meeting for 8:00 a.m. tomorrow."

"Ok Elena, I'll be there."

"Where are you? I can hear traffic noises."

Everyone in the office knew Elena was Del Monica's in-house snitch, "I'm outside a restaurant on Fillmore. Scanlan's having dinner."

"Which place?"

Idle curiosity or something else? "Plump Jack."

"I've heard about it, but I've never been there."

"No, too rich for my budget. See you tomorrow morning," the call forced her feelings of ambivalence back to the surface. She wanted to do the right thing as an agent, but the right thing seemed to be in stark contrast to her Bureau assignment.

The two full wine glasses at the table were hard to ignore. "Jon, I told you I can't have anything to drink."

Jonathan held up his hands in mock surrender, "Alright. I just thought . . . this being our first date . . . it's a Pinot from the Russian River area."

Carmen picked up her glass and inhaled the wine's aroma, "It smells wonderful, but all I need is to be called into the office tonight smelling like a winery."

He smiled and shrugged, "Well, even the most dedicated agents have to eat."

They studiously avoided talking about the investigation as they grazed their way through dinner. As they split a Caesar, Carmen talked about growing up as the only girl among five brothers. She had Jonathan laughing as she told him stories about her attempts to compete with her siblings, all of which were older and considerably bigger.

Jon described his failed attempt to play his way through the PGA's Qualifying School. "I thought I was good enough to make the cut, and to this day I'm not sure exactly what happened. I mean, I lost and the odds weren't great to begin with, but I was one of the top ranked amateurs."

Jonathan described the elimination process in which approximately one thousand entrants compete to earn one of thirty PGA cards issued annually and the right to play on the PGA Tour. "I made it through the first two tournaments which dropped us down to one hundred and fifty-six players. That's when I lost it. The final qualifying stage is six rounds. I was doing well until the third day. Everything seemed to go, my timing, my ability to hit the fairways. Most people will say it's the pressure, and they may be right. Anyway, that's why I teach English lit. rather than going head to head with Tiger."

"Couldn't you try again?"

"Not now. I gave it a second try and didn't fare any better. You have to play every day to keep your game at that level. Now I only play once or twice a week. Q School costs twelve thousand to enter, and at the time, I had to borrow the money from my dad. It's ironic, when I had the right game I didn't have any money, and now, when I'm flush, my game's gone."

Carmen reached across the table and took his hand, "Who knows, maybe in the grand scheme of things everything will work out for the best.

"Who knows? I guess we need to order something for Cal." Jon asked the waiter for a menu and ordered a seafood pasta dish to go. They sat in comfortable silence while they waited for Hulse's dinner to arrive. When it came, they bundled up and walked back into the cool night air. Carmen's hand found Jon's as they strolled back to his apartment.

———

Lawrence was in his element. He cruised through the crowded lobby like a corsair pursuing an unarmed trading vessel. The actor air-kissed and hugged everyone in sight. Lynn Cameron was forced to follow in the small man's wake as he worked the room. She noticed Clarke seemed unusually attentive to a tall blond woman with surgically enhanced bosoms, puffed out lips, and far too much makeup. The agent smiled as she realized she had just described over half the women at the screening. What separated this blond from her doppelgängers was her reaction to Clarke. She draped herself around the actor like a mink stole. At one point, Lynn watched the tall woman's tongue explore the short man's inner ear. Agent Cameron found the display tasteless but not pertinent to her assignment. She was with the actor to keep him alive, not to ward off women who found the man attractive. Lynn noticed her fellow agents scattered around the room. They were not difficult to spot in the sea of hundred-dollar haircuts, nose jobs, and designer gowns.

When the lights dimmed and the crowd began funneling into the theater, Lynn found she was suddenly part of a threesome. The blond, who Lawrence introduced as Claudia, remained attached to the actor in limpet like devotion. Their seats were toward the rear of the theater on the main floor. Lawrence skillfully positioned himself between his official escort and his amorous friend. When the highlights playing on the huge Oscars dimmed and the theater fell into darkness, Lynn was sure she saw Claudia's hand slip toward Lawrence's lap. The thought gave her an involuntary shudder as she continued to scan the theater for possible threats. The team had agreed that the greatest exposure came at the time of their arrival and departure. There was some vulnerability from the sea of people in the lobby, but it was believed there was virtually no credible threat while the film was running. Regardless of the assessment, she continued to observe the audience, knowing her team was also watching from the balcony and from the rear corners of the main floor. Occasionally during the movie, she was distracted by muted moaning noises from her seat-mate that she knew had no connection to the film. Cameron assumed the blond would be traveling back to Topanga Canyon after the event.

Lynn was paying no attention to the movie, and when it suddenly ended, and the credits began playing across the screen she reassessed their exit plan. The Suburban would be waiting at the curb on Wilshire and the team of agents would collapse on the actor and hustle him into the vehicle. Claudia complicated the plan and Cameron was not sure how to adjust. At the very least, she would slow the process and Lynn had no idea what the woman's reaction would be when ten agents began pushing her into the SUV. The lights came on and the audience applauded as if they had just witnessed the second coming. A thin elderly tuxedo clad man walked up the steps at the front of the theater and made his way to the center of the stage. Lynn Cameron was speaking into the miniature microphone attached to her bracelet, telling her detail about Claudia and revising the exit plan as the man on the stage thanked everyone for coming. Several guests glared at the agent as she spoke over the man thanking everyone involved in what he described as an unparalleled artistic achievement.

When the second round of applause subsided, several things happened at once. The protective detail began moving toward Lawrence and Lynn while the thousand theater goers rose to their feet and began making their way out of the facility. Most began shuffling toward the front entrance, but as the side doors opened a significant portion began pouring out those doors.

When they reached the aisle bordering the left side of the theater, Lawrence and Claudia began heading for one of the side doors. Lynn Cameron grabbed the actor's arm, "What do you think you're doing? We're going out the front."

Clarke pulled away from her grasp, "Claudia and I have other plans."

Out of the corner of her eye Cameron could see her fellow agents fighting their way through the departing crowd, "Listen you little shit, you agreed to how this would be handled." Her voice was barely above a hiss, but several guests turned and watched the confrontation.

Lawrence offered the condescending smile he had used so often in his role as a hard-nosed district attorney. "I'm changing the deal. We'll see you in the morning," He turned and began making his way toward the exit with Claudia in tow.

Cameron grabbed the actor's shoulder to hold him back. Under normal circumstances she could subdue the small man in less than a minute. Her problem was the loss of leverage and balance caused by her high heels. She glanced back and saw that her colleagues were making little progress fighting through the stream of guests flowing toward the front of the theater. Clarke was eight feet from the side door when she shifted her grip to his arm and spun the actor around. The effort left her off balance and completely exposed to the right cross that sent her sprawling to the floor. Claudia's punch was not delivered that well or with any significant force but arrived so unexpectedly it achieved a surprisingly effective result.

Lynn Cameron found herself on her back, watching Lawrence and Claudia slip through the door. She pushed away two men trying to help her to her feet, kicked off her heels and frantically searched for her handbag which contained her credentials and her Lady Smith & Wesson, all the while yelling into her microphone. Two of her fellow agents reached her before she found the bag under one of the chairs.

She frantically pointed to the exit, "Stop them! Tackle the little bastard if you have to!"

Lynn began pushing through the remaining departing guests until she was in the driveway that bordered the theater. There were still too many people in front of the agents to make quick progress to the street. When she reached Wilshire, she found her two agents looking up and down the crowded street. Over a thousand guests from the screening were waiting for their limousines while hundreds of fans looked for their favorite celebrities. Finding the diminutive actor was like looking for a needle in a haystack. Tall blonds were also not a rare commodity. They shouldered their way to the line of waiting vehicles. The Bureau's Suburban was double parked on the street with four agents standing outside the vehicle. Cameron motioned the agents over and told them to search the crowd for Clarke.

The man on the third floor trained his weapon on a spot ten feet from the Bureau's Suburban and waited for the actor to be separated from the milling mass of people in front of the theater. He realized something was wrong when he saw the woman who had accompanied Clarke to the screening waving her arms as she talked to the agents by the SUV. Seconds later they all rushed into the crowd, obviously searching for the actor. He began using his Zeiss binoculars to scan the sea of humanity. The process seemed hopeless with all the men looking the same in their tuxedos.

Clarke had asked Claudia to arrange for a limo to pick them up on Wilshire, fifty yards down the street from the theater. As soon as they were able to break free from the crowd, they began making their way up the street. Lawrence was terribly pleased with himself, having outsmarted his Bureau watchdogs. He knew he could have taken Claudia back to his home in the FBI vehicle, but ditching the fascist goons for an evening added a special spice to the adventure. He stopped as he reached the stretch Cadillac and looked back toward the theater and smiled. The Bureau Suburban sat like a lonely child on the street as the agents searched through the crowd. When he turned back to the limo, the driver was standing by the open rear door. Lawrence gave Claudia an affectionate squeeze as she slid into the vehicle.

A movement on the periphery of his vision caught the contract killer's attention. While all the other limousines were queued up in front of the theater a lone limo was positioned well down the block. He wondered why more of the theatergoers had not considered the same solution to the chaotic mess. He had to assume the celebrities wanted to be seen and were willing to tolerate the wait. It was then he recognized Clarke as the actor approached the stretch Cadillac. The assassin had no idea where the tall blond hanging on the actor had come from and could care less. He did not have time to use the laser to measure the distance. He mentally added fifty yards to the distance he had used to sight in his rifle as he shifted the weapon's position on the desk. Lawrence Clarke was bending down to slide into the limo when he squeezed off his shot. The bullet passed through the actor's heart and slammed into the limo's open door.

The assassin ducked below the window, retrieved his brass and began breaking down his weapon before Claudia knew her companion was dead. As soon as they heard the shot, the FBI agents drew their weapons and began searching for the shooter and the victim. Claudia's screams provided one of the answers. Three of the agents raced up the street while the others scanned the surrounding buildings for the source of the shot. The mass of people in front of the Samuel Goldwyn Theater panicked. Some tried to run back into the theater, but most scattered in both directions down Wilshire. With a thousand people running in every direction, the man had no difficulty losing himself in the stampede.

CHAPTER 33

The reaction to Lawrence Clarke's death was exponentially greater than the combined impact of the other four victims. The story eclipsed all other news of the day and extended far beyond the simple reporting of the crime, which in its own right, was sensational. A sniper murdering a well-known actor in Beverly Hills in front of a thousand Hollywood names was everything a journalist or television commentator could hope for. Mix into the pot the fact that he was under FBI protection, was chapter five in *Culprits of the American Culture,* and was, like those featured in chapters one, two, three and four, a vocal critic of the administration. The inclusion of Claudia Kirkland even added sex to the stew.

A reader had to reach page three of their newspaper to find any stories unrelated to the killing and the editorial sections were forced to double their allocated space. While the mainstream media had never been kind to conservative presidents, their collective reaction to Clarke's murder was unprecedented. Charges of incompetence and lack of leadership were replaced with accusations of conspiracy and complicity in the deaths. Demands extended far beyond firing the director of the FBI and all agents and station chiefs that had any involvement in the investigation. Several well-respected journalists wrote that the nation had completely lost confidence in the president and called for Prescott to resign.

The president raised his hand to call the meeting to order. The size of the group again necessitated the use of the Situation Room. Those in attendance sat in groups, isolated by their area of involvement. The White House staff sat on the right side of the table and the Homeland Security and FBI personnel on the left. No one seemed pleased to be in the room.

Prescott was obviously not pleased as he looked around the room, "Alright, first tell us what happened."

William Palacin cleared his throat, "Mr. President, Lawrence Clarke insisted on attending the Hollywood screening. We argued with him, showed him photos of the Carlson crime scene, but we could not talk him out of going. And we had no legal grounds to prohibit his attendance. He agreed to comply with our security procedures which included being accompanied by one of our agents. We were to handle his transportation to and from the event and he agreed to follow our procedures for his entrance and exit from the building. The studio allowed us to place agents in the theater during the screening. Everything went according to the plan until he was inside the theater. Without our knowledge, he arranged to meet a woman named Claudia Kirkland in the theater lobby. During the movie, our agent sat with Clarke and Ms. Kirkland. Clarke had agreed to leave through the theater's front entrance where he would be surrounded by our people, hustled into our vehicle, and driven back to his home.

"When the film ended, Clarke and Ms. Kirkland began to leave by one the building's side doors. When our agent tried to stop him, Ms. Kirkland knocked her down. They were able to slip out the door before our agents could stop them. Over a thousand people attended the event, and they disappeared into the crowd. Mr. Clarke had Ms. Kirkland arrange for a limo to pick them up half a block away. They were getting into the limousine when a shot was fired from an office building across the street, killing Mr. Clarke. No one saw the shooter. A man named Max Dodson was found dead in the office used in the shooting. Apparently, he was working late and surprised the killer."

"Any evidence that can identify the killer?"

"No. We found fibers at the scene but nothing useful."

The national security advisor glared at the FBI director, "One of your experienced agents couldn't stop this short, sixty-two-year-old actor?"

Palacin bristled at the rebuke, "Try it sometime in high heels and an evening dress."

Prescott held up his hand, "This can't deteriorate into a pissing match. We're here to try to figure out what to do next. Director Palacin, I don't hear anything encouraging related to solving these crimes. What about these biblical quotations?"

"There's no way to trace the source of the emails. We have people on it, but it's questionable that they're connected to the killings. Someone has to make a mistake, and so far, they haven't."

"And the guy who wrote this book, *Culprits*?"

"We're on him twenty-four seven. He's definitely not the shooter, and we can't find anything that shows he paid for the hits."

Don MacMillan, the White House spokesman, diverted the conversation down a different path. "What do you want me to tell the press corps?"

The president shrugged, "The truth. The Federal Bureau of Investigation is pursuing every possible lead. Of course, we need to express our sympathy for the victims and their families."

"We need to deny these ridiculous charges in the press that we're connected to or endorsing a program to knockoff all the lefties." This contribution from the president's chief of staff.

Prescott nodded, "Hopefully our denial will be worded somewhat differently."

When the meeting broke up, the president asked the FBI director to remain behind. He motioned for Palacin to sit down, "Bill, this has to be brought to an end."

"I'd like to be more encouraging. We need a break, an informant, a witness, an error on the part of the killer." Palacin had little hope of leaving the room as the director of the FBI.

"You've read the press. They want our heads. I know they're using it as an excuse to come after me and right now the public is agreeing with them. My problem is this is diverting us from our agenda. I can propose legislation all day long and until this is over none of it will go anywhere."

"Do you want my resignation?" the thought of leaving his office in disgrace was galling.

Prescott shook his head, "No, but I do want results. Who is the next person in the book?"

"Barbara Wiehl."

For the first time since hearing of Lawrence Clarke's death the president laughed, "This is going to be interesting."

Palacin nodded, "We tried to provide her with protection earlier. She fought us off with her attorney. I'm flying up to see her as soon as we finish. Perhaps now that she's the next chapter she'll be more cooperative."

"I'd rather wrestle alligators than have to deal with that woman."

"I know, alligators only attack when they're hungry."

———

Jonathan and Carmen heard the news of Lawrence Clarke's death almost simultaneously. They were sitting around Jon's living room watching Cal work on the remaining people on the list when her cell phone went off. She stepped away from the sporadic clatter of the keyboard as she took the call.

"Agent Costello, its Del Monica. Where is Scanlan?"

"In his apartment."

"Are you certain?"

She was tempted to turn the phone over to Jon. "Yes, I'm certain. Why? Did something happen?"

"Lawrence Clarke was shot to death in Los Angeles."

When Del Monica rang off she turned on the television and the three Irregulars watched the coverage of the killing.

CHAPTER 34

William Palacin took a Bureau helicopter to a small airfield outside Hartford. James Pohley, the head of the New York office was waiting for the director's arrival. They shook hands, but neither found the need to speak as they got into the Bureau vehicle and began the short drive to Windsor.

Palacin only knew of Barbara Wiehl by reputation. He never bothered to read her column in the *New York Times* or listen to her when she appeared on political talk shows. He'd asked for a briefing during the flight from Washington and now possessed a few additional facts. Wiehl was forty-eight, married with two children, a daughter out of school and working in Atlanta, and a son attending graduate school at Yale. Her husband, David, practiced corporate law at a large firm in Manhattan. The political views expressed in her column were consistently far left, and the Wiehls were known to be extremely social with their picture frequently appearing in the society columns.

Pohley's assistant had called the Wiehl residence and explained that her boss and Director Palacin wished to speak with Ms. Wiehl. The response had been a grudging acceptance. The Wiehl estate sat on fifteen acres of rolling hillside and was separated from its neighbors by a seven-foot stone wall. They were buzzed in when they announced themselves at the gate. The birch lined driveway curved back into the property fifty yards before the two-story Tudor came into view. If the grounds and home left any doubt regarding the wealth of the residents, a Bentley and a Porsche sitting in the driveway dispelled the misconception.

The doorbell summoned a uniformed maid who greeted them politely and ushered the two men into a formal drawing room. Barbara Wiehl sat in an overstuffed chair and did not bother to rise to meet her guests. A thin man in an expensive suit rose from his chair and stepped forward to meet the arrivals.

"Leonard Silliman, Mrs. Wiehl's attorney."

"William Palacin, and this is James Pohley, the head of our New York office."

Silliman shook each man's hand and offered a wave toward the woman behind him. "Gentlemen, this is Barbara Wiehl." From the introduction the Bureau men almost expected a drum roll.

Wiehl offered a cautious nod but otherwise remained impassive. Palacin saw no reason to beat about the bush. "Mrs. Wiehl, I believe you know why we're here. You're the subject of chapter six in *Culprits of the American Culture,* and I'm sure you're aware of what happened to the people discussed in the first five chapters."

"Yes, you and your Keystone Kops allowed them to be killed," The woman's words had the bite of acid.

The director sighed, "The Bureau was not involved in the first three murders. The fourth victim, Judge Carlson, refused to cooperate. He wouldn't allow our people in his home or permit us to provide secure transportation. Lawrence Clarke was killed because he insisted on attending a movie screening, and at the conclusion of the screening he tried to slip away from our protective team."

"Who created that fiction, the White House speech writers or do you have your own staff of spin artists? Did you read my column today Director Palacin?"

"No, I did not."

"You should. I clearly detailed why you, Prescott, and the entire collection of clowns in the administration are incompetent and should be unemployed."

During the exchange Pohley watched without expression while Silliman seemed to find the conversation highly amusing.

"I thought that was last week's column."

The director's comment caught the columnist off guard. For a brief moment the hint of a smile touched her lips, "Same clowns, different fiasco."

"Mrs. Wiehl, we're here to offer you the protection of the Bureau."

"Mr. Clarke's recent experience doesn't say much for your organization's level of competence."

"I believe I've explained why Lawrence Clarke was killed. We can't force you to accept our protection; it's entirely up to you." Palacin opened his attaché case and extracted a single sheet of paper. "Your political views are well established, Mrs. Wiehl. You have every legal right to refuse to cooperate with the Bureau, as I'm certain Mr. Silliman has advised. We would appreciate a simple, signed statement from you acknowledging your refusal to cooperate."

Leonard Silliman was no longer amused, "Mrs. Wiehl will be making no such statement."

The FBI director ignored the attorney, "Mrs. Wiehl, it's your choice. Work with us and the Bureau will do everything possible to ensure your protection. Refuse, and you're on your own; the Bureau will be issuing a press release to that effect. Perhaps you have more confidence in a private security service. That's entirely up to you."

Silliman stepped forward, "You can't do that. The FBI has an obligation to protect the citizens of this country."

Palacin replaced the sheet of paper in his case, "Not if they're unwilling to cooperate counselor. What is it going to be Mrs. Wiehl? Will you cooperate with our protective team or do you wish to make alternative arrangements?"

The columnist remained silent for a moment. When she finally spoke, her voice had lost it strident edge. "I want the protection of the Bureau."

Silliman raised his hand, "We have a number of conditions."

Palacin shook his head, "No conditions. We do it our way or you're on your own. Clarke demanded attendance at the movie screening. No more demands. The Bureau is not accepting responsibility for Mrs. Wiehl's safety if we don't have total control of the situation."

The director waited for Barbara Wiehl's reaction. When she nodded her head, he turned to James Pohley, "Call in your people."

As they walked back to their car, the director turned to his station chief. "I want you to personally manage this. If you need to borrow people from other regions, you have a blank check. At some point she's going to start insisting on doing things that'll open her up to the killer. Whatever it is the answer's no. If Wiehl gets whacked, we'll both be looking for jobs as security guards at Macys."

While Pohley knew the director was exaggerating about their employment opportunities, he knew the man was not off the mark regarding their pension prospects if Mrs. Wiehl met an untimely end.

————

The email arrived at the Federal Bureau of Investigation communications center only minutes before it was received in the inboxes of the managing editors of the *New York Times*, *Washington Post*, and the *Los Angeles Times*.

Lawrence Curtis Clarke
Have respect unto the covenant, for the dark places of the Earth are
full of the habitations of cruelty.
The Hand of God

Unlike the original communication, the email was instantly transferred to the technical experts assigned to the *Culprits* investigative team. The transmittal was tracked to a cyber café in Tulsa. Ten minutes later the Tulsa police, at the request of the Bureau, had sealed off the café, allowing no one to enter or leave. The Bureau request had not provided a reason for the action but had been sent under the highest priority. Fearing another Oklahoma City disaster, the Tulsa uniforms had secured the facility with guns drawn. The employees and patrons were kneeling on the floor with their hands clasped behind their heads when Bureau personnel finally arrived.

Each of the badly shaken customers and employees was pulled into a back office and questioned extensively. None appeared to have the skills necessary to accomplish the killings or a travel schedule that placed them in the five cities on the dates of the murders. Also, no one appeared to have the financial resources necessary to hire a professional killer. All, however, had the ability to be perpetuating a hoax. During questioning a young woman named Natalie Gutierrez mentioned a customer that had left the café moments before the police arrived. Natalie worked part time as a cashier/waitress while attending a local community college.

She described the customer as a white man of medium height with dark brown hair on the longish side and a full neatly trimmed beard. Natalie had difficulty guessing the man's age because of the beard, eventually placing him somewhere between thirty and forty. She thought he was slightly overweight and had been wearing jeans and a dark blue long sleeve shirt. She said he paid for his coffee and internet service with a twenty.

The agents took possession of the twenty-dollar bills in the register and the computer keyboard the man had used. A technician dusted the area around the terminal, the door handle the man had to touch on his way out, and the counter where he paid his check. When prodded the manager remembered the customer but could offer no additional information. One of the detained customers thought he remembered a gold earring in the man's left ear. The agents on the scene issued an alert through the local and state police, describing the man as a person of interest in a federal crime. The small collection of patrons and employees were transported to the Tulsa police station for additional questioning while their stories were verified.

Later that evening, long after all the café workers and customers had been released, a match was found on one of the twenties and partials from the keyboard. John William Champion suddenly became the focus of interest within the Bureau. Champion had a history of misdemeanor arrests during the late nineties for blocking access to abortion clinics in the southeast. A data search yielded a driver's license issued in Chapel Hills North Carolina six months earlier, but when local police arrived at the apartment complex they found he had not lived there for months and had not provided a forwarding address.

Over the next three days, the Bureau pieced together a comprehensive portrait of Mr. Champion. He was thirty-eight years old, and the only son of Jerome and Ada Champion. John William's mother had passed away four years earlier and his father, now living in Naples Florida, refused to talk to the Bureau's agents. John had been raised in Greenville South Carolina. He was a loner in high school, achieving good enough grades to be accepted into the University of North Carolina on an academic scholarship. His high school classmates described John William as highly intelligent and very strange. While they would scheme how to get their hands on a six pack of long necks, he would try to organize Bible classes. His fundamentalist religious views were beyond the pale, even in a region dominated by Baptists. Without providing an explanation, he dropped out of college after two and a half years. Champion's grades hovered near a four-point average and his professors were surprised when he simply stopped showing up. His academic focus had been in computer sciences.

The man's social security records revealed a history of employment in the Golden Triangle area outside of Raleigh/Durham. Over a period of fifteen years, Champion worked for six different firms and made a great deal of money. Four of the companies were no longer in business, but the two that still had their doors open described John William as brilliant but troubled. He created the elaborate software systems they sold and installed in many of the world's largest corporations, but his lack of social skills and missionary religious zeal eventually counterbalanced his contributions. No one had seen or heard from the man for over two years.

Agents interviewed five of the people arrested with Champion at the abortion clinics. None claimed to have known the man before the protests and they all denied sharing membership with John William in any organization. Three of the protestors mentioned that Champion was the most physically aggressive of the group.

After leaving his last position, John William seemed to vanish in a wisp of smoke.

CHAPTER 35

CNN was the first to break the story, defeating the Bureau's attempt to conduct their manhunt without media involvement. A poor-quality photograph copied from Champion's driver's license presented an average looking white male. The grainy photo, together with the man's full beard and wire rimmed glasses made the image next to useless for identification.

The majority of the media ignored the Bureau's undefined 'person of interest' definition and began calling the man a prime suspect in the killings. John William was a poster boy for the religious right further enhancing his credibility as the killer and making him a juicy target for the mainstream media. Front page stories were augmented with photographs of the murder victims positioned next to Champion's hairy countenance. The cable crime shows dropped whatever sensational murder they had been featuring to devote their hour program to exploring Champion's connection to the killings and to the manhunt.

Liberal politicians piled on, pointing to the evils of religious fanaticism as represented by the country's conservative right. They attempted to define Champion as an ardent supporter of the president even though no one had any idea if the man was registered to vote.

———

It was the first fully attended meeting of the Pacific Avenue Irregulars since Cal Hulse began burrowing into the lives of the list of forty-five. They met at Cal's condo and offered little conversation as they arranged themselves around his dining room table. The whiteboard still dominated one side of the room, but at the moment it was blank. Carmen had given Jonathan a ride over in the Bureau Crown Victoria and sat next to the subject of her surveillance assignment.

Cal sat at the head of the table and did not bother to look up from his notes while he spoke. "None of the forty-five qualify as the professional killer. As a result, we're only looking for someone capable of financing the killings. Age and gender don't enter the picture. The only criteria, besides money that would highlight the person behind the murders, would be motivation. Staying with the money for a moment, the ante goes up with Clarke's death. The estimate had been at least two hundred fifty thousand for the first four killings. The next murder had to be more difficult given the FBI's involvement. If we thought the Wellstone and Carlson assassinations would cost at least seventy-five thousand, the Clarke killing had to be a hundred thousand. That means the person or people financing this had to have spent at least three hundred fifty thousand dollars. We also need to question if they're through. If the assignments to kill continue the payments must continue, probably at an accelerating cost. If we accept this premise, it dramatically reduces the number of people financially capable of funding the assassinations. What do you think?"

Everyone at the table nodded their agreement. The tension in the room was palpable as each of the Irregulars sensed a closure to their efforts. "Alright. That means whoever is behind this can drop five hundred thousand or a million without breathing hard. There were only two names that could satisfy those criteria, a man named Edward Austin Beckwith and a woman named Laura LaCroix. Beckwith owns a majority interest in World Freightways, the nation's largest trucking firm. He's seventy-five, resides in Omaha, and is worth over two hundred million. Beckwith is a heavy contributor to the Republican Party and a lifelong conservative." As Hulse paused, each member of the group weighed the possibility of an aging multimillionaire financing a campaign to kill people he viewed as his political enemies. "Laura LaCroix is worth about eight million on her own, but she also controls the Creighton Trust; a fund worth over four billion. She's the Chairman and President of the trust and has complete discretionary control over the money. She's fifty-six, divorced, and lives in Manhattan. Her politics are extremely to the left, and each year she uses the trust to fund a variety of progressive agendas."

"It has to be Beckwith, look at his politics," Harold was the first to state the obvious.

Jonathan nodded, "He seems to have all the boxes checked. Is there any way we can trace payments from his accounts?"

Cal shook his head, "Bank records aren't easy to access. Also, people with this type of money don't have it sitting around in a checking account at Bank of America. They'll have funds in fifty different institutions including several overseas."

Carmen offered her thoughts, "If we can't look at a money trail, how about his motivation? If he's funding PACs and donating to the Party, we can access those records. Maybe the donations will tell us more about his politics."

Carlos leaned back in his chair. "I think we should turn this over to someone. Create a summary of our findings and send it anonymously to the papers and FBI."

Jonathan stood up, "Think about why we're here. My only connection to these killings is a book I wrote. I've been screwed over by the press and dumped by my employer. What if this poor guy had nothing to do with it?" He looked at Carmen, "Would the Bureau spend time on this based on an anonymous letter?"

"Probably not. I'm sure they're receiving hundreds of communications pointing the finger at someone. Nothing we have rises above circumstantial evidence. We have a rich conservative who bought your book."

"Cal, how fast can we dig up information on Mr. Beckwith's political contributions?"

"If you can give me the organizations, I can do it while you sit here."

No one knew the names of the conservative Political Action

Committees, but a minute on the internet solved the problem. The six Irregulars sat in an uneasy silence while Cal used his laptop to access a dozen public records. After a half hour, he looked up and shrugged. "He gives the NRC about one hundred thousand a year. The president's reelection committee got fifty and the Republican candidates for state office in Nebraska about twenty thousand. I don't see any contribution to a PAC."

"Not exactly your screaming right winger."

Jonathan shook his head, "Thanks for trying guys. Maybe we'll think of another approach tomorrow."

The group looked like they were leaving a funeral home as they filed out of Cal's condo. Jon rode down the hill to his apartment with Carmen. Neither wanted to talk about the investigation's dead end. The meeting had not lasted long, and it was only a little after eight when he opened the door and led her into his unit. Their evenings together had developed into a comfortable routine. When Carmen came on shift, she would join Jon in the apartment. They might watch the news before having dinner, usually preparing something simple at the apartment. Later, they would talk and watch television before she had to return to her car and wait for her replacement. They held hands and kissed, but neither seemed comfortable taking the next step. The disappointing conclusion of the Irregular's efforts seemed to cast a dark shadow over their evening. They stood apart for a moment in Jon's living room before Carmen fell into his arms.

"I'm so sorry. I thought we had it."

He realized she was crying as she buried her face in his chest. "Everything will work out, don't worry," as he tried to reassure her he could hear the hollowness of his words.

Carmen looked up, her face streaked with tears, "Jon, take me to bed."

It was not the scenario he had visualized, but he was not about to argue. He picked her up and carried her into the bedroom. They undressed without haste and were at first cautious in their lovemaking. Their needs began to engulf them, altering their passion from careful and controlled to something much more desperate. Later, as they lay spent, the sadness they had felt earlier returned. Just before twelve, Carmen slipped out of bed and dressed. She leaned down and kissed Jonathan before leaving the apartment. He lay awake for hours thinking about her and where the relationship would take them.

After a few hours of fitful sleep, he forced himself out of bed. A pot of coffee helped him focus on where the investigation had ended. The fact that Edward Beckwith provided rather unremarkable contributions to the Republican Party and its candidates did not mean he was not a right-wing extremist. He could be sending money to right wing militias and South American fascist death squads for all they knew. The more he thought about it, the more convinced Jon became that they had given up too easily. He paced the small apartment waiting until after ten to call Hulse knowing his friend was not an early riser.

"Cal, I think we need to take a harder look at Beckwith. I know you can't access his bank records, but how about his home computer? He's retired so I'm guessing he does everything out of his home. If we could read his emails and look at the payments he authorized, we might not scratch him off the list so quickly."

"Alright, I'll check it out."

"Cal, I don't want this to come back to you. Use my computer."

Hulse thought for a minute. "Ok, but I have a little project I need to finish first. How about one thirty?"

"I'll be here," Jonathan worked on his book for an hour when he hit a wall. Thoughts of Beckwith and Carmen pushed their way into his mind. Nervous energy was flowing through him like an electrical circuit and he knew he needed a diversion. He threw his golf clubs over his shoulder and headed out to Harding Park to hit balls at the driving range. Jon drove across town with a serious young man in another Crown Vic trailing behind.

Two buckets later he felt much better. On the way back to the apartment, he stopped for a sandwich at a deli on Geary. When he reached home, he noticed that the message light was on his machine. He was hoping for a message from Carmen when he began listening to the condescending voice of his literary agent.

"Harvey Bilkin here. Congratulations, Jonathan, *Culprits* will be number eight on the nonfiction best seller list. Tri City recognized they were a bit over their head on this one and they've worked out an agreement with Dell. The third printing will be a five hundred thousand print run in hard cover followed by a six hundred thousand soft cover run."

Jonathan hung up without listening to the rest of the message. He was still sitting in a breakfast room chair trying to absorb his agent's news when the doorbell at the apartment's entrance disturbed his reverie. He buzzed Hulse in and walked to the door to wait for his friend to climb the stairs to his unit.

Cal, ever the athlete, was breathing hard from the one-story climb, "What's up? You look shell shocked."

"*Culprits* just went platinum."

"What are you talking about?"

"I think I almost have as much money as you," Cal gave his friend an odd expression.

"The book will be on the best sellers list. They're running a huge third printing before they go into paperback. I haven't figured it out, but it's a lot of bucks."

"That's nice and you can buy another dinner, but let's see what we can do with Beckwith's computer. I've got another deadline on a program revision for Oracle." Jonathan watched Cal as he began trying to access the Omaha man's system. The programmer's concentration was remarkable. Every so often, he made little noises as he gained progress in his assault or was thwarted in his efforts. In under thirty minutes, Cal leaned back in his chair and smiled, "You know, the barriers this guy put up were strictly amateur hour."

Jonathan pulled a chair next to his friend as he began scrolling through Beckwith's files. The data was remarkably dull. In two hours of digging, the only items of interest were financial records concerning a twenty-eight-year-old woman being maintained by the aging multimillionaire in an upscale building owned by the retired trucking magnate. Since they had no interest in selling the story to the tabloids the information was useless.

Cal stood up and was heading for the door when Jon asked for another try, "I know this is probably a waste of time, but what about Laura LaCroix?"

"What about Laura LaCroix?"

"She's the only other person that made the final cut on the list. Shouldn't we at least take a look?"

"Come on. She's further left than Barbara Lee. What motive would she have to finance a rampage against left wingers?"

"Humor me."

Cal reluctantly returned to his seat before Jonathan's terminal and began working the keyboard. As each security barrier presented itself, Cal became absorbed with the challenge. Thoughts of the Oracle deadline disappeared as he schemed his way into her personal computer's system. Carmen arrived as Cal pushed away from the terminal. The three watched as Cal provided a tour through LaCroix's emails. They proved to be more interesting than Beckwith's, but nothing appeared that touched on the killings.

Jonathan turned to his friend, "Can you hack into the Creighton Trust's computer?"

Hulse shook his head, "Not tonight. I'm way behind schedule on my project, and as it is, I'll have to work most of the night to finish it off."

CHAPTER 36

The lodge at Yosemite was completely booked, so the man, now calling himself James Keller decided to take Carol on a leisurely drive up the coast to Carmel. He rented one of the new Mustang convertibles, lowered the top and began working his way north. It was late afternoon when they reached Santa Barbara. He parked the car near the town center and they strolled hand in hand along the palm lined upscale shopping district. The town's architecture was decidedly Mediterranean which Carol loved. He encouraged her to buy a summer dress that she admired in the window of one of the women's clothing stores.

As the afternoon shadows began to grow, they drove to the Santa Barbara Inn. It was next to the beach, and he had booked a small suite featuring a large balcony overlooking the ocean. They sat and watched couples walking on the beach and the sun as it slipped below the horizon. A scattering of clouds turned the sky into a crimson light-show.

The woman smiled as she reached for her lover's hand, "I love this place. Can we stay forever?"

He returned her smile, "Perhaps someday." He knew it would never happen but did not want to destroy the moment.

Later when they dined at Citronelle, the on-premise restaurant, the wait staff assumed they were another honeymoon couple. He had planned the trip as a reward for the weeks she had endured in the Los Angeles motel room and the brightness of her smile assured the assassin that he had made the right decision.

———

At two in the afternoon on the third Thursday in May, the House Rules Committee, on an eight to seven party line vote, issued a special rule for floor consideration and the debate parameters for the consideration of the censure of President Robert Harris Prescott, the forty-fourth president of the United States. Vermont Representative Paul Menchini, the committee chairman, cited the president's ineptitude and lack of leadership, as evidenced by his failure to stem the rising tide of terrorist attacks around the globe, the nation's estrangement from the world community, and his inability to stop the systematic program of genocide of progressive leaders within the United States. Representative Menchini's statement, made in time to catch the six o'clock network news, concluded with the committee's decision to request a censure resolution from the House Judiciary Committee.

To most insiders it was another day at the zoo. To the mainstream media it was nirvana. The partisan nature of the decision was not mentioned in the feature stories and editorials in the leading newspapers or by the major network commentators. Neither did they discuss the fact that such an "act of censure" had no basis in either the Constitution or the Rules of the House and Senate and was, in effect, the political equivalent of a strongly worded letter.

With the Democratic Party firmly in control of the House of Representatives, there was little doubt that the Judiciary Committee would draft the resolution and send it on to the full House for debate. The full House, operating under the special floor rules set by the House Rules Committee, would gleefully debate and vote on the resolution.

Later that evening in the Oval Office, President Prescott met with his advisors and staff. The president's expression reflected his mood, "We knew this was coming and we all know what it's about. The loyal opposition sees an opportunity to weaken my presidency and in so doing gain ground in the midterm elections and damage my chance at reelection. The question is, how do we respond?"

MacMillan, the White House press secretary spoke up, "We have to label it for what it is, a purely partisan attack that has no rational justification."

"It may have no justification, but it has an impact. Bob's down ten points in the polls," the vice president made no effort to mask his emotions. His long-term ambitions were only viable if Prescott left the White House on a positive note.

Eugene Baronian made a dismissive gesture, "That's today. We still have a long time to go before midterm elections. So far, we've let them define the rules of engagement. We need to go on offense."

Vice President Cummins shook his head, "With what? We can talk about not having car bombs in New York, but every day the public sees Islamic fanatics blowing up something somewhere. And these left-wing killings are playing right into their hands. I think we should dump Palacin."

MacMillan looked at the president, "The House debate over censure will be a show trial. Every Democratic representative is going to use the opportunity to bash Bob. When they finally wind down, they'll vote to censure, and it'll be sent to the Senate where it will die. I agree with Gene, we need something to knock the feet out from under this thing."

Prescott looked around the room, "Every year, politics in this town seems to get dirtier. The public has more respect for pro wrestlers than for politicians, and they should. The wrestlers at least give them what they want. I'm not going to fire Director Palacin. He's a good man trying to do a good job. Finding the people involved in these killings would help our cause, but getting rid of the director won't make that happen." He turned to Richard Owens, the senior speechwriter. "When the press corps try to eat Dan alive tomorrow, I want a lot of arrows in his quiver. Make the case for this being a purely partisan move but give him more than that. Itemize every initiative I've proposed that the House majority has killed. I want them labeled as obstructionists and out of touch with the American mainstream. Hopefully, some of their less controllable leaders will overreact and damage their cause." He stood up, signaling the meeting was over.

———

Hulse was less than his usually cheerful self. The Oracle project had consumed most of the night and his restless mind had chased away attempts at a daytime nap. He had considered putting off the attempt to access the Creighton Trust for a day or two but knew the delay would disappoint his fiend. When he reached Jon's apartment, he found Carmen and Jonathan finishing their takeout Chinese.

"Want some? There's a lot left."

Cal waved off the offer, "Thanks, but no. I'm dog-tired. Let's see what we can do with this trust; then I'm going home and hitting the sheets."

For the next two hours, Hulse worked at slipping past the trust's security barriers. Several times Jonathan and Carmen watched him shake his head as one of his probes failed. He was about to acknowledge defeat when he uncovered a backdoor channel into the system. Cal pushed back his chair and offered his friend a tired high five, "Jesus, whoever put this together installed some serious firewalls"

"But you broke through!"

"It helped that I designed one of the subsystems for Microsoft."

Jonathan was not feeling the optimism he forced into his voice, "Let's see what they have."

The three crowded around the terminal as Cal accessed files. The email files were extensive. After an hour, they were barely through scanning a month of Laura LaCroix's communications. Cal shook his head, "This will take all night. Let's move along and look at the cash disbursements."

The magnitude of some of the expenditures were surprising, even for a trust the size of Creighton. Each disbursement was coded with the assigned expense category. They were able to skip over those that obviously related to categories such as occupancy expenses and reimbursement for travel costs. They stopped when they came across significant outlays that were not as easily defined. They glossed over contributions to known political groups such as Move On and organizations like Air America. Carmen asked Cal to stop as he was scrolling past one of the disbursement records.

"What's this for?"

Cal shrugged, "Another donation to something."

"But what? It's coded for a contribution, but the payment is a wire transfer to an offshore bank."

The expenditure suddenly had the group's attention. Carmen turned to Cal, "Can you do any type of search to see if this type of payment is repeated?"

Cal shook his head, "No. All we can do is look, but let's go back to well before the Fredberg killing and see if we can spot similar transactions."

He took them back to one month before Fredberg was shot. Now that they knew what they were looking for the process moved along quickly. Unfortunately, large payments made to overseas banks occurred with some frequency. Three weeks prior to the killing a fifty-thousand-dollar payment was sent to a numbered account at a Luxemburg bank. During the same week, three other disbursements ranging from thirty to eighty thousand were sent to banks in Thailand, Mexico, and France. Two days after the murder, the same amount was wired to the same bank in Luxemburg. Unlike the Luxemburg transfers the other payments to offshore banks were single payments. Similar disbursements preceded and followed the LaBlanc, Wellstone, and Carlson killings. While the banks changed with each pair of wire transfers the pattern remained constant. Six weeks before Lawrence Clarke was shot, one hundred-fifty thousand was sent to the National Bank of Grand Cayman, followed by a second payment of a hundred-fifty thousand the day after the murder. Hulse was no longer tired.

The programmer sat back and stared at the screen, "Holy shit. She paid for the killings."

Carmen shook her head, "It's not exactly conclusive proof, but the payment pattern works. There could be an innocent explanation, but the transfers seem to fit." She looked away from the screen. "It could be a coincidence; she could be financing the murders, or there could be someone else in the organization behind the killings who has access to the checkbook."

Jonathan could not believe their search was over, "Cal, printout a copy of each transaction record."

Within minutes, the printer tray held copies of the ten financial transactions. Hulse shook his head as he frowned at the screen. "I don't get it. If it is LaCroix, why would an ultraliberal pay a contract killer to knockoff ultraliberals?" No one had an answer.

Jon looked at Carmen, "What should we do now? We can't just sit on this."

"That's the next problem we have to solve. We need to get the information to the Bureau without it coming back to bite us."

"Wouldn't they gloss over the hacking part?"

"Perhaps, but if they don't, we're talking about some serious jail time."

Cal turned to Carmen. "I could scan the copies of the transactions and send them from somewhere that would be impossible to trace, like that cyber café that religious nut was using."

Carmen shrugged, "Maybe, but keep in mind they identified the religious nut through the café. You saw how much money the trust has at her disposal. If we don't handle this right, a dream team collection of lawyers will have this evidence excluded."

Jonathan smiled at his friends. "This can't be that big a problem. Let's call for another meeting of the Irregulars. Maybe one of the other guys will come up with something. Besides they all helped us, and they deserve to know how the investigation ended."

CHAPTER 37

The second day, they continued up 101 past Santa Maria and San Luis Obispo where he branched off onto Highway 1. The drive along the coast was beautiful but slow going, and it was late afternoon when they pulled into the seaside town of Cambria. They had no difficulty finding the bed and breakfast he had lined up over the internet. Their room was small and decorated in a frilly, feminine motif. Carol thought it was precious while he smiled away his distaste.

He did find the Moonstone Beach Bar & Grill to be his type of place. Over an evening cocktail they watched another sunset, this one not as spectacular as the last. Unlike Carol, he rarely drank, believing alcohol to be one more avenue to a mistake. But tonight, he sensed no reason for caution as he ordered a second drink. By the time they finished a bottle of wine with dinner, he was slurring his words. She helped him to the car and up the stairs to their room at the bed & breakfast. He was asleep the moment his back hit the bed.

Carol let him sleep in until ten o'clock when she gently shook him awake. He moaned and opened his eyes while she was waiting with aspirin, juice, and coffee. She found his condition endearing, a moment of vulnerability in an otherwise tightly controlled life. After a shower and more coffee, he still felt like hell. All he really wanted was to go back to bed, but instead he tried to smile as he drove the short distance to the Hearst Castle above San Simeon. They joined a line of tourists as they shuffled through the downstairs portion of the unique structure that had been the home of William Randolph Hearst and the playground of the era's motion picture stars. The assassin tried not to throw up in the Castle's elaborate dining room.

He asked Carol to drive north along the twisting coast highway. They were passing the Mill Creek picnic area in the Los Padres National Park when he told her to pull to the side of the road. He barely had time to step out of the Mustang when he lost the remnants of his evening meal and the small amount of breakfast he had been able to force down. When he was able to get back into the car, he felt considerably better.

The assassin found he was surprisingly hungry when they stopped for a late lunch at the Ventana Inn in Big Sur. He felt better sitting outside in the cool breeze blowing off the ocean. He played it safe with salad and French bread while Carol dug into a cheeseburger. The views were stunning and, as she watched hang gliders float on the airstreams, she never wanted it to end.

They checked into the Highlands Inn and were escorted to a bungalow on the hillside above the main building. He briefly admired the view from the back of the unit before laying down on the bed for a nap. Carol waited until nightfall before waking him. They walked down the hill to the restaurant. Neither was that hungry, so they decided to order appetizers in the bar while they watched the waves, illuminated by spotlights, crash against the rocky shoreline. He ordered tea while Carol sipped chilled Chardonnay. Later that night, after they made love, she dreamt they were together, sitting on the patio of their home overlooking the ocean as they watched the waves break on a sandy beach.

The next morning, he woke early, dressed in running shorts and a tee shirt and slipped out of the unit while Carol as still sleeping. Running on the coast highway seemed like an excellent way to end the day in intensive care so he drove toward Carmel before turning east on Carmel Valley Road. He found a narrower less used road called Robinson Canyon, parked the car, and began his run. He was breathing hard after a mile and knew he had allowed himself to slip out of condition. He pushed himself until he was gasping for breath. He turned and headed back when he began to feel his hamstrings tighten. Carol was pacing the bungalow when he opened the door.

"Where have you been? I was worried."

"I went for a run. I didn't want to wake you."

He felt awkward as she clung to his sweat drenched body. As he held her he thought again how vulnerable she was. When he was able to disengage from her arms he smiled at her beauty, "I have to take a shower."

He had just begun to lather up when the shower door opened, and his lover crowded into the space. "I was lonely." She took the soap from his hand and helped apply it to his body. That day they had a late start sightseeing in Carmel.

On the third day in Monterey, he dropped her off at the room and told her he needed to run an errand. He drove to a parking area opposite the Carmel River Street Bridge, pulled an untraceable cell phone from his pocket and dialed the number he had memorized. He knew the woman featured in chapter six would be completely inaccessible for months and he had no intention of trying to kill her while she was under FBI protection. She would not be as careless as Clarke.

The mechanically distorted voice answered on the first ring, "Where are you?"

He thought for a moment before answering. Theirs was not a relationship of mutual trust. "I'm still on the west coast. Are the religious quotes I've read about in the paper coming from you?"

"Don't be ridiculous. I have another assignment for you," he always found the dismissive voice grating.

"I'm not going to do the sixth while her friends are staying with her," he doubted anyone was listening or that the call could be traced back to him, but he saw no reason to expose himself with more specific information. His employer shared no such restraint.

"It's someone else. I want you to take care of the book's author, Jonathan Scanlan."

The request came as a surprise. He was not a curious man, but the assignment had taken him off guard, "Why?"

There was no response for a moment as his employer debated offering a confidence. "Let us say he has been prying into places that he should not. What is the price?"

The contract killer considered the circumstances. The author would be unguarded and unaware of any danger making him an easy assignment. Conversely his employer had no bargaining leverage. "Two hundred thousand."

"Too high. You could kill the man between having breakfast and lunch. One hundred thousand."

The distorted voice was right, but he knew he held all the cards. "Two hundred thousand or find someone else. I'll start when half is received at the bank. If nothing arrives, I'll assume you've made other arrangements." He ended the call, slipped out of the car and dropped the phone in one of the city's garbage cans.

CHAPTER 38

The Bureau's southeast regional office had run down hundreds of useless leads in the search for John William Champion. Nothing in John William's father's telephone records indicated the two had been in contact for at least a year. It was as if the man had died, a possibility minimized by his recent visit to the cyber café.

Champion's financial records were also a dead end. Several months earlier Champion had liquidated all his investments, including his bank and brokerage accounts. The significant amount of cash seemed to have disappeared at the same time as the brilliant software designer.

It was impossible to keep the lack of progress from the media. The majority of articles and editorials used the unsuccessful search as an opportunity to beat on the Bureau and the president. A few speculated on the man's mysterious disappearance, offering theories that he was a survivalist living off the land in the woods of the Carolinas or was a master criminal now living under a completely new identity.

Even Director Palacin's most ardent supporters were growing weary of the Bureau's inability to find Champion and to halt what the press had labeled 'The Culprit Killings.'

———

They kept the Mustang's top up against the coastal chill as they drove north to San Francisco. Carol and the man, who now called himself Stan Ramey, caught the last remnants of the morning commute when they passed Daly City making their entrance into the city somewhat tedious. A wall of fog blanketed the coastline and obscured the western portions of San Francisco. They broke into tepid sunshine when they made the jog over to 101 and dropped off the freeway onto Van Ness. He patiently made his way across town to Lombard where they checked into a motel prepaying in cash for a week's stay. Before they left Carmel, he had made the call to confirm his bank's receipt of the wire transfer. The Marina District motel was surprisingly expensive but had the advantage of being only blocks away from Scanlan's apartment. After lining up their lodging he drove past Jonathan's residence. The man sitting in the Crown Victoria in front of the building might as well have had a sign in the car's window saying, "Federal Agent on Duty." His employer had neglected to mention that the author was under Bureau protection. Under other circumstances the added complication would require a renegotiated price, but at two hundred thousand he was willing to absorb the slightly higher element of risk.

A single agent following the author around was hardly a challenge in regard to the kill. The problem came in studying the target's habits. Any fool could kill a man. Killing without leaving a trace of evidence was another matter entirely. The key was always careful planning and the agent's presence made that much more complicated. He had been able to study Judge Carlson's habits from his mock plumber's van before the Bureau had arrived on the scene. Even the densest agent would begin to wonder why such a workman's vehicle remained parked on Green Street for days. Following Scanlan around also did not work. Participating in a three-car motorcade would be the same as surrendering to the Bureau.

He dropped Carol off at the motel and drove back up the hill to a street two blocks above the apartment. He parked and walked down Laguna to Green. He was just another resident of the neighborhood returning home after running an errand as he strolled past Jonathan's building. He took no notice of the author's residence or the car and agent parked at the curb. He stayed on Green for two blocks past the building before turning left on Webster to circle back to the Mustang. None of the buildings on Scanlan's block had for rent signs posted which crossed out another possible option. As he made his way back to the motel, he concluded his best alternative was to make the author come to him, as he had with Marc Wellstone. His mind began to consider the type of bait that would appeal to the man.

CHAPTER 39

The Pacific Avenue Irregulars sat around Cal's living room and listened as Jonathan and Hulse described the journey that led to Laura LaCroix and the Creighton Trust. When they finished, no one spoke for several moments as each man absorbed the news.

Greg Stokes shook his head as he looked at Jonathan, "I can't believe it. You actually figured out who's financing the killings."

Jon shook his head, "We all figured it out. Everyone here played a part, but I don't think we can say we know who's behind the murders yet. The payments fit the pattern of the murders, but they're buried among hundreds of other substantial payments; even if they are tied to the killings the trust is worth billions, which must mean a number of people could be authorized to disperse money. We can't be sure Laura LaCroix is involved."

Carlos stared at the ceiling as he tried to sort out the part of the puzzle that did not fit. "I don't get it. You said this woman, LaCroix, is super liberal. Why would someone on the far left want to kill Fredberg, LaBlanc, Carlson, Wellstone, and Clarke? Wouldn't that mean someone else is making the payments?"

"Someone from the far right working at a place like the Creighton Trust? Not an easy trick to pull off."

Carmen shrugged, "Not easy, but not impossible. And maybe that's the whole point. The payments are traced back to the trust, the organization is destroyed, and the country's largest source of funds for the far left disappears. Maybe that's been the main course all the time and killing Wellstone, Carlson, and the others were the appetizers."

Jonathan nodded, "Could be, but we can let the Bureau sort that out. Our last little problem is the question of how we can turn all this over to them without getting burned for hacking into a dozen systems."

Harold Kurtovich lifted one hand and then the other, "Murderer, hacker, hacker, murderer. You've got to be kidding. Do you really think they'd prosecute us for solving the crime of the decade?"

Carmen glanced around the room as she responded, "Probably not, but it's a risk I'm not sure you want to take. I can also guarantee the evidence we've come up with would never see the inside of a courtroom. There isn't a judge in the country that would allow illegally obtained evidence into trial, and without it, there's no case."

Harold spoke for the first time, "There has to be a way."

Jon smiled, "That's why you're all here. Help us figure out how to steer the FBI in the right direction without exposing ourselves and without having the evidence excluded."

Alan raised his hand, "Mail a package to the FBI anonymously."

Carmen answered. "That takes care of the coming back to bite us part, but the information would still be excluded."

Cal shook his head, "This is like one of those riddles. How do you tell them without telling them?"

Carlos looked at the FBI agent, "Couldn't we come up with a story about how you figured it out?"

Carmen laughed, "In the first place, I have trouble picking up my emails and everyone at the office knows it. Besides, without a warrant it would be just as illegal for me to hack into someone's computer as it was for Cal."

Jonathan stood up. "We didn't expect to come up with something tonight. Give it some thought and call us if you think of a solution."

———

He tried to block out the sound of Carol's soaps as he went online and Googled Jonathan Scanlan. He was surprised at the number of references until he remembered that *Culprits of the American Culture* had hit the best sellers list. Most of the information related to the book, but as he continued to dig he was able to gather morsels of background on the author. One book reviewer mentioned Scanlan's golfing success in college and his attempt to qualify for the PGA tour. Another source mentioned the author had been trout fishing in a wilderness area when Fredberg and LaBlanc were killed. He also read about Scanlan's academic credentials and the fact that he was on paid leave from his teaching job at San Francisco State. When he exhausted all references to the author, he closed the laptop and leaned back. The pieces of information were helpful but far from a complete picture of the man. Did he live with anyone? Was he gay or straight, and did he have a girlfriend or boyfriend? Did he have any weaknesses or addictions? What kind of car did he drive, and how did he spend his money? Who were his friends, and did he have a family? He knew his ability to kill Scanlan without leaving a trace would only be possible if he could gain a more complete understanding of the man.

The insipid television program kept intruding into his thoughts. He grabbed his jacket and turned to Carol who seemed mesmerized by the show. "I'll be back in a few minutes." She gave a little wave of acknowledgement without glancing away from the screen as he left the room to walk and think.

CHAPTER 40

The waitress watched the bearded man push away from the counter after he finished his breakfast and walk toward the restrooms with his daypack. She was not a mean-spirited woman, but embedded midwestern values could not accept being scammed. He had that disconnected homeless look even though his clothing was clean. Her suspicions were confirmed when she saw him walk past the restrooms and out the diner's rear door. Shaking her head in disgust, she dialed the police and reported the morning's dine and dash episode.

The police dispatcher radioed one of the town's cruisers, and within minutes Officer Virginia Gionnoni spotted the man walking toward the bus station. She pulled her patrol car to the curb, stepped out of the vehicle, and stood in the man's path.

Gionnoni raised her hand signaling the man to stop, "Hey buddy. Forget something?"

He did not respond. Instead he tried to step around the policewoman. When she grabbed his arm, he swung his daypack hitting her shoulder. The pack was not heavy and the force of the blow not strong enough to cause harm, but the man's resistance was unexpected. Gionnoni lost her grip on his arm as she staggered to the side. He continued walking in an unhurried pace toward the bus station.

Virginia Gionnoni's face flushed with anger as she watched the man start to walk away. She pulled her nightstick from her belt and hit the bearded man behind the knees. He cried out as he dropped to the sidewalk. The patrolwoman pushed him down and struggled to cuff the man's hands behind his back. A second black and white screeched to a stop and Officer Brian Tobin bounded out of the car to help Gionnoni apply her handcuffs.

"What's with this guy?"

Gionnoni shook her head, "The son of a bitch hit me with his pack. He skipped on his check at Carl's. All I was going to do was make him go back and pay."

The man was mumbling to himself as he continued to struggle against his restraints. The two officers pulled him to his feet and walked him to Officer Gionnoni's car. As they pushed him inside he shouted, "You will feel the wrath of God!"

Tobin walked back to the sidewalk and picked up the man's daypack. He smiled as he handed it to Gionnoni, "You don't want to forget his weapon."

Virginia Gionnoni unzipped the pack, expecting to find an unpleasant collection of dirty clothing. She stood staring into the daypack long enough to attract Tobin's curiosity, "What's up?"

She pushed the side of the pack down. When Tobin looked inside he saw a Bible, a copy of *Culprits of the American Culture,* and neatly banded stacks of hundreds and twenties. Both shifted their gaze from the pack to the bearded man talking to himself in the back of the squad car.

Later that day a computer match confirmed they had captured the infamous John William Champion.

———

To no one's surprise, the Judiciary Committee sent the censure resolution to the full House of Representatives stating the condemnation of President Prescott was warranted. The debate that followed was a political food fight. Representatives on the Democratic side of the aisle used the forum to ridicule and belittle the president while their Republican counterparts portrayed the process as a cheap political stunt. The debate lasted three days and made for great theater. The laundry list of accusations from the Democratic representatives included the president's failure of leadership, misleading both Congress and the public on a number of issues, and the deterioration of the country's relationships with traditional allies. The most frequently mentioned failure was a lack of purpose in apprehending the people killing the country's progressive leaders.

Mainstream media treated the process as a somber indictment of a weak and ineffective president and drowned the public in inflammatory sound bites. Rarely was it mentioned that the Republican controlled Senate would never support the resolution. By the end of the House debate, President Prescott had dropped to a forty-three percent approval rating.

The censure process also invigorated the Democratic leadership and aided immensely in fundraisers. The head of the DNC predicted the midterm elections would transfer control of the Senate to his Party and open the door to the possibility of morphing the censure resolution into an impeachment process. The statements of denial by the White House and the Republican leadership rang hallow in the ears of the public.

When news of Champion's capture splashed across the nation's headlines, a number of people gave a sigh of relief. While FBI Director Palacin was pleased that he would see his likeness in fewer political cartoons, the most relieved was Barbara Wiehl. Five minutes after she heard the news, she was on the phone to New York Station Chief James Pohley.

"Agent Pohley, Barbara Wiehl, I understand your people have this man Champion."

"That's correct. John William Champion was taken into custody in Medina Ohio."

"Then it's over. Your agents can leave my home."

"That wouldn't be wise, Mrs. Wiehl. All we know is Champion sent at least one of the 'Hand of God' emails. We have nothing else connecting him to the murders."

"Wait a minute!" the columnist shouted into the phone. "He's your suspect! Everyone knows he's the one. He's a right wing religious fanatic, taunting the police with those emails." Wiehl was so irate she knocked over her chair as she pushed away from her in-home workstation.

"Mrs. Wiehl, the man is being questioned as we speak, and the Bureau considers him a person of interest. The media has speculated on his guilt, but we have never issued a statement saying we consider him a suspect."

"Don't play games with me. We both know he's guilty, and that means you can pull your people out of here."

"We're not playing games Mrs. Wiehl, and at this moment I have no idea if he's involved in the killings or just likes to send strange emails. Remember what Director Palacin said. If you throw our agents off your property, the Bureau will be issuing a statement that you're refusing our protection. Think about it Mrs. Wiehl, if Champion had nothing to do with the murders and the killer reads you've rejected our protection . . ."

The columnist hissed into the phone, "I hate you, assholes."

"Yes, I know, Mrs. Wiehl. I read your column, but the agents stay." Station Chief Pohley had to jerk the receiver away from his ear as Barbara Wiehl slammed the phone into its cradle.

CHAPTER 41

The man with Stanley Ramey's driver's license and credit card in his wallet drove out 19th Avenue to San Francisco State University. The college was situated about a mile from the Pacific Ocean in the southwestern corner of the city, which typically meant on a nice day the students and faculty needed to bundle up against the cool ocean winds. Today was no exception. Young men and women pushing off the Muni at the Holloway stop on 19th were well shielded from the cold.

He turned right on Holloway and followed the road bordering the southern edge of the campus until he found a parking space. He locked the car, now a less memorable Taurus to replace the Mustang, as he walked on campus. He followed the signs to the Administrative Building where he picked up a map of the facility. For the next hour he walked the campus, studying the access routes and parking areas relative to the Administrative Building. Drawing Scanlan to a bogus meeting would be as simple as a phone call. The problem was setting up the kill zone. Without facility privileges the man could park on 19th, on Holloway, Font, or in one of the public lots. Without knowing where the author would park, the contract killer had no way to know where to set up shop. As he walked back to his car he began developing an alternative plan.

———

Jonathan had rejected all but two requests for interviews knowing most were attempts to subtlety draw him into a discussion of the killings. The exceptions were the book reviewer for the *San Francisco Chronicle* in the hope she would be mildly partisan for a hometown boy and Nicholas Abenroth from the *New York Times*. *The Times* reviewer was a matter of simple necessity. Like the Roman Caesars, Abenroth could determine your fate by a thumbs-up or a thumbs down. Jon thought things were going well with Allie Rhine from *The Chronicle* until she mentioned she considered him a fascist right-wing swine responsible for the murders of five of the greatest people to have ever walked the face of the earth. The brief remainder of the interview deteriorated into a creative variety of insults.

He hoped things would go better with Abenroth. *The Times* reviewer suggested they meet at his suite at the St Francis. Jonathan felt like he was appearing before a tribunal as he and the trailing Crown Victoria from the Bureau parked in the underground hotel lot. He knew *Culprits* was not selling because of his brilliantly crafted prose or eloquent analysis. Circumstances beyond his control had shoved it into the flavor of the month. He also believed the book was well written and an honest presentation of the destructive impact of certain influential people on the American society. With that thought and the knowledge that the person he was about to meet controlled his future as an author, he knocked on the door of room 820.

A short balding man in slacks and a dress shirt with an opening at the neck greeted Jonathan at the door. "Nick Abenroth," the man smiled as he extended his hand.

Jon instantly warmed to the man while a hidden voice murmured something that sounded like buyer beware. Abenroth's eyes radiated intelligence as his face crinkled into an engaging smile. "Mr. Scanlan, a distinct pleasure," this from a man who could probably have lunch with Norman Mailer any given afternoon.

"Please call me Jon."

Abenroth led Jonathan into the sitting area of the suite. "Can I offer you anything? Water, coffee?"

Jonathan smiled as he settled onto the sofa. "Thank you, no. I'm fine."

"*Culprits of the American Culture* seems to have captured the country's imagination." Abenroth invested neither praise nor criticism into the comment.

"Nick, let's be honest. The only reason it's selling is because some wacko decided to use it to start killing people."

The small man seemed taken aback by the comment, "I know the numbers haven't been released yet, but next week it's moving into the number two slot."

Jonathan smiled. "That's great. Nick, what brings you to San Francisco, certainly not just to bask in the radiance of a brilliant author."

Abenroth laughed, "No. My sister and her family live in Menlo Park and I was overdue for a visit. We chat for a little while, I write a profile and *The Times* pays for my trip."

"Well, let's not keep your sister waiting. What would you like to know?" Abenroth was a skilled interviewer and for the next hour he led Jonathan through a synopsis of his life. He seemed particularly interested in Jon's attempt to join the PGA tour. When the reviewer closed his notebook and leaned back in his chair, Jonathan was surprised none of the man's questions touched on the murders.

"So, what's next for Jonathan Scanlan?"

"What else, another book."

"Can I ask what it's about?"

"The origin of political correctness and how it evolved into today's usage in America."

"Interesting concept." While Abenroth's expression was difficult to read, Jonathan had the impression the reviewer was hoping for a more confrontational project. As Jon waited for the elevator to take him to the hotel garage, he mulled over Abenroth's reaction to the new book and wondered if he was about to be trashed in the reviewer's profile.

Jonathan picked up his mail in the building's lobby on his way back to his apartment. Before *Culprits* became nationally known, his mail slot typically contained a bill and a few pieces of junk mail. Even though he never released his address, fans, critics, and hundreds of people who wanted to help him invest his newfound wealth found a way to his mailbox. Nearly every day the mail carrier dropped off a plastic tub filled with envelopes. Once inside his unit, he set the tub on the counter and placed a wastebasket on the floor next to his chair. The unsolicited credit card applications, junk mail, and opportunities to invest went into the can unopened. He set aside any bills and created a second stack of correspondence from readers. Jonathan was about to drop one of the envelopes into the trash when the logo and return address caught his eye. He tore it open and found a gift certificate in his name from the Lodge at Pebble Beach. It covered one nights lodging for two, dinner, and a round of golf. An enclosed note read 'from your friends at Dell Publishing.'

He smiled at the thought of spending a night at Pebble with Carmen until he realized that would only be possible if the Bureau called off their surveillance. While Jonathan could now afford to stay at the Lodge and play the course most considered the best in the United States, he would never spend that kind of money to play a round of golf. He went on line and checked the Northern California Golf Association directory. A round at Pebble was four hundred and twenty-five with another fifty if the guest wanted to use a cart. Jon had played the course twice when he was on Cal's golf team and he did not have to pay the bill. He wanted to call and thank his new publisher for the generous gift, but no name was mentioned on the card.

He was as happy as a young boy on Christmas morning as he reread the gift certificate.

CHAPTER 42

John William Champion stared into distant sights that only he could see as the interrogator pushed away from the table in frustration. They had been questioning the handcuffed man for five hours and knew no more about Champion's movements or involvement in the case than when the bearded man was first led into the interrogation room. The lead interrogator had used all his tricks, threats and promises, understanding and outrage to no avail. Occasionally, John William would turn to the man across the table and appear to listen to his offer of leniency or an angry demand before returning his gaze beyond the confines of the room. He had not reacted when he was read his Miranda rights or asked if he wanted counsel.

John William had only spoken twice since his arrival, both times providing quotes from the Bible and Apocryphal. The first quotation had been from the Book of Jubilees and the second from the Apocryphal Book of Enoch. When he did speak, his tone, if not his subject matter, was matter of fact and without emotion. "And I measured out the whole earth, its mountains, and all hills, fields, trees, stones, rivers, all existing things I wrote down, the height from earth to the seventh heaven, and downwards to the very lowest hell, and the judgment-place, and the very great, open and weeping hell."

The behavioral team and researchers at Quantico were as frustrated

as the interrogator in their efforts to place the quotations in the context
of the investigation. They rejected the easy conclusion that Champion
was completely delusional. He had evaded capture for over a month and
had been cognitive enough to go to a cyber café and send his emails to
the press and the Bureau. The consensus was John William was jerking
them around.

———

When Carmen arrived at the apartment, Jonathan showed her the gift
certificate. "That's very thoughtful of them. When are you going?"

"I thought of holding off until the surveillance was, over and we
could go down together."

"That's sweet, but who knows how long that's going to be. I think a
change of scenery would be good for you. Give Cal a call."

———

He waited a few days after Scanlan had received the gift certificate
before he called the Lodge. "Good morning, this is Harold Warner with
Dell Publishing. We had you send one of our clients, Jonathan Scanlan, a
gift certificate for lodging, dining, and golf. Could you tell us if he's
booked the date he'll be with you? We want to surprise him with a few
other gifts during his stay."

He smiled as he noted the date, "Thank you, you've been most
kind."

There was a great deal to accomplish in the next six days.

CHAPTER 43

They took Jonathan's Jeep for the ride down to Carmel. The weather was cooperating with blue skies and temperatures in the high 70s. It was just after two when they pulled up to the gatehouse at the entrance to the 17 Mile Drive. Jonathan glanced in his rearview mirror at the Bureau car nosed in behind him. He was curious how the team assigned to his surveillance was going to handle the new situation. With the exception of Carmen, they had not known where he was going or for how long. Jon doubted the upscale Lodge would be allowing the agent behind him to park his Crown Victoria in front of the hotel. He realized if he were a nicer person he would have mentioned his overnight trip to one of Carmen's coworkers.

The two vehicles wound down the two-lane road toward the ocean. The hillside was at first a lush dense growth of pines, scattered oaks and heavy ground cover. After a few miles, the elaborate homes began to appear; many of them with gates to insure their privacy. The golf course and ocean came into view before they could see the Lodge. Jonathan noticed the Bureau car lagged back as he pulled in front of the hotel. He could see the driver talking on his cell phone as Jon opened the Jeep's rear door for the bellman to pull out their bags and his set of clubs.

After they checked in and had their bags delivered to their room, Jonathan took a shuttle to the driving range to hit a few balls. Cal, who refused to play the game, was content to wander through the hotel and nearby shops. When Jon returned, he found his friend sitting in a comfortable chair in the lobby reading a book on astrophysics.

"Have you ever heard of Clancy or Grisham?"

"No. Have they published in astrophysics?" This said without a trace of sarcasm.

Jonathan shook his head and laughed, "Let's have a beer."

A few beers at the 19th Hole transitioned into dinner at Club XIX. Cal was the least imaginative eater Jonathan had ever encountered. A Caesar salad, hold the anchovies, steak cooked just past medium, a baked potato and an ice cream sundae for dessert. Jonathan, on the other hand, considered dining in a fine restaurant as an opportunity to explore, especially if he did not have to pick up the check. He started with a soft-shell crab appetizer accompanied with a glass of Rombauer Chardonnay before moving on to poached salmon from one of Oregon's rivers in a dill sauce. Hoping the gift certificate included wine, he ordered a bottle of Rochioli Pinot Noir from the Russian River area. Jon knew the Pinot was a little light for Cal's steak, but he did not think his friend, who knew less about wine than Jonathan knew about astrophysics, could tell the difference.

When Jonathan's appetizer arrived, Cal stared at it in mock horror, "What the hell is that, deep fried tarantula?"

Jon smiled at his friend's reaction, "Not easy to find on a menu."

The conversation over dinner bounced over a potpourri of subjects, most of which related to sports. UC's inability to best rival USC in football, the quality of the Forty-Niner's draft picks, whether the Warriors would ever make the playoffs, and how to categorize Barry Bond's tainted home run record carried the two friends to dessert. Cal was about to consume a large spoonful of ice cream when he glanced at Jonathan.

"I haven't seen any signs of your new wealth. No new Porsche or BMW, no trips to Monaco, or an exclusive resort in Thailand. What are you doing with the loot?"

Jonathan shrugged, "Nothing."

"What's nothing? You mean it's just sitting in your checking account?"

Jon was embarrassed by his friend's question, "It's not like I've had the money for ages. I haven't been spending it because I can't think of anything I need."

"What about buying a condo like mine?"

"Maybe, I really haven't given it any thought."

Cal shifted his focus back to his sundae. When he looked up, he sensed his friend's discomfort. "When we get back to the room I'll give you my broker's number. If nothing else, shove the money into Treasury bills. At least you'll be making a little interest."

After dinner they tried to watch television in the room but found nothing that captured both their interests. Both men read until lights out; Cal was engrossed in the physics of stellar phenomena while Jonathan followed Harry Potter's most recent adventures.

———

He checked them into a motel in Pacific Grove, an oceanside town on the north end of the famous 17 Mile Drive. He left Carol in front of the television and drove to the nearby Marina. The boating supply house on Central had a number of used boats for sale, some their own and some on consignment from customers. After an hour of haggling, he was the owner of a twenty-foot Wellcraft with a 140 horsepower Johnson motor. When he paid in cash, the supply house manager was so pleased he threw in the trailer and a month's free berthing.

His next stop was one of the local dive shops where he purchased a wetsuit, mask, fins, and a waterproof pack. He declined the manager's sales pitch for a tank and regulator, explaining he was already equipped. He returned to the motel to find Carol still firmly entrenched in front of the television. Out of desperation, he suggested they catch an early dinner.

The sun was beginning to set when he dropped Carol off at the motel and made his way back to the marina. His key gave him access to the locked gate as he carried his wetsuit, fins and pack to the boat. A few boat owners were cleaning up after a day's run or sharing a cocktail with friends as he threw his gear in and cast off, but none seemed interested in the new boating enthusiast. The motor gave a deep rumble as he reversed out of the berth and slowly powered his way out of the yacht harbor.

He opened the engine up when he cleared the marina but was forced to throttle back when heavy chop began slamming into the hull. He kept the throttle at three quarter speed knowing there was no hurry. The sun had set as he powered out of the marina, but there was no problem following the coast. Lights from the homes and businesses illuminated the seaside towns and the reflection from the moon and stars cast a silver sheen on the water. He kept well clear of the rocky shoreline as he rounded Point Pinos and passed Asilomar State Beach. He eased back on his speed when he spotted Cypress Point and nosed closer to the shoreline. A scattering of boats anchored in the cove made his destination easy to find. He anchored a hundred yards from the nearest boat and used no lights as he slipped into his new wetsuit. It did not appear anyone was aboard the sail and motorboats in the cove, but there was no reason to attract attention. Once in his fins and mask, he picked up his pack, slid quietly into the water and moved effortlessly toward the shore.

When he reached the rocky shore, he removed his mask, fins, and wetsuit. He quickly dressed in the clothing he had stored in the waterproof pack. His black sweatshirt, dark blue jeans, and baseball cap made him just another shadow in the night. If somehow, he was discovered he was a guest of one of the locals out for an evening stroll on the golf course.

He stowed the pack now containing his wetsuit, fins, and mask and climbed the bluff running along the ocean. The assassin paused at the top and looked in both directions. No one appeared to be in sight. He began working south, away from the Lodge. He was disappointed with what he found. There was virtually no heavy cover on the ocean side of the course. The rough, consisting of no more than long grass, ran to the edge of the bluff. Here and there a bush or a few trees interrupted the ocean view, but not enough cover to set up shop and wait for the author.

There was adequate cover on the eastern edge of the course but that meant after the kill he would have to run across open fairways to reach the ocean and the boat. The idea of using a boat had come to him when he realized how easy it would be for the authorities to close off the 17 Mile Drive exits. As he retraced his path back toward the Lodge he began to question that decision. At the sound of voices, he stood motionless and listened. He thought he heard a man and a woman talking. His alternatives were to try to drop out of sight over the bluff or simply walk along as a man on a late-night stroll. He immediately rejected hiding below the cliff as there was no way to know if at this point along the bluff the slope down to the water was gradual or a sheer twenty-foot drop. He pulled his cap lower, put his hands in his pockets and began walking toward the couple.

They were no more than fifteen feet away when the woman made a startled noise. The young man flinched then covered his reaction by placing his arm around his companion.

"Sorry, I didn't mean to startle you."

"What are you doing?" he could hear the fear in the young man's voice.

"I imagine the same thing you're doing here. Taking a walk."

The couple watched him for a moment before walking away. He continued toward the Lodge until he saw the configuration of the eighteenth fairway. The assassin turned and walked back along the course, this time hugging the eastern edge. A few large homes overlooked the course, but at several points only wooded hillside bordered the property. He turned away from the course, crossed the 17 Mile Drive, and hiked up the hillside. Much of the terrain was covered with pines with little undergrowth. When he was approximately three hundred yards from the fairway, he began moving latterly to the course and working his way across the hillside. His night vision was excellent, but twice he slipped on the thick bed of pine needles. He was above the ninth fairway when he found a site that satisfied his needs. Thick brush offered perfect cover and a gap between the pines allowed an unobstructed view of the fairway.

The lack of heavy vegetation along the bluff forced him to alter his original plan which was to arrive by boat, kill the author from a site near the ocean, and escape by boat. He assumed other golfers would see him as he made his way from the course to the boat, but they would be powerless to stop him; even if one had a cell phone and called the police he would be well away before they could arrive. The powerboat could cover the ten-mile run in under twenty minutes in moderate seas which would not allow enough time for a Coast Guard intercept even if they were in the area.

He spent no time lamenting the need to alter his plan. His years of experience had taught him to view each environment objectively and adjust as the circumstances dictated. That was why he had come to Carmel two days before the author would play his round of golf. As he worked his way down the hill, he wondered if Carol was still watching television.

CHAPTER 44

Jonathan left Cal to his own devices and took the shuttle to the driving range. A brisk wind off the ocean had the morning golfers in wind shirts and sweaters. He hit balls for twenty minutes before shifting to practicing his short pitches and putts. Jon checked in with the starter thirty minutes before his tee time and went to have a cup of coffee. He had not seen his FBI companions since his arrival and assumed they would not be following him around the course.

At ten minutes before his tee time he shouldered his bag and walked to the first tee. The starter introduced Jonathan to his partner; he was a middle-aged man named Hugh Doyle from Portland Oregon. Doyle was a heavy set and outgoing with an Irishman's red hair and the pale complexion that never tanned.

Jon preferred to walk the course while Hugh drove a cart. The starter gave them the course rules and pin placements while they waited for the threesome in front to finish their second shots. Jonathan led off as he was playing from the blues, while Doyle indicated he would play from the golds. Jon decided control was the better part of valor and went with a three wood and landed the ball in the middle of the fairway between the one hundred and one hundred-fifty-yard markers. Hugh went with his driver and sailed his ball out of bounds to the left. Without hesitation he teed up a second ball and this time managed to find the rough on the left.

Doyle proved to be a pleasant man, but a better companion than golfer. He claimed to be a twelve handicap, which Jonathan considered unlikely. By the sixth hole, Jonathan wondered how many balls Hugh had in his bag. If anything, Jonathan's game, which hovered around par, seemed to intimidate his playing partner. At one point, Jon smiled as Doyle tried to crush a drive, "I see you're a follower of Daly, grip it and rip it."

Hugh turned to Jon, "Think I'm trying to put too much into my swing?"

Jonathan shrugged, "This is a tough course. Even Tiger tees off with a three wood on some of these holes."

Jon wasn't sure if Doyle appreciated his suggestion, but he noticed the man was scaling back on his swing and clubbing down on some of his shots. The result was a marked improvement in Hugh's game and scores that approached bogie golf. Jonathan's companion was a regional sales manager for one of Microsoft's divisions and he enjoyed chatting when he had the opportunity. Since Jon was able to stroll up the fairways while Hugh was restricted to the ninety-degree cart path rule those opportunities appeared on the tee boxes and greens. When Doyle asked what Jonathan did for a living, he told the Oregonian he taught English lit. in college. The last thing he wanted was a probing discussion over *Culprits*.

While he might have wished for a less talkative golfing partner, Jonathan was enjoying the day. He made a mental note to track down the individual at Dell Publishing that had allowed him to experience this perfect outing.

———

He paid his visitor's fee at the gate and drove the Taurus down the winding road to Pebble in the late afternoon. The area's remarkable beauty was lost on the assassin as he continued past the Lodge to a parking area near the driving range. He walked back to the Lodge and browsed through the on-premise shops to kill time and to hopefully catch a glimpse of his prey. His vigilance was rewarded when a tall, dark haired man wearing a black wind shirt walked across the hotel lobby toward a smaller man reading a book. In his tourist mode the assassin was wearing khakis, loafers, and a plaid shirt under a light jacket. At nightfall, he walked back to the car, slipped a daypack on, and took a metal case from the trunk. He knew the case might attract attention, but it was the risk of being remembered, not of being stopped. He walked up the road until he was even with the ninth fairway. He shot a glance in both directions to confirm no one was in sight before turning up the hill and into the cover of the trees. As soon as he reached cover, he stripped down to his underwear and into the black sweatshirt and jeans. He placed his tourist outfit in the daypack and settled in for the night. When the evening chill descended, he slipped the black lightweight jacket he had worn earlier over his sweatshirt. A black knit wool cap added camouflage and reduced his body's heat loss; it was not a significant concern with the temperatures predicted to stay in the fifties.

He woke at the first light of dawn. A call to the pro shop the day before had confirmed the author's ten o'clock tee time. He assumed it would take Scanlan nearly two hours to play his way to the ninth fairway. His early years of Special Forces training had instilled the ability to lay motionless for hours. He did not bother to set up his rifle until ten thirty. The Barrett M82A1 had been sighted in at two hundred yards before he knew the distance to the kill zone and time had not allowed him to return to the range to make the adjustment for the longer shot. The barrel nestled in a sniper's short legged bipod to improve stability. The one element that caused him concern was the suppressor screwed onto the end of the barrel. Without the silencer, the muzzle blast would give his position to the Bureau agents protecting the author. Their pistols would be ineffective at the three-hundred-yard range, but they could give chase and complicate his escape. The problem was the suppressor's impact on the accuracy of the weapon. It was an unknown that he had no way to test. He decided to go for center mass rather than a head shot.

At eleven, he began studying each of the players progressing up the fairway through his scope. As he watched a golfer in tan pants and an orange sweater walk up to his ball, he realized the homework he had been able to do on the author was extremely limited. Beyond his brief view of the man the prior day his visual knowledge of Scanlan was limited to a photo from the man's book cover and two from newspaper articles. The circumstances of the man's protection and where he lived had not allowed the assassin to study how he walked, his mannerisms, or how he looked in different settings. This realization hit home when he watched a foursome make their way up the fairway. They all looked alike. They all wore the same stupid preppy type outfits. Dockers, sweaters, wind shirts, and vests were everywhere. They all wore caps or visors and sunglasses.

As he studied the passing players he became more confident. Most of the men were older than the author and few approached Scanlan's six-foot two height, athletic build, and pro quality golf swing. Even if the man wore sunglasses and a cap the assassin was confident he would recognize his target. Keeping these criteria in mind, he began focusing on the taller Caucasian men with dark hair and athletic builds.

At eleven forty-five he had his man. He watched the player stop at his ball which was resting in the middle of the fairway just before the two-hundred-yard marker. The assassin knew little about golf, but he had spent the morning watching golfers walk to their balls, the majority of which were either in the rough or far behind this man's drive. He could see longish dark hair below the tall man's baseball cap. The contract killer's position only allowed him to see the author in profile and, when he took a fluid practice swing before addressing his ball, his back was turned to the hillside.

The assassin was not given to indecision. Within minutes, the man would hit his ball and move past the killer's narrow tunnel of vision between the trees. He controlled his breathing, rested the crosshairs at a point slightly above the man's back, and softly squeezed the trigger. He watched the player collapse seconds before he picked up his casing and began breaking down his weapon. The assassin moved swiftly across the hillside, using the trees for cover, and was out of sight in thirty seconds. He walked quickly to his car, threw the case and daypack on the backseat and was leaving the parking area as the police headed toward the golf course. He drove at a conservative speed toward the Pacific Grove exit. He had just driven past the entrance to the Inn at Spanish Bay when the first police cruiser passed with siren blaring and lights flashing. At one time, he considered parking the Taurus at one of the observation parking areas along the road and have Carol pick him up in the boat. He rejected the idea when he realized there were no protected areas for bringing the boat to shore along the route and Carol was hardly a skilled powerboat operator.

He tried to control his heartbeat and breathing as he stayed within the speed limit. There was no guarantee the police would close off the exits, but there was also no guarantee that they would not. If he found a line of cars backed up at the Pacific Grove gate, his alternative plan was to turn around, drive back a half mile and park the car. He had wiped it clean of prints and vacuumed it thoroughly the day before in the off chance it could be tied to the killing, and his hands were encased in latex gloves. He recognized there was an unfortunate amount of ad lib that would then have to occur as he would then have to push through the hillside until he could breakout somewhere in Pacific Grove. None of these desperate measures came to pass as the Taurus drove through the unobstructed gate and made its way through the streets of Pacific Grove to the motel.

He turned on the all-news station as they drove north to San Francisco International. Murders were a daily phenomenon in the Bay Area, warranting only brief mentions on the radio or in the local papers. The killing of a man on the fairway at Pebble Beach, an enclave of wealth and privilege, was another matter. The additional seasoning to the dish was the media's conclusion it was a professional hit and not a crime of passion. The name of the victim was being withheld pending notification of relatives, but the man in the Taurus did not need that irrelevant piece of information.

CHAPTER 45

Jonathan stood on the tee box, waiting for the threesome in front to hit their second shot. Hugh Doyle was talking about a course he had played in Mesquite Nevada when Jon saw one of the players on the fairway collapse. His first thought was heart attack or stroke. He ran to Doyle's cart, jumped in, and floored the small vehicle. His partner, not understanding what was happening, yelled for Jon to stop. When Jonathan was within fifty yards of the fallen man, he cut across the fairway bouncing violently over the dips and crests of the course. The man's two partners were standing over their companion lying face down on the grass.

The bullet hole was obscured by the man's black wind shirt. When Jonathan gently rolled the man over, blood from the exit wound made one of the man's friends gasp and turn away. There was little question; the golfer was dead.

When Jonathan looked more closely he saw the entry wound in the man's back. Jon turned and looked for the shooter but saw nothing. He glanced at the two men staring numbly at their friend. "I think he's been shot. Do either of you guys have a cell phone?"

One man nodded and ran to his cart. A minute later he returned and handed the phone to Jonathan. He dialed 911, gave his name, and told the woman on the other line what had happened. When she tried to solicit more information he cut her off, "Look, just get someone out here. He's on the fairway of the ninth hole at Pebble." He hung up, handed the phone to its owner, and went back to Hugh's cart. Doyle was walking up the fairway when Jonathan reached him.

"What's going on?"

"The man over there's dead. I think he's been shot."

"Shot? That's crazy."

Jonathan studied the wooded hillside, looking for movement, "I can't argue with you there."

"What do we do now?"

Jon shrugged, "I guess we wait for the police."

Hugh gave Jonathan an odd expression, "You don't seem very rattled."

"You should walk a mile in my shoes."

Hugh Doyle distanced himself from Jonathan as they waited for the police.

———

He stopped in Santa Cruz and shoved the weapon far down in a dumpster behind a Shell service station. They turned in the Taurus at the rental agency and took the Alamo shuttle to San Francisco International's north terminal. The man paused outside the terminal and dialed the number he was to use after completing his current assignment. Within seconds, the mechanically altered voice was on the line.

"I've taken care of business. Have the balance of my payment sent to my account."

"I need verification. How and where?"

He did not believe it prudent to discuss specifics over an open line, even if the cell phone could never be traced back to him. "The same type of tools was used as in the prior job and the location was Carmel."

"We'll use the same phones for another day. I'll call to verify the transfer."

He walked into the terminal and joined Carol in the line for United.

Frank Cala left the interrogation room and studied Champion through the one-way window. Their suspect sat placidly by the table, his body was relaxed, and his mind was focused on something beyond the confines of the Bureau office. Other than offering occasional biblical quotations the man had not responded to any of the questions asked by the interrogation team. Champion's behavior was so unlike any man or woman Cala had ever questioned that the lead interrogator, flown in from Quantico, found it impossible to draw any conclusions. John William had not asked for an attorney, declared his innocence or guilt, or even shown signs of mental illness. He appeared comfortable in his new environment, accepting without comment his confinement in a cell and the meals the agents provided; although, he did whisper a blessing to himself before eating.

"So, what do you think?"

Cala continued to watch Champion as he responded to the chief of station's question, "I think he's either playing us or he couldn't tell you what planet he's on."

"That narrows it down."

Cala shrugged, "What do you want me to say? It isn't just that he hasn't answered our questions; he hasn't responded to our questions. No change of expression, no change in body language, nothing. It's like trying to get a reaction out of my Honda."

"What about door number two? He's not responding because he's delusional."

"Possibly, but he's been with us three days and we've seen none of the classic symptoms. He doesn't talk to himself or go on rants about voices in his head. He's fastidious with his personal hygiene and we know he sent the emails which would require a certain level of cognitive thinking."

"He seems happy to be with us, but we can't hold him forever. Shoplifting is a misdemeanor, and charging him with assaulting a police officer is a bit of a stretch. The Bureau's going to take another hit if we have to cut him loose and it turns out he's involved."

"What about booking him under the terrorist statutes?"

The chief of station considered the suggestion for a few minutes, "We'd need a friendly judge, but I don't see a problem there." He thought for another minute, "I like it. It gives us all the time we need to break him."

CHAPTER 46

When the agent assigned to watch Jonathan appeared at the golf course, the police questioning ratcheted up considerably. Few people involved in law enforcement believed in coincidences, but try as they might they could find no evidence to tie Jon to the killing. He had no connection to the victim, an attorney from Fresno, and from the Bureau's point of view the dead man was not mentioned in *Culprits*. The Carmel police were outwardly unhappy when they questioned Hugh Doyle who reluctantly confirmed that his playing partner could not have shot the victim.

The golf course swarmed with investigators and crime scene technicians for the balance of the day. When Jonathan was eventually released from questioning, he found a crowd of reporters outside the Lodge interviewing anyone with the slightest knowledge of the day's tragedy. He pushed through without responding to their requests for an interview and found Cal waiting in the entry with their luggage. They called for Jonathan's Jeep to be brought around and waited inside the lobby, away from the media.

A man in a gray suit who had been talking to other guests approached the two men. "Mr. Scanlan, Mr. Hulse, Michael Nelson. I'm the manager of the hotel. I understand, Mr. Scanlan, you were on the course when this terrible thing happened."

Jonathan really did not want to answer more questions, but he also did not wish to be rude. "Yes, I was playing behind the man who was killed."

"How very awful. I want to apologize on behalf of the Lodge. Such a thing has never happened before. Please accept a complimentary one-night stay and a round of golf as our way of apologizing for this terrible experience."

"That's very kind of you."

Nelson handed Jonathan his card, "Please call and let me know when you would like to return."

Cal listened to his friend describe the shooting on the ride back to the city. "I know this is a strange thing to ask, but the guy who was shot didn't happen to be someone you wrote about in *Culprits*?"

Jonathan shook his head, "Never saw him before. I talked to one of his friends while we waited for the cops. He said the guy's name was Phil Sundell. All three were lawyers from a firm in Fresno."

"Criminal defense lawyers?"

"No, I thought of that too. Sundell just did corporate work."

"Weird."

Jonathan could not agree more.

Jon drove back to his apartment after dropping his friend off and barely had time to unpack when Carmen arrived. She threw her arms around him and hugged him. "When I first heard about the shooting I was sure it was you. I was in the office when the report came in and all they said was a golfer was shot and killed on the course at Pebble Beach. I went into the ladies' room and threw up. We didn't learn the man's identity for at least an hour."

"He was in a threesome playing in front of us."

For several minutes Carmen clung to him, her face buried in his chest. When she eased her grip and looked up, her face was streaked with tears. "I was afraid I'd lost you. I was going crazy and I couldn't talk to anyone. It was the longest hour of my life."

Jonathan was not sure what to say, "I'm sorry you had to go through that. I would have called, but I didn't have my cell phone with me and then the police questioned me for hours." In truth, with everything going on, he had not thought to call, but that did not seem to be the right thing to say.

"That hour, before the man was identified, made me realize what you mean to me. Jonathan, I love you."

A flood of warmth and confusion flowed through Jonathan. Commitment was not his middle name, yet he knew he wanted the diminutive FBI agent in his life. Jon paused for a moment as Carmen waited for a response, "I love you too."

They moved to the bedroom without haste and undressed each other. When they made love, they did so without a sense of urgency, as if this would now be as much a part of their lives as breathing. Later, when Carmen had to leave he watched her dress and thought of the changes a few words were going to make on his life.

———

The protocol was simple. After each assignment they would each discard the disposal cell phone they had been using and acquire a new one. Each would provide the other with the new untraceable cell numbers by email. The email addresses also were untraceable. Their conversations occurred only when it was absolutely necessary. The contract killer found such a conversation necessary when he was informed his bank had not received the second half of his fee for removing the author. He stepped out to the porch of his farmhouse to make the call.

The phone rang several times before he heard the distorted voice of his employer.

He saw no reason to exchange pleasantries, "The money hasn't been received by the bank."

"Yes, and Scanlan is still alive."

He could not believe the author could have survived the shot. His mind played back the image of the man crumpling to the grass. He wondered if this was to have been the last kill and if his employer was playing games with his final payment, "That's hard to believe. I saw where he was hit."

"I'm sure you did, but the man wasn't Scanlan. You killed Philip Sundell, an attorney from Fresno."

For a moment he said nothing as he remembered how difficult it had been to identify the target. His employer said nothing as he swore into the phone, knowing he was cursing himself, "I have to go back."

"I could not have said it better myself." The next thing he heard was the dial tone.

CHAPTER 47

Jonathan was up early; his collage of thoughts was too persistent to allow him a restful sleep. He glanced out the window to see the first streaks of daylight and noticed an empty space where the Bureau's Crown Victoria was normally parked. After starting a pot of coffee, he put on a robe and went downstairs to retrieve his newspaper. The ever-present vehicle and agent were nowhere in sight.

He sat at his breakfast table with his coffee and juice and glanced through the paper. The killing at Pebble Beach dominated the front page. The article profiling the victim, Philip Sundell, described him as a thirty-four-year-old attorney from Fresno. He was married with two children and was a junior partner in a regional firm that focused on corporate law. His family and fellow attorneys told police they knew of no one who would wish to harm the man. The feature article describing the crime speculated on a random killing and compared the shooting to the Malvo/Muhammad murders that terrorized the Washington DC area years earlier.

Most of the articles in the paper stressed the contrast between the violence of the crime and the bucolic setting of the crime scene. Two men shot to death in Oakland the prior night rated a two-inch column on page three of one of the inside sections of the paper. Jonathan was refilling his mug when he saw the envelope that had contained his gift certificate. While his Pebble Beach outing had not turned out to be everything he had hoped for, the gift had been extremely generous, and a pang of guilt made him realize he had not thanked his benefactor. Information gave him the main number at Dell and the receptionist who answered routed his call to the senior editor of the nonfiction division, a woman named Jacqueline Lehman.

"Mr. Scanlan, I'm so glad you called. We're all thrilled by how well *Culprits* is doing. Congratulations."

"Thank you, Ms. Lehman. I'm calling to thank you for your generous gift."

There was a moment of silence before Jacqueline Lehman responded, "I'm afraid I don't understand, Mr. Scanlan. What gift would that be?"

"A night's stay at the Lodge at Pebble Beach, dinner, and a round of golf. Perhaps it came from someone else at Dell."

"Are you sure it came from us?"

"The card said, from your friends at Dell Publishing."

Lehman paused again before replying, "As I said, Mr. Scanlan, we're very pleased with the sales of your book. I have to say I don't know anything about such a gift and to my knowledge, Dell has never authorized anything like this."

"Dell's a huge publishing house, perhaps it came from someone in public relations or marketing."

"Perhaps. Well . . . I hope you enjoyed the gift."

Jonathan was not about to mention the dead golfer. "It was wonderful." Something in Jacqueline's voice prodded his curiosity, "Ms. Lehman, would a gift of this magnitude have to come out of your budget?"

Lehman was reluctant to discuss internal processes with an author, but the question had already occurred to her. "Normally yes, but I suppose there could be an exception."

Jonathan could tell that the woman was anxious to get off the line, "Well, I hope I'm not creating a problem for someone who was so generous."

When the conversation with the puzzled Ms. Lehman ended, Jonathan remained at the breakfast table trying to make sense of what the Dell editor had said. If the gift had been an expensive pen or even dinner at a nice restaurant it could easily fly under Ms. Lehman's radar, but the Pebble Beach outing had to cost close to fifteen hundred dollars. That had to raise a few flags. Perhaps someone junior to Lehman was carried away by the amount of money *Culprits* was bringing in the door and went over the line out of gratitude. He was wondering if he had just damaged his benefactor's career when the phone rang.

"Good morning, I hope I didn't wake you." Carmen was definitely in a positive mood.

Jonathan had to smile, "No, I've been up for a while. You sound rather chipper. What's up?"

"Well, two things. I don't know if you noticed, but you no longer have your friendly FBI agent stationed outside your door."

"My neighbors will be happy to get the parking space back. What happened?"

"Nothing really. I guess they finally decided watching you day and night wasn't worth the cost which, from an entirely personal prospective, I would have to disagree. They might have decided the Bible guy they have back east is going to be the answer."

"Ok, so what's the other thing?"

"I have a few days off."

"What do you have planned, going shopping?"

"Very funny, I have an appointment to have my hair done at ten. I'll come by when I'm finished."

"Great. Can I ask for a favor?"

"Of course, what do you need?"

"I know this sounds a little morbid, but could you get a copy of the autopsy report on the guy that got shot, Philip Sundell?"

"I guess so. Why?"

"I'm working up a theory. Humor me, I'll tell you when I see you."

Jonathan spent the balance of the morning restlessly pacing his apartment. He considered working on the new book, but other thoughts kept pushing their way into his mind. Ever since his interview with Nick Abenroth, Jon would go online and scan the *New York Times* for a mention of their interview. This morning his vigilance was rewarded. He clicked onto the review and was pleasantly surprised to find it generally complimentary. Aside from a few comments designed to reinforce the critic's liberal heritage, Abenroth found *Culprits* to be a thoughtful, literate, and polished project. He was equally flattering in his comments regarding Jonathan, who he referred to as a rising star in the literary world. The critic's last opinion was that Jonathan would be well served to bring his considerable talents to the world of fiction.

Jon printed the review then leaned back in his chair and considered Abenroth's suggestion. He remembered Nick's reaction to the origin and application of political correctness and wondered if it would be worth taking another run at fiction. Jonathan's thoughts were interrupted by Carmen's arrival. He had assumed the hour appointment at the hairdresser would mean a dramatic change in hair style. When he opened his apartment door, Carmen's hair appeared to be unchanged.

"Your hair looks great." No fool he.

"Sweetie, if our first evening free of surveillance worries is going to be spent looking at pictures of a dead man, I may start reconsidering my options." Carmen tried to keep from smiling as she tossed a file folder on the coffee table.

Jonathan picked up the folder and studied the findings of the autopsy. "You're a skilled Federal Bureau of Investigation agent. Phil Sundell was a half inch taller than I am. He had dark brown hair cut long, had the same physical build as me, and the newspaper said he was an eight-handicap golfer."

Carmen slouched in one of the living room chairs and looked at Jon. "Alright, but what does his handicap have to do with anything?"

"The swing. Let's assume the killer knew I was almost a PGA level golfer. He wasn't about to whack someone hacking at the ball. Another big thing, we were both wearing black wind shirts, tan pants, and sunglasses."

Carmen stood up and stared at Jon, "You think you were the intended victim?"

"Clarke and Carlson were shot at long range by a professional. The shot that hit Sundell had to come from the hillside about three hundred yards away. I wasn't that far away, and I never heard the shot, which probably means a silencer. Sound familiar?" Jonathan pressed his point when Carmen did not respond. "I'm the link that ties this back to *Culprits*."

"But why? They go down the list killing each person featured in your book and then what? They change course and go after you? Why would they do that?"

"I have no idea, but it makes sense, sort of anyway. What do you think?"

Carmen moved over and wrapped her arms around Jonathan. "I think it scares the hell out of me. The killer murdered Clarke while the Bureau was protecting him, and I have trouble believing Del Monica is willing to give you the same type of coverage as the actor. What are we going to do?"

"Tell your friends everything we know."

"What about the hacking?"

Jonathan laughed, "Not much of a threat compared to being killed by a professional assassin. Think about it, if the Bureau knows everything I know, why would they want me dead?"

"Why was Fredberg killed? Why were La Blanc, Carlson, Wellstone, and Clarke murdered? We have no idea what's driving these people. There's no guarantee going to the Bureau would stop them."

"What's the name of the person over your boss?"

"Helen Hanavan." Jonathan could hear the reluctance in Carmen's voice.

"Didn't you say she was more reasonable than what's his name, Del Monica?"

"I've never really dealt with her, but that's the word."

"Can you give me her number?"

Carmen glanced at Jonathan for a moment before pulling her cell phone out of her purse and dialing a number. She walked over to the counter by the kitchen and scribbled on a pad by Jon's telephone. When she put away her cell she pointed to the pad, "That's her direct number."

Jonathan picked up his phone and dialed the regional director. He had expected to hear a recording and was surprised when the woman answered, "Helen Hanavan."

"Regional Director Hanavan, this is Jonathan Scanlan. I have information that should help your investigation. Can we meet?"

"How did you get this number Mr. Scanlan?"

"Can we meet?"

There was a moment's pause, "It would be more convenient for you to meet with the head of our San Francisco office, Ross Del Monica."

"I don't wish to meet with Del Monica, I want to meet with you."

"Might I ask why?" Jonathan could read little in the regional director's voice.

"Ross Del Monica is an asshole, and it's doubtful he has the cognitive skills necessary to understand what I have to say."

He thought he heard Hanavan suppress a chuckle, "I'll be in Los Angeles tomorrow. We can meet at the Bureau offices at 11000 Wilshire. Can you be there at one thirty?"

"One thirty it is."

When he put down the phone, he found Carmen shaking her head and smiling. "I liked the subtle way you avoided meeting with Del Monica."

"Let's go get something to eat, I'm starving."

The smile disappeared, "Whoa big boy. Think about it. You're suggesting we stroll down to Union Street as if nothing has happened. If you're now the killer's target, you might as well wear a tee shirt with a big bull's-eye on the front."

Jonathan sat down as the realization hit him. "He has to know where I live."

"He doesn't know where I live. Pack enough for a few days."

Carmen followed Jonathan into the bedroom and thought about their next move as he packed a small suitcase. "Is there any way out of this building besides the front door?"

"Not really. There's a small backyard, but it doesn't go anywhere."

"It's fenced in?" Jonathan nodded as he stuffed two pairs of sox into the case. "How high is the fence?"

"I don't know, maybe six feet."

"Alright. It's doubtful the killer knows what I look like and, even if he's figured out I'm with the Bureau, there's no reason for him to follow me. I'll take the suitcase to my car. You go to the backyard and hop over the fence that separates you from the property on Union Street. Go through that building, and I'll pick you up on Union."

"You think this is really necessary?"

Carmen gave Jonathan a look of mild exasperation. "Only if you're right about Carmel. Carlson, Clarke, and the guy on the golf course were all shot from long range. You'd be completely exposed if you just walked out the front door."

Jon nodded as he zipped the suitcase closed. He went into the living room and stuffed stacks of papers into a briefcase. Jonathan carried them down to the entry, handed both to Carmen, and watched her leave the building. He waited a few minutes before making his way to the small laundry room and out into the backyard. The wooden fence surrounding the yard was six feet in height and offered no purchase for his hands or feet. Jonathan made a halfhearted attempt to pull himself over before realizing the futility of the effort. He went back into the apartment house and looked for something to stand on. He found a wooden box containing cleaning supplies in a utility closet. He emptied the carton, carried it to the fence and stood on it. With the extra foot of height, he was able to boost himself up until he was straddling the fence. Jonathan lost his grip as he tried to lower himself into his neighbor's yard, slipped and fell into a rose bush. His jeans were muddied from the soft earth and he found blood on his face from a long scratch. He brushed himself off and went to the building's rear door only to find it locked.

He stood still, staring at the locked door, feeling completely ridiculous. He glanced at his building and considered scaling the fence back to his yard until Carmen's words came back to him. Jonathan decided looking stupid was better than looking dead. His neighbor's side of the fence had two by fours bracing it a foot off the ground and just below the top making scaling it much easier. He went to the east side of the yard and glanced into the rear of the next property. The center of the yard was cemented with a border of plants along the fence line. A patio table, four chairs, and a barbecue occupied one corner. Jonathan climbed the fence and dropped into the backyard. He walked quickly to the rear door only to find it also locked. He pulled one of the chairs to the edge of the fence on the east side, stood on it and heaved himself to the top of the fence. Without hesitation, he dropped into the area behind the next building. When he stood up, he found a Hispanic man in a white apron staring at him.

It took Jonathan a moment to figure out where he was. He had just fallen into the yard behind the Bus Stop, a sports bar on the corner of Union and Laguna. Thinking things were going from bad to worse Jonathan smiled at the man. "Hi, how are you doing?"

The man continued to stare at Jon without expression. "Buenas dias." When Jonathan began walking toward the back door of the bar the man moved to block his path.

The last thing Jonathan wanted was a scuffle with this man. "Look, there's this girl I've been seeing . . . her boyfriend's this really big guy."

Suddenly, the man's face broke into a wide grin, "He do that to you?" He pointed to Jonathan's bloody cheek.

When Jon nodded, the man stepped aside and pointed at the back door. Jonathan hustled through the backroom, the bar, and out onto the sidewalk. Carmen was double parked in front of the building that now had a crushed rose bush in its backyard.

Carmen looked at Jonathan's dirty clothing and the scratch on his cheek. "I can't leave you alone for a minute, can I?"

Jonathan's initial flush of anger was replaced with the image of his absurd flight over the neighborhood fences. "Can we stop and pick up something to eat?"

Carmen watched her rearview mirror for a possible tail, "Yes dear, but only if you promise to behave yourself."

CHAPTER 48

The flight back to San Francisco did little to improve his mood, and the two-hour delay on their connection in Denver did not help. He had never before killed the wrong target. Morality did not enter into his self-recrimination. He prided himself on his meticulous preparation, and shooting the wrong man was the type of mistake only an amateur would make. As he glanced through the in-flight magazine, he questioned whether he was losing the edge, the finely tuned combination of skills and experience that had carried him into his forties without leaving behind the slightest trace of evidence.

The concept of retirement seemed so foreign to him. He knew he could not sit around his home while Carol watched the soaps. He had no hobbies outside of his work and could not see himself developing an interest in golf or tennis. For over twenty years he had killed people, first for his country and then for money. Not exactly the profile of a people person. Besides Carol, the two things that held his interest were weapons and exotic automobiles. While his current lifestyle allowed him to gratify his attraction to rifles and pistols, his interest in unique cars was restricted to the occasional automotive magazine. He closed his eyes and tried to visualize being out of the game. What surprised him was for the first time in his life he could see himself in a different role.

They checked into a different motel on Lombard where he installed Carol in front of the television and went to pick up his weapons. The rifles used to kill Joseph Carlson and Phil Sundell had been purchased from a contact in Rio Vista, a small town east of San Francisco. His current buy, like the prior two, were arranged by email. In each case, he prepaid with an untraceable money order. His emailed instructions included where his purchase was to be delivered and the name he would be using when he picked up his order. He had no intention of allowing his appearance to be known to a black-market arms dealer. The now brown-haired assassin had a nostalgic thought as he remembered the pre 9/11 days when he could fly with his weapons in his checked luggage. Today's order was waiting for him at a mail drop in the nearby town of Fairfield under the name of Henry Donaldson.

During the uneventful drive out of the city and up Highway 80 to Fairfield, the contract killer's mind strayed to Jonathan Scanlan. Over the years he had learned to depersonalize his targets. They represented degrees of difficulty, not individuals. He neither viewed them as mothers and fathers, sons and daughters, nor did he consider the wreckage of the lives he left in his wake. Scanlan intruded into his thoughts through *Culprits*. In the beginning, he only read the chapters related to his prey to gain a greater understanding of their vulnerabilities. By the time he finished reading the chapter on Lawrence Clarke, he was hooked. He finished the book in three days, which for him was an Olympic record. He was so engrossed he actually went back and reread several chapters. While he considered himself apolitical and had not voted in an election since he was in the military, he found himself agreeing with the author. He identified with the hypocrisy and abuses of power, with the end justifies the means rationalizations, and the opinion that social, business, and political leaders of questionable integrity were defining the nation's moral compass. He accepted the author's premise that the people described in the book were systematically tearing away the country's moral fiber in an attempt to install their vision of a secular, socialistic society. The contract killer knew he was going to regret killing Scanlan.

He picked up the case containing another Barrett without difficulty.

A second package left for Henry Donaldson contained a Sig-Sauer nine-millimeter, ammunition, and suppressors for both weapons. He caught the evening commute traffic on the way back into the city and did not reach the motel until after seven. The room was empty. He paced the confined space for half an hour before his patience ran out. He walked out to the street and looked in both directions. Most of the businesses to the east seemed to be motels, apartments, and retail operations closed for the evening. He turned to the west and began checking the restaurants on the north side of Lombard. It was Thursday evening, the weather was mild, and the young and restless were out on the town. He pushed his way through eight establishments before deciding Carol would not have walked further from the motel. He crossed the street and began working the bars and restaurants along the south side of Lombard. She was sitting at the bar at a Mexican restaurant named La Barca. He stood at the entrance to the bar and watched Carol and the man seated on the stool beside her for a moment. He could tell immediately she had been drinking heavily. The man with his hand on her leg was big. He had the body of a regular at Gold's Gym; he was at least six four, two-fifty, and without question, a serious lifter. The man slouched forward on his stool with casual arrogance, his body and expression relaying his confidence.

The contract killer paused for a moment to consider the best way to extradite Carol from the bar. A physical confrontation with the man at the bar was not an option. There was no question which man would prevail in such a contest. He could kill or incapacitate the large man in seconds, but an altercation would probably mean the police and the Henry Donaldson's identity would never survive a serious inquiry. When the assassin moved to the bar he dragged one leg. He put his hand on Carol's shoulder. "Let's go home, honey."

Carol barely responded, but the big man next to her was not as reserved, "Buzz off, asshole."

The killer stepped back, again dragging his right leg. He also slouched, diminishing his size and physical presence. "Sir, Carol here is my wife." He drew out each word in a rural Arkansas accent.

"I don't see any ring. We're having a real good time. Why don't you take off before you get hurt?"

The assassin raised his hand in a defensive gesture, "Look, I can't fight you. I lost one leg in the first Gulf War and I'm not a big guy like you. I just want to take my wife home."

They had attracted the attention of several people in the bar, including the bartender, "Hey, we don't want any trouble in here."

A man seated on the other side of Carol looked at the lifter. "What are you going to do, beat up a one-legged war veteran so you can get in his wife's pants?"

The big man's confidence was rapidly eroding, "You don't know this guy's her husband."

The contract killer moved closer to Carol, "Tell the man we're together."

Carol turned awkwardly on her stool. Her eyes were having difficulty focusing. After a moment she gave her lover a drunken smile, "Hi baby. I got lonely."

The lifter made a derisive noise, threw money on the bar, and pushed his way out of the restaurant. The assassin picked up Carol's purse and eased her off the stool. She was unsteady but able to walk with minimal assistance. He continued dragging his leg until they were on the sidewalk several buildings away from the restaurant.

When they were back at the motel he undressed her and tucked her under the covers. When she fell into a deep sleep, he went to his car and drove by the author's apartment building. The normally present Crown Victoria was absent, but that probably meant Scanlan was out for the evening. He considered the same limited options that were available on his prior reconnaissance. As he drove back to the motel, he decided to use the same technique that had worked so effectively on Bernie Fredberg. He knew there was a greater chance of discovery than had been present in New York. Fredberg's building had the anonymity of size. In a complex of over forty condominiums, particularly in Manhattan, no one knew their neighbor. In the author's small, three story Victorian apartment building that would not be the case. There was also the possibility of being seen by the agent stationed outside the structure.

He began considering ways to minimize his risk as he drove back to the motel.

———

Jonathan did not know what to expect. Her apartment could be anything from Holiday Inn utilitarian to a testament to Martha Stewart. The answer leaned more toward the Ikea end of the spectrum. The featureless four-story building on Bryant seemed fairly new and Carmen's third floor unit faced Bryant and offered an uninspiring view of the structural supports to Highway 80 as it fed into the Bay Bridge. The area was a mix of commercial and residential properties in an area stylishly referred to as China Basin. The district underwent a renaissance when SBC Park, still referred to by the natives as Pac Bell, was built. Rents and property values rose exponentially the closer one came to The Embarcadero that ringed the city along the bay.

Her one-bedroom unit was saved from hotel room blandness by framed photographs on nearly every flat surface. Jonathan dropped his bag and wandered around the living room looking at what he assumed were family pictures. Carmen listened to messages on her machine before joining Jon on a virtual tour of her family.

Carmen smiled and gave the apartment a dismissive wave of her hand, "Not exactly the Ritz."

"It's fine. Come on, you've seen my place. Do you think it's alright to go out? I'm starving."

"We weren't followed. If the bad guys are watching your apartment they'd have to assume you're at home. We just have to stay away from Cow Hollow and the Marina."

"Let's go down to Gordon Biersch, I'd do anything for a beer and a hamburger."

"Anything?"

"Name your price."

Carmen laughed, "I'll collect later, after we get the poor boy something to eat. But first I think you need to slip into something a little less torn and tattered."

Jonathan glanced down at his torn shirt and muddy jeans, "I'll just be a minute."

Fifteen minutes later they were walking down to the microbrewery/restaurant.

CHAPTER 49

Carmen drove Jonathan to the airport for a ten o'clock flight. They had decided that it made more sense for him to make the short trip alone since they could not disclose her involvement in the investigation. The United flight left on time and an hour later the plane was taxiing to its gate at Los Angeles International. He took a cab to the Federal Building in Los Angeles and arrived early enough to have a sandwich at a nearby deli. At one fifteen, Jonathan was waiting in the sixth-floor lobby for his appointment.

A woman in a gray business suit opened a side door and walked towards him, "Mr. Scanlan?"

Jonathan guessed the woman to be in her late forties. "Yes, Regional Director Hanavan?"

She gave Jon a perfunctory handshake without replying, turned and led the way into the Bureau offices. When they reached a conference room Hanavan motioned him toward one of the chairs. "You said you had information that might be helpful to our investigation. What information would that be, Mr. Scanlan?"

"I'm fine, Director Hanavan. No problems on the flight down, but thank you for asking." Jonathan offered Hanavan a pleasant, non-confrontational expression.

The regional director looked away for a moment before redirecting her gaze on Jon. "Alright. I apologize if I was abrupt. It's been a long day. Actually, it's been a long spring."

"Well, perhaps I can improve your day. I don't know where the Bureau is on the investigation other than what the papers say about this man Champion, so some of what I'm going to tell you may be redundant information."

"Is this going to take long, Mr. Scanlan?" Jonathan hoped Hanavan's obvious impatience would be tempered by her need to achieve progress in the case.

"Yes, it is." Jonathan pushed into his description of the assumptions made by the Irregulars before the woman could object to his hijacking her afternoon. "We all know the killer is a professional. We believe, given the proficiency shown with a variety of weapons, someone who served in an elite branch of one of our domestic services."

"Why domestic? Why not from Britain, France, or Israel? There are a dozen countries with elite units."

"Could be, but why hire someone from another country when we have so many highly trained former servicemen with no language challenges and no problem understanding our culture. But let's put this point aside. It doesn't have any bearing on the rest of our investigation."

"You keep saying, our and we, Mr. Scanlan. Who represents the we?"

Jonathan looked at Helen Hanavan for a moment. "Do you want to know our conclusions?" He continued when Hanavan did not respond. "When *Culprits* was first published, the initial print run was only ten thousand copies. Let's say we agree Fredberg, and the killings that followed, were contract murders. Bernie Fredberg was killed on April 28th. We believe the killer took somewhere between ten to fourteen days to travel to Manhattan, study the victim, and to plan the crime. We estimate it would take the person behind the killings at least four days to locate the assassin, negotiate the price and transfer the funds used to finance the murder. Logic dictates the killer's employer purchased a copy of *Culprits* before they contacted the assassin. Following the bouncing ball, this means the person financing these killings had to have purchased the book sometime between March 31st, when the first copy was sold, and April 10th."

He paused to study the regional director. Jon could read the intelligence in her green eyes but nothing more. "In that time period only two thousand copies were sold. We were able to obtain a list of all credit card purchases made during that time period. We then estimated how much a contract killer with this level of skill would require to assassinate high profile people. Our guess was fifty thousand each for Fredberg and La Blanc, seventy-five thousand each for Wellstone and Clarkson. Clarke would possibly go as high as a hundred thousand."

"Why the escalating prices?"

Jonathan was not sure if the question was a test of their logic or an honest inquiry. "Fredberg and La Blanc had no protection. Wellstone had his own, private, security team. The Bureau was carefully watching Clarkson, and Clarke was under a security blanket. We assume the price goes up proportionate to the amount of risk involved. If we add up the estimated payments, the employer put out approximately half a million to kill five liberals. Not a lot of people have this kind of financial depth. Financial information was pulled on the list of people who bought *Culprits* during the ten-day time period and only two had the resources to finance this type of program, Edward Austin Beckwith and Laura LaCroix. Beckwith owns World Freightways and is a big conservative contributor. LaCroix is the chairman and president of Creighton Trust, which is a huge contributor to left wing causes.

"Our initial reaction was to focus on Beckwith because of his political leanings, but when we dug into his records we found nothing interesting in his contributions. Nothing came up when we looked into LaCroix's accounts, but we did find a history of payments to overseas banks that matched the dates of the killings when the Creighton Trust account was examined."

"Can I ask how this account information was obtained?"

Jonathan removed a stack of printouts from his briefcase and pushed it across the table. "No, you may not. Regional Director Hanavan, has this same information been developed by the Bureau?"

"I can't answer that."

Jonathan met Hanavan's stare without blinking, "Two days ago, a man named Phil Sundell was shot while golfing on the Pebble Beach

Golf Course. The shot came from a silenced weapon positioned about three hundred yards from the victim. The shooter vanished after the killing, leaving no trace evidence for the police. Does this have a familiar ring?"

"The murdered man had no connection to your book."

"No, but I have a connection to my book."

Helen Hanavan was obviously not seeing where this was going, "What are you talking about?

"I was playing the course behind Sundell. He and I share the same height, weight, hair color and we are both very good golfers. I believe I was the intended victim."

"I agree it's a bizarre coincidence, but I don't see a connection. The murders were people discussed in your book. You're the author."

"I received a gift certificate from my publisher for dinner, a night's stay, and a round of golf at Pebble. When I called Dell, the nonfiction editor told me she knew nothing about the certificate which had to cost over a thousand dollars. Didn't I read in the paper Wellstone received a bogus invitation to meet with someone at the Pacific Union Club?"

Helen Hanavan pushed away from the table and walked to the conference room windows to give herself time to think. "Why would the focus change from the people in your book to you?"

Jonathan pointed to the stack of papers on the table. "What if our excursion into the Creighton data base was detected and traced back to my computer?"

She moved away from the window, placed her hands on the table and leaned forward. "You've made a number of assumptions that might or might not be accurate. What if the killer is doing this on his own? What if your book was a cash purchase?"

"Those are both valid possibilities."

"And even if your conclusions are correct, I can't use any of this." Hanavan waved her hand toward the papers. "First, most if not all of the information was obtained illegally. Second, it's all circumstantial evidence based on broad assumptions. No judge in the country would issue a warrant based on this data." When she saw Jonathan's expression her face softened. "Please don't misinterpret what I'm saying. I'm not saying you're wrong. There's a good chance you're right. And in answer to your earlier question, no, the Bureau hasn't pursued this line of inquiry."

Jonathan recognized the regional director was throwing him a bone, but one with little meat on it. He slouched back in his chair and glanced at the stack of data he had thought might end the killings. "So, what happens next? The FBI sits back and waits for the killer to make a mistake?"

Hanavan shook her head, "No, there are things we can do. We can start looking at the trust and Laura LaCroix. People don't look in the yellow pages for a killer. Perhaps we can find a lead there. I do have a problem with motive. You said the Creighton Trust is a major contributor to liberal causes. Why finance the murders of prominent left-wing leaders when you share their philosophy?"

"I have no idea."

"If the man shot at Pebble Beach was mistaken for you, we have to assume they'll try again. The Bureau can offer you protection."

Jonathan stood up and began pacing the room. "I'm all in favor of not being this guy's next trophy, but what if it takes months or years to bring this to an end? What if you never find enough evidence to bring anyone to trial?"

"There's the Witness Protection Program. We could arrange a new identity, a new life."

Jonathan stopped and faced Hanavan, "I appreciate the offer and maybe that's what I'll eventually have to do, but I like my life as it is and I'm willing to take a chance to keep it that way. I have an idea that might draw them out."

"This isn't television where we burst into the room just before the killer shoots you. I can't agree to put you at risk."

Jon smiled as he sat back in his chair, "No, I know you can't, but you also can't stop me. Let me tell you what I have in mind and perhaps we can work something out."

Regional Director Hanavan listened with obvious skepticism as Jonathan described his plan.

CHAPTER 50

He promised to take Carol out for a nice dinner when he finished his work if she agreed to stay in the motel. She was hung over enough from the prior evening's outing that her agreement was not much of a sacrifice. The previous night he had purchased enough food and bottled water to keep her from having to go out for two days. His first stop was a hardware store on Fillmore to buy painter's coveralls, two cans of paint, a drop cloth, brushes, and rollers. It was midmorning, early enough to find parking a half block from Jonathan's building.

The Schlage lock on the entry door took less than a minute to pick. One of his problems was solved when he saw the author's name on the mail slot for apartment 2B. He lugged his painting gear up the stairs, set the paint cans on the hallway floor, covered both hands in surgical latex gloves, and knocked on Jonathan's door. His left hand held a box of rollers and brushes while his right gripped the silenced automatic in his deep coverall pocket. He knocked a second time without response. The contract killer set the box on the floor and went to work on the lock. When he heard the click he turned the knob with his left hand and stepped inside. His right scanned the room with the Sig-Sauer. Seeing the living room empty he moved quickly to the bedroom and bathroom, finding both equally devoid of the author.

The assassin placed the pistol back in his pocket and returned to the hallway where he retrieved his painting equipment. He carried the cans, brushes and rollers into the apartment and set them on the floor near the door. It had always proved helpful to understand the person he was being paid to kill, to know their interests, passions, and fears. He studied the apartment, and beyond the piles of books stacked on the floor and on several of the tables, he saw nothing of the man he would soon kill. A few family photos showed an attractive family at the seashore and another in ski garb with snow covered mountains in the distance. Fly rods and reels in the closet and golf clubs propped against the wall in the bedroom confirmed the man's interests.

The refrigerator was bachelor empty. A hopeful bottle of Chardonnay waiting for a cooperative date, packets of cold meats, processed cheeses and a six pack of Heineken completed the inventory. He could not tell from his survey of the bedroom whether Scanlan was away on an errand or would be gone for an extended period of time. The assassin pulled a chair to a position where it could not be seen from the doorway and made himself comfortable.

Carmen circled the arrival level at San Francisco International until she saw Jonathan standing by the curb. The sight of him gave her a thrill and she wondered if it was the newness of their relationship or if the feeling would last. When he called to confirm his arrival time, he had told her the meeting with Helen Hanavan had gone well, but he had not elaborated. He had promised to give her all the details when he was home.

Jonathan had barely buckled up when Carmen began pressing, "Ok, what did Hanavan say?"

"She said we might be right, but the Bureau can't use the information for reasons we all know. They'll try to figure out how someone at a nonprofit trust could figure out where to go to line up a contract killer."

"Did she offer you protection?"

"She asked if I wanted protection. She also mentioned the Witness Protection Program."

Carmen glanced away from the road, "And?"

"And I suggested something else." Jonathan avoided Carmen's gaze, knowing what he was about to say was not going to be well received. "I want to rattle Laura LaCroix and her friends at the trust. I want them to make a mistake with the Bureau watching."

Carmen turned her eyes back to the road and did not immediately respond. When she did speak Jonathan could hear the undertone of pleading in her voice. "You're going to get yourself killed Jonathan. Accept the offer of protection by the Bureau or even witness protection. We know of seven people that have been murdered counting the CPA in Los Angeles and the unlucky golfer. This isn't some *Diagnosis Murder* episode where the hero always prevails."

"Look, I'm not trying to be a hero. I just want this to go away. I want my life back. If I thought the FBI was close to catching these people, I could live with Bureau protection, but I'm not. Hanavan said she couldn't get a warrant to dig into the trust. And look how well the Bureau's protection worked for Judge Carlson and Lawrence Clarke."

Carmen veered over to the right lane and took the Silver exit. She said nothing as she drove; her hands were locked in a death grip on the steering wheel. After a few blocks, she turned into the parking lot of a 7-Eleven. Tears streaked her face as she jerked the car into a slot, slammed the shift into park, and turned off the engine. She pounded on the steering wheel with her small fists before leaning forward and burying her face in her arms. "You men, you're all so stupid."

Jonathan did not think it prudent to respond. After a moment she looked up, her face distorted in aguish. "I finally found someone I can love, and you want to go and get killed."

"I don't want to get killed. I know, you told me Carlson basically refused protection and Clarke exposed himself when he insisted on going to the opening. Sooner or later I'm going to make a mistake that'll make me vulnerable or someone on my protection team will screw up. If I make them come out in the open, we have a chance of stopping this forever. And I'm not refusing protection, just how the protection works."

"What do you mean?"

"I'll have agents with me all the time, but they'll look like my friends, not like they're guarding me. One of them will even play the part of my girlfriend."

Carmen rubbed her eyes and looked away. "Did Hanavan say who that would be?"

I told her the only agent I'd seen that was attractive enough to be believable was Agent Carmen Costello."

A smile forced its way to Carmen's lips, "And what did she say?"

"She mentioned another woman, I think the name was Tracy Brayton, out of the Los Angeles office. I told her I was sure Brayton was a fine agent, but we met when you first connected the killings to *Culprits* and I wanted you for the job. I think she believes I have a hidden case of the hots for you."

Carmen shook her head and laughed, "I think I met Brayton. You might want to reconsider. Blond, big chest . . ."

"Well, I guess I could go back and interview."

"Alright, alright, I'm only half as pissed at you as I was a few minutes ago. I still think this is a dumb idea, but how do you plan to draw out the bad guys?"

"Take the fight to them. Fly to New York and visit the Creighton Trust. Show up at Aureole while Ms. LaCroix is having lunch, things like that."

"What do you think the contract killer is going to be doing while you're strolling around the streets of Manhattan?"

"While we're strolling around the streets of Manhattan, I imagine he'll be trying to get to me, but that's my point. It's harder to hit a moving target. With the exception of Winnie La Blanc all his kills have been carefully set up. He either springs a trap and waits for his victim to walk into it, like he did with Wellstone and with me, or he lays in wait and shoots when his target arrives. You can't do that if there's no pattern and your target is constantly on the move."

"La Blanc maybe the exception, but a notable one."

"I agree. That's why you and your FBI friends will be around."

Carmen started the car and drove out of the parking lot, "There are a lot of things that could go wrong."

"I know, but they could also go wrong if we sit around and wait for the killer to see an opening. The bad guys aren't used to playing defense."

"So, what do we do now?" Jonathan was pleased to see the shift in Carmen's thinking.

"We go home and pack. I booked us on an eight a.m. flight into JFK tomorrow morning."

"We'll stop at Stonestown. You can pick up whatever you need."

"Why don't we swing by my place?"

"For the same reason you were hopping over backyard fences yesterday. You said it yourself, it's harder to hit a moving target."

Jonathan put his hands up to surrender, "Alright, I leave all matters related to security in your capable hands. What do you want to do after our little shopping binge?"

"Let's pick up something for dinner. I don't have anything at the apartment. Then I thought we could iron out the bugs in these girlfriend/ boyfriend roles we're going to have to play."

"And what happens if I don't get it right?"

"You have to do it over and over again until you have it perfected."

CHAPTER 51

At three in the morning he accepted the fact that the author was not coming home. He left with his painting gear as quietly as possible and returned to the motel. The television was on, and Carol was asleep. He turned off the set, undressed, and slipped into bed without waking her. He was mentally prepared to wait day after day in Scanlan's apartment until the author returned. His concern was Carol. How long would she sit in the motel watching television and eating sandwiches? If the author was gone for several days, the odds were good that Carol would wander off in search of companionship and beverages.

As he lay in bed he considered sending her back to the farm in eastern Tennessee, but that too carried its risks. He thought of Carol as a fragile and delicate flower, exotically beautiful, but only capable of surviving in a rigorously controlled environment. He wondered for the hundredth time if he could maintain such an environment.

They dozed and read their way across the country. Ross Del Monica had tried to stop Carmen's involvement but had eventually acquiesced when Helen Hanavan made it clear she had approved the agent's participation.

Carmen was sure the real reason for Del Monica's objection was his exclusion from what he had called a ridiculous sideshow.

It was after seven when their taxi dropped them off not far from Broadway and Times Square at the Paramount Hotel. Jonathan had decided on the boutique hotel for reasons of location and price. He did not realize it was one of Philippe Starck's unique projects. They wandered around the lobby admiring the colorful overstuffed chairs and tables made from split logs before checking in. Jon had to laugh when Carmen complained that the blue light in their elevator made her look terrible. Their room carried the same theme with the end table, lights, and other furnishings; all were products of the designer's imagination.

Carmen looked around as she began unpacking, "I feel like I'm in some kind of theme park."

"But it's fun."

She stopped, nodded, and smiled, "Yeah, I like it. So, what's the plan for tomorrow?"

"Laura LaCroix and a man named Gordon Croll, who's the number two guy at the trust, are having a lunch meeting with three people from PETA. I've booked us at a nearby table."

"Alright, I have to ask. How did you know where they're going?"

"Cal spent a few minutes in her online day-timer."

"Why do I even ask?"

Before they went out to dinner, Carmen called the New York office and told the head of the office, James Pohley, about their lunch plans. The warm evening temperature invited them to walk in search of somewhere to eat. The streets were crowded, and the first few restaurants they tried had over an hour wait for a table. When they turned off the main thoroughfares and into the side streets, they found an Italian place named Angelo's with tables available. When their pasta arrived, they found out why. The food was inedible. After a few valiant mouthfuls of the pastiest linguini he had ever eaten, Jonathan asked for the check. They wandered back to the hotel and settled for room service cheeseburgers and an early night.

They woke up late not having adjusted to the three-hour time difference. Carmen ordered coffee while Jonathan hustled into the shower. They arrived with few minutes to spare for their meeting with Pohley at the nearby Marriott. They were glancing around the lobby when a compact man in his late fifties approached.

"Mr. Scanlan? I'm Jim Pohley."

Jonathan shook the man's hand and introduced him to Carmen. Pohley led them to a private area he had secured near the hotel's circulating pond. When they were comfortably seated the senior agent gave Jon a look of curiosity. "I have to say this is a strange game you're playing, Mr. Scanlan."

Jon shrugged, "Please call me Jonathan. What can I tell you? I'm hoping if I push hard enough they'll make a mistake."

"I know. I had a long conversation with Helen Hanavan. Frankly, I'm surprised she went along with this."

"I really didn't give her a choice. I told her I was going ahead on my own if the Bureau refused to work with me." Jonathan wondered if the agent's close-cut hair and military bearing were an affectation or if he had spent time in the service.

It was Pohley's turn to shrug, "Anyway, I've assigned a team to shadow you and to watch the LaCroix woman. You have to understand I can't guarantee your safety."

"I know that. What about monitoring her communication? If she panics she's going to call in the contract killer."

Pohley shook his head, "We'd have to have a warrant and right now we don't have grounds. We're going to try to pick up her conversations with a parabolic microphone, but that only works if she's outside."

"Shouldn't I meet your team?"

"No. It's better you don't know who they are." He turned to Carmen, "How are you feeling about all this?"

"I'll be fine," she hoped her nerves were not obvious.

"Are you wired?"

At first Carmen thought he was asking if she was on edge. "No. I didn't have time to check out that kind of equipment before we left San Francisco." In truth she had not considered the need.

Pohley pulled two miniature transmitters from his briefcase. He handed one to Carmen and the other to Jonathan. "They have a range of about a half mile. You don't have to do anything to activate them, they're already on. Jonathan, why don't you attach it to the inside of your collar?" He waited while Jonathan and Carmen secured the transmitting devices. "Well, I guess it's show time. We won't be in the restaurant today, by the way. It would be too obvious, and I don't have the budget." When neither Carmen nor Jonathan laughed he smiled. "Agency humor." He picked up his briefcase and stood up. "When we need to meet, we'll use the Marriott. The Bureau's taken a room, 403, which we'll keep as long as necessary. Good luck." Pohley walked away without looking back.

Picholine was the type of expensive restaurant that catered to well-heeled business clientele and intentionally hovered below the radar of the tourists. Jonathan's sport coat and slacks stood out like a beacon in a sea of gray and dark blue business suits. They had just been seated and handed their menus when Laura LaCroix, Gordon Croll, and the people from PETA threaded their way to a nearby table. Jonathan studied the thin woman in her tailored business suit as he pretended to read his menu. Her narrow face and severe features made her appear older than her fifty-six years and the expression etched in the lines of her face made it apparent Ms. LaCroix found the world to be a serious place. Croll, on the other hand, was all smiles and good cheer. The number two banana at Creighton was a heavy set, animated man in his mid-forties. Jon could not hear what Croll was saying, but from the expressions on the faces of the woman and two men from PETA, it appeared to be an amusing story.

Jon waited until the man finished his tale and received obligatory chuckles from the PETA people before he placed his napkin on the table, stood up, and walked over the LaCroix's table. "Ms. LaCroix, I'm Jonathan Scanlan." Confusion swept over Laura LaCroix's features, quickly replaced with the flush of anger. Jon was focusing on LaCroix, but he could see Croll's startled expression out of the corner of his eye. "Did you finance the murders of Bernie Fredberg, Winnie La Blanc, and the others referred to as the *Culprits* killings?"

Croll started to stand up and the PETA people stared at Jonathan as if he was a space alien, but it was LaCroix who held his attention.

Pure hatred distorted her features, "You're the author of that awful book."

"Yes, I am," he turned to Gordon Croll for a moment. "Sit down, Mr. Croll."

Jonathan again focused on Laura LaCroix. "Confession is good for the soul, Ms. LaCroix."

"Get out of here," the words were hissed more than spoken.

Jonathan could see the maître d' hurrying toward the table. "I know where the money came from for the killings and I'm not going away." He walked back to the table and collected Carmen as the maître d' attempted to placate LaCroix and Croll. They left the restaurant before the officious little man in the tuxedo could tell them to leave.

Carmen linked her arm around Jonathan's as they walked away from the restaurant. "That was fun. What's next in store for lovely Laura?"

"She's scheduled to attend a gallery opening in the Village this evening. I thought we might broaden our cultural horizons and stop by."

"Marvelous, now let's see if we can actually have lunch, I'm starving."

———

He had the cell phone set on mute. He remained seated in the corner of Jonathan's living room as he pulled the vibrating device out of his coveralls. Since only one person had the number there was no mystery over who was calling.

"Where are you?" the distorted voice did not appear to be in a pleasant mood.

"In the man's apartment."

"Unfortunately, he's in New York."

"In Manhattan? How do you know?"

There was the briefest pause, "Never mind, I just know."

"Where is he staying?"

"I don't know, but get out here immediately."

"I can't just walk the streets looking for him."

"It's your job to find him."

"No, it's my job to kill him." The imperious nature of his employer was starting to really tick him off. "I've spent too much money on this guy. I'll wait for him to come home."

"I'll tell you what you will and will not do."

He closed the phone without responding, replaced the chair in its original position, gathered his paints and other materials, and left the apartment. As he drove back to the motel he considered his alternatives.

CHAPTER 52

The gallery opening was by invitation, but with a thin turnout, no one was being checked at the door. Jonathan and Carmen paused at each piece as they worked through the showroom. He accepted a glass of Champaign while Carmen stayed with water. The haute couture for the art crowd appeared to be everything black, which as at the restaurant, segregated Carmen and Jonathan as outsiders. The gallery seemed to specialize in large, incomprehensible pieces that patrons would study to find hidden meaning. They were halfway through the second room when Laura LaCroix appeared on the arm of a young man.

The man, clad in a tight black turtleneck and equally form fitting black pants, was fawning over the chairman of Creighton Trust. Jonathan and Carmen hung back and watched the interaction between LaCroix and the man who was clearly thirty years her junior. After watching several patrons stop the young man to discuss different paintings it became obvious he had created the large oils hanging in the room. Jonathan examined the card resting in a holder by one of the pieces. It was titled "Sunlight in Palestine" by Julio Delucchi and the price of the oil was listed at ten thousand dollars.

Jonathan stepped back and viewed the piece from the middle of the room. To him it was a jumble of thickly applied colors without form or reason. He glanced at Carmen, "I think this would go well on your living room wall."

"Can't you see the anguish of the artist in the primary colors and the background swirls indicating his search for identity?"

When Jonathan stared at her in disbelief she laughed, "Gotcha. It's one the most hideous pieces I've ever seen. A blind man wouldn't buy it."

"Well, Ms. LaCroix is buying something." The young artist was hanging onto the older woman as a drowning man might grip a life preserver. "Let's add a little spice to the show."

Julio was pointing out the hidden mysteries of one of his pieces when Jon and Carmen moved in behind the couple. Jonathan leaned forward and whispered in LaCroix's ear, "Why is a lefty like you paying to have your liberal friends killed?"

Laura LaCroix dropped her glass of Champaign as she spun around to face her accuser. "You! What are you doing here? You're stalking me!"

Jonathan smiled, "No, just a happy coincidence, like those payments from the Creighton Trust that coincide with the dates of the killings."

Julio Delucchi's initial expression of confusion transformed to one of rage as he realized the man insulting LaCroix was ruining his showing, and more importantly, his chance to sell his works to Laura. He tried to push Jonathan, but the bigger man brushed his hands away. The enraged artist took a wild swing at Jon, who ducked away from the blow. When Julio's fist connected with Laura LaCroix's temple, the chairman and president of Creighton Trust dropped to the parquet floor like a sack of potatoes. Unaware of the damage he had inflicted on his patron, Julio took another swing at Jon who blocked the blow, stepped inside, and hit the artist as hard as he could in the stomach. A woman in the room screamed as Delucchi gripped his abdomen and dropped to his knees. Jon was vaguely aware of someone with a camera to his right.

For a moment Jonathan and Carmen stood over the couple. "You sure know how to spice up an art show."

"Perhaps we should leave," Jonathan said as he took Carmen's hand and began walking toward the exit. The woman hired to photograph the event tracked their movements across the room. Before they could make the door, they saw the police.

Several of the men and women in the room pointed at Jonathan. The two uniforms saw the unconscious woman sprawled ungainly across the showroom floor and the young man rolling in pain beside her. The muscular black patrolman pushed Jon against the wall and began frisking him for a weapon. When Carmen tried to intercede the second patrolman pushed her away. "Step away unless you want a ride to the station with your boyfriend."

Carmen stepped back and let the officers handcuff Jonathan. She let them lead Jon out of the gallery to their patrol car. Just before they were about to stuff him into the car's rear seat she moved between them and the patrol car's rear door. The black policeman glared at her. "Lady, move away or be booked for obstruction."

Carmen held up her identification card, "Special Agent Carmen Costello. Screw with me and you'll be writing tickets in Bedford Stuyvesant."

The white cop could not believe what he was seeing. "What is this shit? Why didn't you identify yourself when we came in?"

Carmen smiled sweetly. "Have you two ever heard of something called undercover?" When neither of the patrolmen answered her rhetorical question, she pushed on. "Uncuff my partner." When they hesitated she barked, "Now!"

The patrolman saw the lay of the land, uncuffed Jonathan and tried to minimize the damage. "Nobody said anything about a federal investigation going on down here."

Carmen was enjoying the moment. "It's not our job to keep you informed. By the way, the guy on the floor holding his stomach was the attacker. Take a look at the video from the photographer."

Carmen and Jonathan walked away as an ambulance pulled up to deal with the unconscious LaCroix and the reviving artist. They hailed a cab on Bleecker Street, gave him the name of their hotel and settled into their seats. Jonathan was as subdued as Carmen was energized. "That was really, really fun."

"A schoolyard fight. I was hoping she'd say something we could use."

"You have to understand, for someone who mainly brings coffee to the meetings and has to act like Del Monica's toady, this was a life enriching experience."

Jonathan forced a smile, "I'm happy when you're happy. Let hope Ms. LaCroix confesses when they bring her around. Should she be a bit reticent when she comes to; we may have rung out our string."

His petite companion was not willing to be let down. "Honey, I have a good feeling about this."

As they headed back to the Paramount, Jonathan hoped Carmen's vibes were based in reality.

CHAPTER 53

The television in the Tennessee farmhouse was turned to a show that chronicled the activities of the entertainment industry's beautiful people. The program absorbed Carol as it offered glimpses into the lives of young actors and actresses the assassin had never heard of. He had paused to see what she was watching when quite a different picture filled the screen.

The voice of the program's host followed the action as a young man in black took a roundhouse swing at a taller man in a sport coat. "And just to prove not all the excitement occurs in Hollywood. Film from the opening of the Lighthouse Gallery in the Village has featured artist Julio Delucchi taking on best-selling author Jonathan Scanlan. As you can see, Julio would be wise to deal with his critics in a more cerebral manner." The screen shifted to the picture of a woman being carried out of the gallery on a stretcher. "The woman caught up in the melee has been identified as art patron Laura LaCroix. Ms. LaCroix apparently suffered a concussion but is expected to make a full recovery. We understand the police are looking into the matter, but no charges have been filed at this time."

For a moment he stood still, absorbing what he had just seen. Perhaps the author would not be so difficult to locate in Manhattan. The contract killer had collected Carol at the motel and caught the first available flight back home. He was convinced his employer's demands were ridiculous and that their relationship had ended. In light of the art gallery story, he began making a mental list of what he would need for the trip.

———

Fortunately for the White House, the public has a short memory. Several weeks had passed since the Clarke killing and news of the series of murders had slipped off the front pages. The holiday period in killings reinforced the belief that law enforcement had their man in John William Champion and the Bureau saw no benefit in linking Phil Sundell's murder to the list of progressive leaders.

The president's political adversaries were not as forgetful. Prescott sat in an alcove in the Oval Office and watched the evening news and commentary on Fox. Since taking the oath of office, he limited himself to one cocktail an evening. Tonight's old fashion was shared with his chief of staff as they watched Senator Robert Mallory blame the president for everything from global warming to the spread of AIDS in Africa. The Massachusetts senator pounded the rostrum, waved his arms and shouted as he debased the head of state.

Prescott took a sip of his drink and pointed at the screen. "I'm surprised Bobby hasn't had a heart attack by now."

Gene Baronian shook his head, "Mallory gives out heart attacks. Kidney failure may be another matter."

"I thought he stopped drinking."

"Every evening. On a happier note, the polls are looking a little better."

"Don't count your chickens before they're hatched. Palacin doesn't think the man they have in custody is the killer. All it's going to take is another well-known liberal being murdered and the firestorm will be burning brighter than ever."

"I think the whole censure thing hurt them more than it helped them."

"A nice thought, but I'm afraid it's not true. Negative advertising works in political races and that's exactly what this was all about. It doesn't matter if the accusations are true, say them often enough and people will start believing you. It's the old 'you can fool all of the people some of the time and some of the people all of the time.'"

Baronian turned his attention back to the television, realizing the president was in no mood to hear a pep talk.

———

The hotel lobby was crowded with arriving visitors and guests organizing themselves for an evening on the town. Carmen and Jonathan made their way up the asymmetrical staircase to the mezzanine bar and a table overlooking the lobby. With drinks in hand they watched the ebb and flow of the milling guests as each considered the day's events.

Jonathan shrugged as he continued to watch the people below, "I guess I was hoping for too much. LaCroix's out of reach in the hospital, and you can bet we won't be able to get near her when she's released. I don't know what we can do next to apply pressure."

Carmen reached over and covered his hand in hers. "This isn't like the old *Perry Mason* shows where the killer breaks down on the stand and confesses. These people are smart, but even smart people make mistakes."

"You're right. I just don't know what thread we could pull next."

Carmen sipped her drink, her mind wandering down hypothetical avenues. "Our problem is how we obtained the records of payments from the trust. What if we could get our hands on another copy in a way that would open the door for a warrant from the Bureau?"

"How would we do that?"

"They would have to be turned over to us by someone at Creighton."

"Why would they do that?"

Carmen shrugged, "All types of reasons. We could throw out the threat of their involvement in a criminal enterprise, maybe they don't like LaCroix, and it would be their way of sticking it to her. Then there's old fashioned bribery."

"Wouldn't the records be off limits if they were obtained through bribery?"

"They're not privileged like they're coming from a doctor or someone's attorney, but maybe you're right. It might have to be structured so it's not exactly a bribe."

Jonathan pushed the idea along. "The right person would have to be someone with access to the accounts payable records but not anyone too senior at the trust. I can't see Croll or whoever is the CFO selling out over a vague threat or money."

Carmen smiled as she watched her energized friend, "So how do we find out the name of someone in accounts payable?"

Jonathan picked up his cell phone and dialed a familiar number, "We ask the keyboard wizard to do a little more digging."

CHAPTER 54

They drove from the farm to Virginia and took the train into Manhattan. With virtually no security on the train system, he was able to bring along his own weapons. Killing the author was already turning out to be an expensive task. Carol read the *Enquirer* and movie magazines while he reread *Culprits* for the second time. Several of the men in their car stole furtive glances at Carol, which he no longer resented.

When they reached Grand Central Station, they took a cab to a Holiday Inn on the west side. The room was clean, functional and ridiculously expensive. He picked up a copy of *The Times* and thumbed through it looking for an article on the dustup in the Village. He found a brief article, but it offered no new information. He sighed as he picked up the telephone and began dialing every major hotel in the city. By eight, he had covered the major names as Carol complained that she was hungry. The woman at the reception desk recommended a steak house two blocks away.

Carol paused over her prime rib and studied the man she loved, "Are we going to keep doing this forever?"

He thought for a moment before he answered. He had never lied to Carol, but he was not sure if he knew the truth. "No, not forever. There are times I want to get out of the business, but the thought frightens me."

"Nothing frightens you," she made the statement as if it was an established law of science.

"I'm frightened by not knowing what I'd do. Sitting around the farmhouse day after day would drive me crazy."

"We could travel."

The concept of traveling for pleasure seemed odd to him. All his travels had been work related. "I guess, but what would I do when we aren't traveling?"

"There has to be something you could do to keep your interest besides . . . you know."

He hesitated for a moment, not wanting to appear ready to make a commitment he could not keep, "I've always liked exotic cars."

Carol's smile brightened the room, "I know you like to watch the races. Is that what you mean? Racing cars?"

He shrugged, "I don't know. I'm just saying it's something I've always liked."

Carol went back to her dinner, pleased with the possibility of a change in their lives. When they were back in their room, he began working through the yellow pages, calling the lesser known hotels while Carol watched television. He quit for the evening after working through the hotels starting with the letter K.

He was awake early, thoughts of his conversation with Carol still cascading through his mind. He dressed quietly careful not to wake her and went down to the lobby. He drank coffee and tried to read the paper but found himself unable to concentrate on the news of the day. He watched his fellow guests as they left for their meetings and sales calls and wondered if he could be like them, an ordinary citizen leading an ordinary life. When he felt it was late enough, he went back to the room, waking Carol as he unlocked the door.

He handed her a latte, returned to the telephone book, and began calling hotels. It was after ten when he dialed the Paramount.

"Good morning. I'd like to speak with one of your guests, Jonathan Scanlan."

He hung up at the sound of the first ring.

————

Cal Hulse's exploration into the Creighton database had produced the names of two women in accounts payable and a credit check showed one of the women, Maria Santos, to be heavily in debt. Her address was on East 152nd in the Bronx. They assumed she would be at work in Manhattan until evening, leaving them with a free day.

Jonathan was glancing through pamphlets of tourist information in the room. "You know what I've always wanted to do? Go out to the Statue of Liberty."

Carmen pulled the drapes open and looked at a narrow slice of the sky between the neighboring buildings. "It looks like a great day. Let's do it."

They picked up coffee at a nearby Starbucks, stopped at an ATM, and cabbed down to Battery Park. Jon felt like he was on a family vacation as he and Carmen stood in line for tickets surrounded by dozens of young families and children. The ride out to Liberty Island was brief and crowded. Most of the passengers lined the rail to watch Lady Liberty as the boat crossed the Upper Bay

The weather cooperated with a warm wind blowing off the water and only a slight chop on the bay. When they arrived Carmen and Jonathan held back and let the eager passengers leave the ferry before they debarked. The scale of the monument was impressive. They held hands as they walked around the base for a while. Later they climbed the interior stairs and looked back at the city. Jonathan thought of the arriving immigrants as they turned toward Ellis Island.

The ferry back to Battery Park was less crowded and they were able to stand by the rail and watch Manhattan approach. They stopped for a late lunch at a café near Washington Square Park and observed the students from NYU pass on the sidewalk. They walked down 5th until the Empire State Building where they caught a cab for the rest of the way back to the Marriott. Carmen knocked on the door of room 403.

When a soft looking man in shirtsleeves answered she assumed she had the wrong room.

"Is James Pohley here?"

The man motioned them into the room, "He was here earlier. My name is Lyons, I'm in communications."

"We thought we'd check in. Has anything happened on your end?"

He shook his head and put on a pair of earphones that were attached to an array of electronic gear. "As far as we know Laura LaCroix is still hearing bells," He smiled and looked back at Jonathan. "We enjoyed your subtlety at the gallery. By the way, the agents we have tailing you wanted to thank you for the trip out to the statue."

Carmen motioned toward the door. "Let us know if anything pops."

As they walked back to the Paramount, Jonathan glanced at his watch, "Still a little early to head out to the Bronx."

"Why don't we go up to the room and work on our team building?"

Jonathan smiled as he took the petite agent's hand after he removed the Bureau's transmitting device.

CHAPTER 55

He sat in the lobby reading a paper and watching the guests and Nehru jacketed employees as they went about their business. The vagaries of style and fashion had never interested him, and he found his surroundings absurd. Philippe Starck's originality that touched every facet of the hotel's furniture, lighting fixtures, and décor was lost on the man who purchased his clothing from LL Bean and his furniture through the Sears catalogue. He assumed Carol would be captivated by what he considered ridiculous. When he felt he could no longer keep his position without drawing attention from the hotel staff, he moved to a small table in the mezzanine bar and ordered a beer.

He was still nursing his beer and nearly through his second reading of *Culprits* when he saw Jonathan and the small attractive woman he had seen outside the author's apartment. He watched as they walked through the lobby to the bank of elevators. The contract killer remembered the woman sitting in a Crown Victoria in front of Scanlan's building. She did not bare the stamp of the typical Bureau agent, but he had no doubt regarding her employer.

He thought about the possible need to kill the woman. Her gender meant nothing to him, nor did the fact that she carried a weapon and was well trained in its use. It was just a complication he would prefer to avoid. As he finished his beer, he considered how he might separate the agent from the focus of her assignment.

———

Traffic was horrendous and the ride out to the Bronx was longer than they anticipated. As Jonathan watched several near collisions, he decided he would rather jump out of a plane without a chute than try to drive in Manhattan. Maria Santos' apartment was housed in a five story, nondescript building huddled in a row of singularly unremarkable structures. They found her name taped to the mailbox for 4D. The elevator creaked and moaned as if they were the last burden it would ever carry. A narrow hallway smelling of overcooked food brought Carmen and Jonathan to the apartment door. Since Carmen was the one with the credentials, they decided she should take the lead.

Her knock brought a woman's narrow face to the slender gap between the door and its frame. A sturdy chain spanned the opening. "Maria Santos?"

The woman's expression was a blend of annoyance and apprehension, "What do you want?"

Carmen extended her credentials. "FBI, Ms. Santos. We want to speak with you." They could hear the sound of a television and children's voices in the background.

"What about?" her tone was defiant, but they could see the edge of fear in her eyes.

Carmen put on her best no bullshit expression. "Open the door Ms. Santos. We only want to talk to you."

"I've done nothing wrong. Go away."

Jonathan turned toward Carmen as he began dialing his cell phone. "I'll get Harrington to bring out a protective witness warrant for her and someone from Child Welfare to take care of the kids."

Maria's voice climbed several octaves, "What are you talking about? What do you mean 'someone to take care of the kids'?" Jonathan noticed her Spanish accent became more pronounced under stress.

He kept his voice impassive. "If you're not going to cooperate with us, we have no choice but to get a warrant and drag your ass down to our office. Child Services will take your children until we're finished."

The door slammed closed and for a moment Carmen and Jonathan believed Santos had called their bluff. When they heard the chain being released, their thoughts became more positive. The door opened to reveal a small woman who looked older than her thirty-three years. Without speaking, she lead them through a small living room where a boy of about ten and a girl slightly younger were watching cartoons and into an eating area off the kitchen. She sat down heavily at the table without offering her guests a seat. "Alright. Now what do you want?"

Carmen opened a file folder and spoke without looking at Santos. "You work in accounts payable at Creighton Trust. We want to know who at the trust authorized these payments." She took a printout from the folder and pushed it across the table.

The small woman glanced at the record, shrugged and turned away, "I have no idea."

Jonathan leaned across the table, his face inches from the woman's. "Beep. Wrong answer. You didn't even bother to look at the printout. One more try Maria before I make the phone calls. We think these payments are tied to five murders. We're not about to let you shine us on." He roughly shoved the papers closer to Santos.

This time she bent over the records, examining the highlighted lines. When she looked up all signs of defiance had evaporated. "I don't know. We make hundreds of payments every week."

Jonathan moved away from the table and let Carmen make the next move. "But you can find out who authorized the payments, can't you?"

The woman was clearly rattled, "I guess so."

Jonathan did not wish to offer her any slack. "You're in accounts payable. We know you can. We'll be back tomorrow evening at the same time. We expect to see printouts showing who authorized the payments. He started to leave, then turned back. "By the way, there's a twenty-thousand-dollar reward for the person that helps break this case. If you provide the records and they give us what we need the money's yours."

When they were in the elevator groaning their way to the first floor Carmen gave Jonathan a puzzled look, "There's no reward."

"Yes, there is. If she comes up with the information we want, I'll pay her."

———

The man currently calling himself Nicholas Stapp wanted to follow the couple from the hotel but could not do so without calling attention to himself. The old "follow that cab" routine hardly worked when you planned to kill the man you were following. While Jonathan and Carmen were visiting Maria Santos, he culled through the want ads and two hours later he was the proud owner of a used Yamaha motorcycle.

When he returned to the Holiday Inn with his new purchase, Carol was sitting in the chair by the small writing desk. She was dressed in a knee length tan skirt and a white sleeveless blouse, the dressiest outfit she had packed. She answered his questioning expression with a look of determination, "We're going to dinner and the theater."

He shook his head and extended his arms in a plea for understanding, "Honey, we're here on business."

Carol did not waver, "We're always somewhere on business. Even businessmen have to take time off. We have tickets on will call for Chicago. We'll catch dinner after the show."

"I can't stop what I'm doing and go to the theater."

"Why not? Were you going to finish everything tonight?" Carol had difficulty articulating the end product of her lover's vocation.

"No, but I need to plan what I'm going to do tomorrow."

She stood up and pointed toward the closet, "Hurry up, if you're going to change. We don't have much time."

He paused for a moment before waving his arms in mock surrender. As he changed he wondered if he preferred the inert, soap opera watching Carol or the new, more demanding manifestation.

CHAPTER 56

Jonathan awoke to a mild headache. It was the product of an evening laced with more than his normal intake of beer and wine. A long shower and a room service pot of coffee almost put his keel back in the water. Carmen was wrapped in a one of the hotel robes reading the Times when he asked how she wanted to spend the day. "There's a Jacqueline Kennedy exhibit at the Metropolitan Museum that might be fun."

Jon feigned interest. "That sounds good or we could always take in a ballgame. The Mets are playing the Dodgers." He could tell from her expression she was less than thrilled at the suggestion.

"It looks like the weather's going to be great today. Let's walk around Central Park and people watch." Jonathan agreed to the compromise solution without hesitation.

It was midmorning by the time they began walking up 7th toward Columbus Circle and Central Park South. The southern boundary of the park was only ten blocks from the hotel, but they were long blocks and neither Carmen nor Jonathan had bothered to pack comfortable walking shoes. They entered the park on the southeast corner, known to few as Scholars' Gate, and skirted past the children's zoo and the parents herding their children toward the Carousel.

Assassin Nicholas Stapp stayed a half block behind the author and his FBI escort as they plodded their way up 7ᵗʰ Avenue. The male and female agents trailing behind could not have been more obvious. He assumed the most junior of the local office had been assigned this remedial task. He followed the procession into the park at the Wien Walk entrance. He stopped briefly at a vendor stand for a cup of coffee. He had to admit it was a glorious day and he wondered if it made any difference to the man who was about to die.

The balmy weather had attracted New Yorkers to the park like bees to honey. Carmen and Jonathan held hands as they strolled along the circuitous paths, enjoying the day. For a while they rested on a bench near the William Shakespeare statue and watched the passage of walkers, runners, and hard bodied young men and women on roller blades. New foliage filled the trees and shrubs with lush abundance and new plantings added a riot of color. They had no difficulty spotting the agents assigned to their surveillance as they were the only people wearing coats to conceal their weapons.

Sheep Meadow was a patchwork of sunbathers and picnickers. Jon and Carmen threaded their way across the vast lawn toward Tavern on the Green. They had considered catching an early lunch at the famous restaurant but were discouraged when they saw the line of people waiting to enter. They left the park and crossed Central Park West in search of something to eat. A deli on W 66ᵗʰ provided the solution. They carried their sandwiches and sodas back into the park looking for a quiet spot to sit down and eat. Jonathan and Carmen pushed on past Adventure Playground and the play area's herd of squealing, running children. They found their peaceful oasis at Cherry Hill. The sounds of the city could not penetrate the area's seclusion and only a few people were sunbathing or reading.

"Who would have thought we're in the middle of the city?" Carmen looked out at the lake as she worked on her sandwich.

The cherry trees in springtime bloom reminded Jonathan of trips to the Japanese Tea Garden in Golden Gate Park when he was a child, "It's a beautiful setting."

"When all this is over, do you want to go back to teaching?"

Jonathan shrugged and looked away. "I don't know. It's fun when you're working with students that are really interested, but most of the time they're only there to pick up some credits and check off a mandatory course. What about you? Do you plan to stay with the Bureau until retirement?"

"I've been so busy, first in training and now just trying to keep my superior off my back, I haven't given it any thought."

He took a sip of soda and stood up, "I need to use the restroom. I think we passed one over there." Jon pointed down the path they had taken.

"I'll come along."

He waved her off, "Stay and finish your sandwich, I'll only be a minute." He nodded toward the man and woman on a bench thirty yards away. "Besides, I'm sure I'll have company."

The man in jeans and a tee shirt watched Jonathan leave the woman and walk away from the lake. The young man, who had been seated a short distance away, left the woman he was with and followed the author. Nicholas Stapp picked up his daypack and began moving in the same general direction. He stayed off the path, keeping parallel to his target as he considered his options. He preferred not to kill the agent protecting the author, but it appeared to be an unfortunate necessity. As the three men moved away from Cherry Hill, they encountered more and more people along the path and sunbathing on the lawns. The assassin had no desire to commit a double homicide in front of thirty or forty witnesses. When he saw Scanlan walk into the restroom, his problem was solved. He felt the comfortable weight of his Browning Hi-Power at the bottom of his daypack as he walked toward the facility.

CHAPTER 57

Special Agent Mitchell Dougherty took up position at the side of the restroom where he could see the entrance. James Pohley had made it clear their role was to watch and protect Agent Costello and Scanlan, and that it did not matter if they were obvious. Dougherty was sweating heavily from the heat of the day and the hike from the author's hotel. He desperately wanted to take off his jacket, but he knew the nine-millimeter Beretta on his hip would attract too much attention. He also did not wish to watch the author relieve himself, but when he saw a muscular man in a tee shirt and jeans enter the small structure he decided he had no choice.

Like all public restrooms the odors were less than pleasant. The agent saw Scanlan stepping away from a urinal as the man in the tee shirt began to pull something from his daypack. He was a second slow as he recognized the shape of a pistol. The silencer attached to the barrel delayed the man an extra second as he pulled it clear of the pack. Dougherty shouted, "Stop," as he went for the gun on his hip. Then everything seemed to happen in slow motion.

The restroom was of average size with two sinks, two urinals and two stalls, but in the violent confrontation that followed it was like a bar fight in a phone booth. The man with the silenced automatic was amazingly fast. Before Dougherty could clear his pistol, the man spun in a half circle and brought the Browning down hard just above the agent's right ear. As the assassin began to turn back to Jonathan, one of the stall doors flew open, hitting his elbow and sending the gun flying across the room. A short, overweight man in a Hawaiian shirt and unzipped walking shorts burst out of the enclosure screaming for help.

The man with closely cropped blond hair was partially blocking the exit as Jonathan lowered his shoulder and bolted for the door. His shoulder hit the man, spinning him sideways, as Jon raced through the door and out into Central Park. The middle-aged man in the Hawaiian shirt was right behind, yelling for help.

The contract killer scrambled to his feet, retrieved his weapon, threw it into his pack and hurried out of the men's room. He knew the author was momentarily beyond his grasp, and his only priority was escape. He pointed toward the restroom entrance and called out to the people standing near the structure. "There's a man with a gun. Run!" The cluster of people who had been watching the men exiting the restroom scattered in every direction. In less than three minutes, the killer was on Park Avenue West hailing a taxi.

Jonathan sprinted up the path expecting to feel the impact of a bullet any second. He was a hundred yards from the restroom when he turned to see if he was being pursued. The blond-haired man was nowhere in sight. He went directly to the female agent seated on a bench in sight of Carmen. "A man just tried to kill me in the restroom. He hurt the agent you were with, call an ambulance."

Carmen hurried over as the woman began speaking into a cell phone as she ran toward the restroom, "What happened?"

"A guy came into the john. He had a gun and would have shot me if the agent we had with us hadn't walked in. He hit her partner." Jonathan was not sure if he was making sense. "There was another guy in one of the stalls. He panicked, and the stall door slammed into the guy with the gun. I'm not sure what happened then, I just ran."

Carmen fought to control her emotions. Her voice was surprisingly calm. "What did he look like?"

"Close cut blond hair, about five ten or eleven, pretty well built. I would guess late thirties."

"What was he wearing?"

"Jeans and a gray tee shirt. It said something on the front, but I don't know what."

Carmen pulled the cell phone from her purse and relayed the information to James Pohley as they walked back to the men's room. A crowd of curious onlookers had encircled the building, held back by a mounted policeman. The man in the Hawaiian shirt was gesturing wildly and talking to anyone who would listen. Several uniformed police arrived moments before the ambulance. Two helped the mounted policeman secure the scene while another began questioning the man who had been in the stall. Two others circulated among the crowd, looking for witnesses. Carmen and Jonathan stayed on the outside fringe of the onlookers.

They watched as the paramedics wheeled the gurney with the unconscious agent out of the restroom and into an ambulance. His partner climbed in the back of the vehicle for the ride to the hospital. It was then that the media arrived. Unable to bring their vans into the park, they were forced to lug their portable units over hill and dale to the site. The reporters from the local television stations competed with the police for statements that would fill slots in the evening news. Jonathan foolishly thought he might escape the limelight until he saw the man in the colorful shirt pointing in his direction.

One of the uniformed policemen reached Jonathan only seconds before the cameras and reporters. "Were you in the men's room at the time of the attack?"

Carmen stepped close to the man, flashed her credentials and spoke softly enough not to be picked up by the microphones thrust in their direction. "Can we talk about this away from the media?"

The cop nodded and led Carmen and Jonathan inside the perimeter of the crime scene. He turned to Carmen, "Alright, what's the story?"

"We believe the man with the gun is the one they're calling the *Culprits* killer."

The patrolman took a step back as if he had been physically struck by Carmen's statement. "No shit?" When Carmen offered a weak smile in response, the uniform waved toward the middle-aged man now garnering his fifteen minutes of fame in front of the cameras. "The guy over there says he was the target."

Jonathan stepped into the conversation, "Let's keep it that way."

The patrolman gave Jon a quizzical look, "Who are you?"

"Jonathan Scanlan."

The name obviously did not ring a bell as the uniform wrote it in his notebook, "What's your connection to the shooter?"

Carmen pushed her way between the two men, "Officer, the Bureau is taking jurisdiction over this crime."

Jonathan watched the patrolman bristle, "Saying it doesn't make it so lady."

"What if I say it, officer?" they turned to find James Pohley standing behind them. He offered his credentials. "I'm in charge of the Bureau's New York office."

The patrolman pocketed his notebook and turned away in disgust. Pohley waited until the patrolman was out of hearing. "So, what happened?"

Jonathan described everything he could remember about the incident and the man with the gun. We'll have a sketch artist sent over to the Marriott." He glanced at his watch. "Can you be there in an hour?"

They nodded, "Do you need us here for anything else?"

Pohley shook his head, "The forensic team is on its way. Did you see him touch anything?"

"No. Maybe the door handle." As they walked away the day did not seem as bright and sunny. Jonathan gave an involuntary shudder as they walked past the Eagles and Prey statue depicting two eagles devouring a goat.

———

He seethed in silence as he switched cabs three times before having the taxi stop several blocks from the Holiday Inn. He expected the FBI agent, but how did he miss the man in the stall? He had taken a quick glance under the doors to the stalls and had somehow missed the man's feet. There was no question that he was losing it. Not only had he failed, but for the first time in his life someone other than Carol knew what he looked like.

He willed himself to be calm. In addition to the author and the man in the Hawaiian shirt, a number of people had seen him leaving the restroom. Within hours, a composite drawing would be circulating among law enforcement agencies in the area. The good news was he had nothing distinctive that would make identification easy. No scars or tattoos that would separate him from the crowd. As a blond haired white man of average height, he was Mr. Average in a city of over eight million.

Carol was watching television when he walked through the room and into the bathroom. He emerged, and the blond hair was gone replaced by dark brown. He dressed in a loose-fitting shirt to hide his physique and added dark framed glasses with clear lenses.

Carol looked away from her program, "Are we leaving New York?"

"We will be as soon as I get rid of the motorcycle. Line up train tickets back to Virginia. I'll be back in about an hour."

As Carol began packing she whispered a prayer that this was their last business trip.

CHAPTER 58

It was after four when the sketch artist left their hotel. Jonathan's tone was less than optimistic. "Did you see the sketch? The guy looks like half of America."

"Well, we can eliminate all the NBA players."

Jonathan smiled, "Let's go see the charming Maria Santos. Maybe we can put this together from the other side. What have you heard about the agent that was hit?"

"Severe concussion, but they said he's going to recover completely."

"Good, I didn't want another killing on my conscience."

Carmen went over to Jon and took his face in her hands, "Don't say that. You didn't kill the man in Carmel. The person we're after did that."

Jonathan did not say anything, but Carmen knew she had not lifted the burden of guilt he still carried. The trip to the Bronx was as long and expensive as they remembered. The elevator labored its way to the fourth floor and tonight the hallway reeked with the pungent odor of curry. Carmen's knock brought the narrow face of Ms. Santos to the door. She released the chain and they followed her through the living room to the breakfast table. The Santos children were again watching television.

Carmen saw no reason for polite conversation, "Do you have the records of the transactions we discussed?"

The woman's features took on an expression of cunning, "What about the twenty thousand?"

Jonathan shook his head, "I told you the information has to break the case. If it does the money's yours."

Maria's eyes narrowed in determination, "Twenty thousand dollars if you want to see the records."

Carmen put as much steel in her voice as she could muster. "Withholding evidence is a felony, Ms. Santos. We aren't going to give you twenty thousand dollars for what may be useless information. You're going to have to trust us on this."

"Like I trusted the man who fathered my children when he said he was just going out for a beer! No. I want the money up front."

Jonathan shook his head, "That isn't the deal and besides, I don't carry around twenty thousand in cash."

"Then come back when you have the money."

Jonathan considered searching the apartment but decided against the idea. While they were not dealing with a brilliant mind, she was probably smart enough to keep the material out of their reach. "Alright. Tomorrow you call in sick. We'll be here at eleven."

"I have to go to work. I've already used up my sick leave."

Carmen leaned over the seated woman, her face inches from the would-be blackmailer. "Listen, for twenty thousand dollars you're going to lose a day's pay. Any more bullshit from you and I'm arresting you for obstruction of justice, concealing evidence, and anything else I can think of."

They watched the fight leave the woman's eyes, "Alright, tomorrow at eleven."

Carmen broke the silence on the cab ride back to the hotel, "Are you really going to give her the money if the records are useless?"

"No. Your main squeeze may occasionally be dense, but I'm not that stupid." He took her hand. "Let's have a couple of drinks and order room service. After today, I need a quiet evening."

———

They were at the Grand Central Station when his cell phone rang. He stepped away from Carol to take the call. The mechanically altered voice wasted no time on pleasantries. "You failed again."

He did not bother to answer the accusation, "I'm leaving New York. I was seen by too many people."

"You will do no such thing. You will stay and complete your assignment."

He laughed at the demand, "Or what? The risks aren't worth the reward. Our business relationship is finished."

"Or what? Perhaps the answer is the world learns the truth about David Quinn." When there was no answer the mechanical voice pressed on. "Are you surprised I know your real name? It's amazing what you can find out if you have enough money. Did you think it was impossible to follow the money transfers all the way to the Grand Caymans, or did you believe your banker was incorruptible?"

For the first time in his life David Quinn was at the edge of panic, "What do you want?"

"I want Jonathan Scanlan dead."

"And then?"

"And then you will do what I tell you to do. I expect your next appointment will be with Barbara Wiehl. By the way, that's a lovely little piece of property you have in Tennessee."

Quinn closed the phone and stood on the in the middle of hundreds of people without seeing beyond the images in his mind. After a moment he turned back to Carol, "I was wrong. Our business here isn't quite finished."

CHAPTER 59

The money was waiting for Jonathan when he arrived at the bank. A few months ago, a request for twenty thousand in cash would have been the source of a few chuckles around the water cooler but with most of the revenue from *Culprits* sitting idly in a checking account the financial institution fell over themselves to comply with his request.

They had stopped at a store and purchased a cheap tote bag for the currency's short journey to the Bronx. Their third cab ride to the account payable clerk's apartment was no more interesting that the prior two. Neither Carmen nor Jonathan noticed another fine late spring day.

Maria Santos opened the door without greeting, turned, and walked down the short hallway into the living room. The children were nowhere in sight as the small woman stood in the middle of the room. "You have the money?"

Jonathan walked over to a low coffee table and dumped the contents of the tote bag onto the table's glass surface. "Now it's your turn. Give us the printouts."

Santos seemed to hesitate for a moment before leaving the room. Carmen eased her hand into her shoulder bag until she found the familiar grip of her Smith & Wesson automatic. The chance that the woman would try use force to take the money was remote but not impossible. She relaxed when the accounting clerk returned with a file folder. Santos set the folder on the table next to the pile of money.

Jonathan picked up the folder and pulled out several sheets of paper. He held them so Carmen could see the details of the money transfers. A code number appeared following the word 'authorized.' "Who authorized these transactions?"

Santos was staring at the uneven pile of currency. "You have the printouts. That was the arrangement."

Carmen stepped between Santos and the money. "Maria, Maria, Maria. You just don't get it. We already knew about the transactions. The money was for documents showing the person who authorized the transfers."

Maria shouted, "No, you have your printouts," and moved to pick up the cash. Carmen spun Santos around, took a pair of handcuffs from her bag and applied them to the accounting clerk's wrists. Maria started crying. Between sobs she said, "You lied to me."

Jonathan pointed to the money. "You have two choices Maria. You can either be taken into custody as a material witness, lose your job, and never see a dime of the money on the table, or you can tell us who authorized the transfers, keep the money and your job."

She could not keep her eyes from the pile of cash, "I'll lose my job if I tell you."

Carmen was growing tired of the woman's antics. "You heard the choices. Tell us who approved the transactions, or I promise you I'll personally tell Laura La Croix you gave us the printouts."

Santos whispered something that they could not hear, "Louder, Maria." Jonathan glanced at Carmen when the woman repeated the name.

CHAPTER 60

Both were lost in thought during the cab ride back into Manhattan. It seemed hard to believe their journey was over. Carmen wondered if their relationship would survive once they shifted back to their normal lives. Divorce rates and broken relationships among FBI field agents were not encouraging statistics, and then there was the money. How long would it take before Jonathan succumbed to the temptations of wealth and the beautiful women that seemed to always be on the arm of a rich man?

Jonathan silently wondered if Carmen would drift away as she became consumed with her next assignment, perhaps one that took her away from San Francisco. He thought it odd that instead of feeling satisfied with the answer to their investigation he felt adrift, without purpose.

Carmen called James Pohley and related the news as the taxi wound its way past Central Park. When she ended the call, she turned to Jon. "Pohley is going to stop by the hotel as soon as he can. He's on his way back from DC right now."

"I don't know about you, but I could use a drink."

"Great minds think alike."

As soon as they were back at the Paramount, they made their way up the winding staircase to the mezzanine bar and one of the tables overlooking the lobby. Jonathan ordered a draft and Carmen a glass of Chardonnay. A couple followed them into the bar and took a nearby table. The man had heavy framed glasses and was wearing a conservative business suit while the strikingly beautiful woman he was with wore a white blouse and tan skirt. Jonathan thought the woman looked like a younger version of Sophia Loren.

Jonathan's expression was somber as he turned his attention back to Carmen. "I guess I should be happy it's over, but I can't shake the feeling our relationship is somehow tied to the investigation and I don't want that to end."

She reached across the small table and took his hand, "Our relationship is something we control. It only has to end if that's what we want."

He forced an uneasy smile and changed the subject, "Why do you think he did it?"

"We may never know for sure. When he's arrested he'll lawyer up and claim the payments are no more than an odd coincidence, but I have a theory. What impact did the killings have on the country?"

Jonathan wasn't sure what Carmen meant, "Everyone was angry. Five well known liberals were no longer out doing their liberal thing."

Carmen shook her head, "I know you considered the five victims to be significant players or you wouldn't have mentioned them in your book, but like you once said, you featured the most important progressives at the end of *Culprits* which means the people in the early chapters weren't as influential. But what happened politically?"

"There were a lot of angry speeches condemning the FBI."

"And the administration," Carmen continued her thought when Jonathan nodded agreement. "Five liberals are murdered in the same sequence as they appear in *Culprits*. With each killing the criticism escalates in Congress and in the media. The president's approval rating sinks like a stone and his Party is in danger of continuing to lose control of the House of Representatives at the midterm elections. Prescott loses his bid when he comes up for reelection and we have a complete reversal of power in Washington."

"If you're right, my book really didn't have anything to do with the killings."

"It added spice to the story which helped the media frenzy and it made the Bureau look stupid which further weakened the administration."

Jonathan had trouble absorbing the implications of Carmen's theory. "Who would do such a thing? This assumes a dedicated liberal would hire a professional killer to knock off five prominent lefties to create bad press for the conservatives?"

Carmen gave Jon a condescending smile. "Five inconsequential sacrifices to put your people at the helm of the government? Is that such a stretch? And in answer to your question, someone who is amoral, someone who believes the end justifies the means, and then sleeps well at night."

Jonathan finished his beer and looked out toward the lobby. "Jesus. I have to believe you're right, but the idea that someone could have people killed for political gain seems bazaar."

"Does the term coup d'état come to mind?"

"I'll be right back, I have to go to the bathroom."

A moment after Jonathan left the table, the man seated nearby left his companion and followed the author to the restroom. The strikingly beautiful woman he had been with put forty dollars on the table, picked up the copy of *The Enquirer* she had been reading, and made her way out of the bar, across the lobby, and out of the hotel.

Jonathan was relieving himself in Philippe Starck's uniquely designed urinal when he heard the sound of someone entering the men's room. Suddenly the muzzle of a silenced pistol was pressed against the back of his head.

"What is the name of the person who paid for the killings?" The accent was vaguely southern, which Jon realized was now useless information.

Jonathan could not move from his frozen position. He thought of how ridiculous he would appear in crime scene photos with one hand holding his private part, "No."

"What do you mean, no?" The man with a gun at the back of his head seemed genuinely surprised by Jon's response.

"You're going to kill me whether I tell you the name of the man behind the killings or not. Why would I help you?" At this point Jonathan had finished his business and zipped up. It was a minor victory, but he found satisfaction in knowing he would be discovered in a less embarrassing mode.

There was a pause before the man responded, "Mr. Scanlan, if you tell me the name of the man who commissioned the killings, I will not shoot you. You may accept this, or you may not; that is your decision. But, as soon as another person enters this restroom, I will have no choice but to kill you," the man spoke in a reasonable, emotionless voice.

Jonathan's first thought went to Carmen's comment. The man who orchestrated the murders, which most probably would shortly include his own, would bring in a dream team of attorneys and quite possibly beat the charges. If he was about to die, perhaps he could bring about a measure of street justice, "Gordon Croll."

"Who the hell is Gordon Croll?"

The situation was approaching the theater of the ridiculous, "What do you want? I just gave you the name of your employer. Did the payment for the last killing start out being sent to the National Bank of Bern?"

Jonathan assumed that someone would open the restroom door any moment and he would be dead. After another pause the southern voice answered, "Yes."

Jon sighed. "Croll is the second banana at an organization called the Creighton Trust."

"My opinion may not be important to you, Mr. Scanlan, but I think your book is great," a second later the world disappeared as Jonathan collapsed on the restroom floor.

CHAPTER 61

The bright light seemed to penetrate straight to his brain bringing searing pain. Everything in the room was white and for a moment Jonathan wondered if he was dead, waiting in some celestial way station for a decision as to his eventual disposition. When he tried to sit up, the room tilted wildly; he had to fight off a wave of nausea. It was then that he realized he was in a hospital bed. A blood pressure monitor periodically tightened and relaxed on his arm, and a faint beeping noise measured his heart rate. He nervously began probing his body with his free hand, exploring for injuries. Heavy bandages encased the back of his head, and his vision was unfocused. He fell asleep before he could find the call button to summon a nurse or doctor.

The next time he awoke Jonathan noticed someone in the room. A blinding bolt of pain made him gasp as he shifted in the bed to see his visitor. A hand came to rest on his shoulder, and a familiar voice offered assurances. "Don't move. You're going to be alright, but you have a severe concussion."

He patted Carmen's hand and tried to focus on her tear-streaked face, "What happened? I remember going to the men's room, but after that my memory's a blur."

"Someone struck you from behind. When you didn't come back, I had one of the hotel staff go in and look for you. You were on the floor in one of the stalls."

Jonathan managed a grim smile, "Welcome to the Big Apple, just don't go to the men's room."

"Jon, you weren't robbed."

"I don't get it."

Carmen bent down and kissed him, "Don't worry about it. Rest and get well. You've had a major trauma, but the doctor said the effects would fade away. He didn't say anything about memory loss, but I wouldn't be surprised if that comes back too."

"What's happening with Croll?"

Carmen shook her head. "Pretty much what we guessed. As soon as he was questioned he demanded a lawyer and refused to talk. The trust issued a statement saying Mr. Croll is an upstanding citizen, they stand behind him one hundred percent, and his prosecution is politically motivated."

"How long have I been out?"

"About eight hours. The doctors could have brought you around earlier, but the CAT scans didn't show anything serious, and they decided to keep you sedated. Honey, you had me so worried."

"Do they have any idea how long I'm going to have to stay in here?"

"No, it's in the hands of the doctors, and they won't say. Try to get some sleep. I have another meeting with Pohley. I'll come back when we finish."

Jonathan floated in and out of consciousness during the night. At one point he looked over to see Carmen dozing in one of the visitor's chairs. He wondered if his inability to become fully alert was a function of his injury or the medication he had been given. The pain in his head had lessened to a dull throb. Carmen awoke and moved to his side.

"How are you doing?"

"The double vision's gone. I have a slight headache, but otherwise I feel fine. Any word on when I'll be released?"

"The doctor said he wanted to take another look at you, but it sounds like you'll be out today."

Carmen helped him adjust the bed into a semi upright position and bought Jon a paperback from the hospital gift shop. The hours dragged as they read and waited for the doctor to catch them on his rounds. Jonathan felt like he was waiting for a delayed flight at an airport gate. When the neurologist finally arrived, he proved to be an energetic man of Filipino decent with a bag full of one-liners.

Jonathan interrupted the man's second joke, this one relating to twelve lawyers captured by terrorists. "Doctor, I don't want to be rude, but when can I leave?"

The small man smiled, "Right after I finish my joke."

Twenty minutes later, a nurse wheeled Jonathan to the administrative offices to ensure his medical coverage and credit cards measured up to the financial task. His insurance and bank account passed muster, and by noon Carmen and Jonathan were in a taxi on the way back to the Paramount. Jon's head was heavily bandaged where the laceration caused by the blow had been treated. He felt like an extra from a Civil War movie.

As they were pulling up to the entrance, Jonathan turned to Carmen, "Something just came to me. I think I remember what happened in the restroom. The man who attacked me asked me the name of the person who paid for the killings."

Carmen grabbed Jonathan's arm. Her voice shook with emotion, "You were attacked by the killer?"

Unlike Carmen, Jonathan felt disconnected from his experience, as if he had observed a violent act performed in a play. "It had to be. At first, I wouldn't tell him anything," he paused, embarrassed by the balance of his memory.

Carmen turned Jonathan towards her, her face reflecting a cauldron on fear and anticipation, "And then what, Jon?"

"He said he wouldn't kill me if I told him the name," Jonathan twisted away from Carmen, his face flushed with shame. "I assumed he was going to kill me, and Croll would have the money to skate, and . . . and I was afraid. I gave him Croll's name."

While the driver waited impatiently for his fare to be paid, Carmen sat back in the taxi's fabric seat and considered Jonathan's recollection.

CHAPTER 62

David Quinn watched the house for over an hour before moving across the expansive lawn and patio area. The night air was heavy with the first signs of summer's humidity and the insects that most enjoy the damp warmth were active. He paid them no attention as watched the movements within the stately home. It was a large Tudor. The back of the structure was heavily endowed with small panes of glass set in French doors and stylish windows. Lights were on in most of the rooms allowing him to follow the family as they moved through their evening rituals. Barbara Croll was the first to retire.

Her husband moved to his study and turned on the television to view the evening news. The voice of the CNN commentator drowned out the faint metallic noise as one of the French doors was forced open. The exclusive community was virtually devoid of crime, and Gordon Croll, like most of his neighbors, was lax in the use of his alarm system.

The assassin moved noiselessly through the home, ignoring the Persian carpets and fine art adorning the walls. The door to the study was partly open, and he slipped inside as silently as a shadow. Croll was sipping from a crystal glass as he sat on a massive leather sofa, his feet propped up on a hassock. Quinn closed the door and moved across the room until he came in sight of the seated man. He held his silenced pistol at his side; his hands were encased in surgical gloves.

"Good evening Mr. Croll."

The heavyset man on the sofa stared dumbly at his visitor. "I heard a theory about the motivation driving the killings. It goes something like this. It was all done to discredit the administration and to shift the political pendulum to the liberal agenda. Was that correct?"

When Gordon Croll did not reply the man pointed his automatic at the big man's left knee. "You'll answer, or I'll shoot your kneecap. Trust me, it's quite painful, and you will never play tennis again."

Beads of sweat ran down Croll's face even though the room was quite cool, "Yes, but why are you here?"

Quinn ignored the man's question, "Why did you use the book, *Culprits*? Was it just to add a little mystery to the killings? To attract more media attention?"

Croll had moved his feet off the hassock and was seated in a more upright position. Quinn could smell the man's fear, "I can pay you. I have money here."

Quinn shook his head and fired the weapon. The sound was little more than a pop. Croll cried out and clutched his knee. At the last second, Quinn had shifted his arm and the bullet created a harmless hole in the soft leather an inch from Croll's leg. "You're not a very good listener, Mr. Croll. I asked a question. Why use the book?"

The big man could hardly form sentences, "I came across it by chance. I knew it would distract the police and that the media would love it."

"You're an ultraliberal. Didn't you have a problem having me kill people who thought the same way you did?"

"A few pawns had to be sacrificed. We're talking about the future of the country. Prescott is a joke, and all he's done is cater to his big business cronies. His policies are killing the environment, and he squanders the economy building a war machine. He has to be stopped!" Croll's righteous anger absorbed much of the man's fear.

Quinn lowered his pistol, "Alright, I've been seen, and I have to disappear. You said you had money here."

Croll stood on unsteady legs and moved to one of the paintings in the study. He pulled it away from the wall to reveal a small safe. He glanced nervously back at the man he had hired to kill five people before turning the tumblers and opening the safe. He pulled out several stacks of currency, piling them on a side table.

"One more thing. Who else knows my real name?"

Gordon Croll seemed surprised by the question. "Of course, I've told no one."

"You know, I'm really a conservative at heart." The nine-millimeter round hit the Creighton Trust executive in the forehead between his two puzzled eyes. Quinn stepped over the dead man to empty the balance of the currency from the safe. He took a small recording device from his pocket and placed it on the dead man's chest. Three minutes later he was on his way back to Manhattan to pick up Carol. He decided to surprise her with a few months in Santa Barbara as a retirement vacation.

CHAPTER 63

The interrogator from Homeland watched John William Champion as he walked out of the facility. Champion stopped and looked back, as if reluctant to leave the building where he had been held. John William squinted into the bright sunlight as he threw his daypack over his shoulder and began walking toward the bus stop.

The security guard at the exit turned to the interrogator, "So he just walks away?"

The man shook his head. "We never really had a reason to hold him. You know, the entire time he was here the only time he spoke was to recite some biblical passage. We couldn't keep him just because he's nuts."

———

Carmen and Jonathan were in the terminal waiting for their flight when her cell phone rang. She listened without speaking for several minutes before ending the call, "That was Pohley. Gordon Croll was shot and killed in his home last night. His home safe had been emptied out and the police initially thought the motive was robbery, but then they found a tape recorder. They don't know if it belonged to Croll or the shooter, but the entire conversation prior to the killing was recorded. Croll admitted to financing the murders."

"Did he say why?"

"Pretty much what we guessed. He called them sacrificial pawns in his plan to discredit the president and his administration."

Jonathan looked out toward the tarmac and taxiing aircraft, "And it was working."

Carmen took his hand. "*Was* is the active word. When the recording's released the political backlash is going to be enormous." She stared at her companion for a moment before speaking, her face reflecting her discomfort. "You may not want to talk about this right now and I'd understand, but why do you think the killer let you live? He tried to shoot you in Carmel and in Central Park. Why did he just knock you unconscious at the hotel?"

Jonathan's fingers touched the pad at the back of his head. "I just remember bits and pieces before I went out, but I think he said something about liking my book."

Neither spoke as each explored their own thoughts. Carmen was the first to break the silence, "Imagine, spared by a literary critic."

Jonathan could not help but smile, "And the rarest bird of all, a critic with a conservative bent. I'm really anxious to get home and start my next project."

"The one about political correctness?"

Jon shook his head, "No, I'm thinking of a story about a man who hires a killer to knockoff prominent liberal leaders in order to discredit the conservative administration and shift the direction of the country's politics. Against unbelievable odds an intrepid couple foil the plot. Think it has a chance?"

"Maybe you should see if they kept your position open at State."

ABOUT THE AUTHOR

Barry Solloway was born and raised in San Francisco. He has lived in Los Gatos, Marin, and Napa Ca. He and his wife, their furry child, Jake, a chocolate lab, are now transplanted to Henderson Nevada, where they enjoy an active social life and enjoy the dining scene and all that Las Vegas has to offer. He has two daughters that still live in northern California.

To his mother's great discomfort, as a teenager, he worked 4 summers as an ordinary seaman in the merchant marine, and 2 summers at casinos in Nevada. He took a year off between achieving his bachelors and master's degrees and hitchhiked all over Europe. These adventures contributed to his life experiences.

The author obtained bachelors and master's degrees from San Jose State University and managed businesses in Silicon Valley. Barry Solloway's passions beyond his family, writing, and reading is an avid interest in the American political scene.

THANK YOU READER

Thank you for reading, and I sincerely hope you enjoyed my book. As an independently published author, I rely on you the reader to spread the word. So if you enjoyed the book please tell your friends and family, and if it isn't too much trouble, I would appreciate a brief review. They help authors out. Thanks again.

My best to you and yours.

Barry